Gerald Rochelle is a writer, editor and philosophical practitioner. His PhD was on the unreality of time. He has published books on time, general philosophy, ethics, grief, and the nature of self as well as editing S.V. Keeling's Time and Duration. In addition to Forewords and Introductions to important reprints, he has published essays, reviews and bibliographies, edited a well-known Philosophical Journal and published seventeen novels in various genres.

Also by Gerald Rochelle

Cold Blood

Blood of the Flock

Saying Goodbye: Grief from Beginning to End

APLtF—A Philosopher Learns to Fly

Beyond Within

Well of Souls

"I am"

Doing Philosophy

Behind Time

The life and philosophy of J.McT.E McTaggart 1866-1925

An Introduction to Philosophy in Schools Book I

Ethics Matter: An Introduction to Philosophy in Schools Book II

As Parvus Potentes

Piano People

THE LAST DAY OF SOCRATES

by

Gerald Rochelle

Not Equal Press

Not Equal Press

www.doingphilosophy.uk

www.geraldrrochelle.com

www.notequalpress.com

First published 2021

Not Equal Press

ISBN 9798757548289

For and because of Ws—beyond and within

'…and so the world runs away.'

Edward Senior

CHAPTER 1

In the beginning (of it all)—God (himself) and gGod

'So, here we are, the two of us,' said God (himself).The other one of the two shuffled a little uneasily, continuing his state of not knowing by being not even sure where they were, nor (as he had no experience of others anyway) what the concept of "the two of us" actually meant. 'You may be a little confused at the moment...' Yes, he was—more than a little. '...suddenly appearing from nowhere like this, wondering who it is of the two of us that's wondering about appearing from nowhere like this, and wondering who it is of the two of us that's doing the wondering about who it is of the two of us that's wondering. But that will soon pass—the wondering, that is. It's probably mostly passed already.' He stared hard at the other, obviously hoping for a response. The other nodded unconvincingly, paused and nodded again for emphasis (of the nod itself). 'Ah! Thought so. That's what comes of being a god!'

That made the other prick up his ears.

'God?' he asked, seemingly wakened from his confused torpor if not his wondering, as well as being surprised, in these obviously early stages, at trying out his powers of speech and hearing the result of them.

'Yes. A god! Ah, you hadn't got that far yet had you, on the wondering front. I suppose it's a lot to take in all at once—especially when you're new to things. Yes, you're a god. I've just made you. Well, I say "just made you"; I did "just make you", yes, but I don't mean I "just made you" in the sense of having "just made you" on a whim. Whim! Perish the thought! What I mean

And they both nodded, though the sense of clarity, logic and general good sense of it all in truth rested more with God (himself) than with gGod.

'Now,' continued God (himself). gGod sat forward. 'One of the recurring problems for God, that is for *me*…Oh, I could just add here that even though I am God (myself) ("God (myself)" being my true name in full), between the two of us we don't need to use any formality of address; none of these reverent and capitalised "He"'s and "Me"s—just plain "he" and "me" and so on will do perfectly well for me. I've no time for the manners of reverence for myself, even though obviously I created them.' gGod raised his eyebrows, suspecting that he didn't actually share God (himself)'s view on this, but pushing this to the back of his mind and going along with it. 'Good. Now where was I? Of course, one of my recurring concerns (apart from the suspicion of the contents of unperceived dark corners and what untidiness they might hide in their darkness) is the specific problem of good—of good and evil. And on this subject I want to feel that you're sufficiently briefed so that…' He turned to gGod and nodded emphatically, '…you do not get mixed up about acting properly as you go along. With me so far? gGod?' gGod nodded, quite obviously not having the slightest clue what God (himself) was talking about. 'It's a big subject that runs into all corners of creation—the lightest and the darkest.' He paused to take another, this time rather too prolonged and clearly forced laugh. 'And I like to think that I've taken most of the problems into account—that I've weighed up the potential balance between good and evil in all possible worlds. There are, of course, no other *true* worlds except this one, but it is always possible to *imagine* different worlds. Dark corners! As I always say, "If you can imagine it, then it's possible. And even if you can't imagine it, it's still possible—even likely!" Anyway, to this end I created you, gGod, with an eye on the furtherance of the good. And, as far as I can tell, you seem to have turned out, well more or less…' He pursed his lips as if struggling to find the right words. '…(more or less)…fine.' He put his hand to his mouth and gave a forced cough. 'I have given you free will as well, so things should never get boring. Because of this, you might make some mistakes, but at the same time I'm sure you'll learn from them and, with good always in your mind, will improve as you go on. But, and there's always a downside, isn't there, you will I'm sure come across things that aren't all that good. The other side to "good", which I call "evil", is an unavoidable outcome of good in the first place (a little bit like "light" and "dark"). Indeed, from what I've seen so far in my creational activities, it seems a sort of unavoidable outcome of being—a consequence of anything that's created. As I said, I'm afraid that if there's one side, then there will always be another side; and in the case of good it's the downside—the bad side. At the same time, and this might make it seem a bit less troubling, I have to say I do wonder if there is such a thing as *truly* good or *truly* evil anyway. I'm more inclined (perhaps a bit wishfully, I accept that) to think that it's more likely to be only *apparently* good and *apparently* evil. I don't know what you think?' gGod didn't offer anything—he was still thinking about reverent capitalisation of the initial letters of pronouns. 'Anyway,' obviously not suffering from lack of feedback, God (himself) continued. 'Whether it's true or apparent, evil is necessary for some good in just the same way that good is necessary for some evil. Evil is necessary in order to *define* good, though good does not *derive* from evil. Ah!' he said, staring fixedly at gGod. 'And I can see that you realise that there is another element in play; both good and evil demand…' He paused in the hope of encouraging a response but got none. He waited, but still got none.'Yes! You have it! "Possibility"! In order to work, "possibility" is *essential*. Evil is only possible if there is something of good against which it can be set or measured, and so with good. You want an example?' gGod hadn't invited one and had no intention of trying for one. 'Very well. For example, how can there be (the good of) compassion if there is no suffering to be witnessed by the possibly compassionate? And how can there be suffering unless there is the possibility of the (good) absence of suffering against which *it* can be set? No getting out of that one, eh?' Profoundly, no reply. 'So, I think that just about wraps it up. Any questions?'

gGod looked at God (himself) blankly. The terms and the setting out of the example had completely finished him off.

'No,' he said blandly, though (showing admirable persistence) he was somehow toying with the idea of coming up with an example of his own. But even after trying, nothing came to mind and he said nothing.

'Good, so gGod, I wish you well. Be thoughtful. Get on with the creating. And of course the perceiving.' gGod tipped his head sideways in a questioning sort of way. 'Oh, on perception! Just in case I didn't make it absolutely clear, let me emphasise that in order for created things properly to exist they must be "perceived". If it's not perceived then it doesn't exist! You'll get the hang of it. All in a god's work! Poking into those dark corners!' No response from gGod. God (himself) shrugged. Then laughed. 'And the light ones! Don't forget the light ones.' He laughed again, this time fidgeting in a way that clearly heralded his need to move on. 'And don't let anything I've said cause you to hold back on using your powers—yes, you've got plenty of them; creating and so forth. It can be very rewarding being a god. Remember though, the more you create the more perceptive attention you will have to give to things as there will be more created things to give your attention to—to "perceive". And the more created things there are, the more will be the contest between the good and the not so good, real or apparent, absolute or not; problems with mistakes and consequences and the mutual reliance of the good and not so good. But nothing to worry about. Good. Now, is there anything else?'

gGod widened his eyes, lifted his eyebrows and, suddenly discovering newfound methods of expression, tipped a wink (the format of which he'd just created) to God (himself). God (himself) looked puzzled—(obviously); he'd never come across a wink before. Encouraged by the success of the wink and now persisting with his novel ways, gGod mouthed something to God (himself). God (himself) failed to pick up the meaning—he thought it might have been something to do with goldfish but (surprisingly) wasn't really sure what goldfish were. gGod leant forward and, feeling a surge of his reflective powers and ways of expressing them, spoke into God (himself)'s ear in a whisper.

'A word in your shell-like, if I may. Just a private word… with you, God (yourself),' he said, now unashamedly taking hold of God (himself)'s elbow.

God (himself) allowed (God) himself to be drawn aside.

'What is it?' asked God (himself), feeling a little presumed upon. It was one thing asking if there was anything else, but in light of feedback he'd received so far, quite another being taken up on the invitation—and being physically drawn aside.

'Well, I've been set thinking by what you've been saying.'

'Yes?' said God (himself) looking a little concerned that he might be asked something that he would struggle to answer and so something that would hold him back from getting going on the things that were pressing on him to get going on.

'Well, I wonder if you could clarify your meaning over a few things?'

'Of course,' said God (himself) now looking positively disconcerted.

'Well, I wonder if you'd care to explain the meaning of some of the words you've been using?'

'Go on.'

'I need some more explanation on what you mean exactly by the terms: good, not good, real, apparent, consequences, mistakes, reliant, absolute. I've got others, but these are my main concern at the moment.'

God (himself) shook his head. It was obvious that for a moment he was stuck for the next step. Then, after a great deal of silent consideration, he spoke.

'You sound a bit like Socrates.'

'Who?'

'Socrates was… is…well…will be ("god-time" and all that), a great thinker, and a great questioner.

'Oh,' replied gGod, very confused by the tenses and not yet tuned in to the *B*-series (meaning 'before and after") anomalies of "god-time".

'Now, gGod...' God (himself), having started too early on his reply, hesitated, went into some deep thought, arrived at an idea, then disappeared.

CHAPTER 2

A little after the beginning (of it all)—God (himself) and gGod again

'gGod, something has come to my notice,' said God (himself), looking decidedly concerned. 'Something that is more than a little concerning.'

gGod looked puzzled and more than a little concerned himself.

God (himself) continued.

'It seems as though some of the ethical stuff that I expected to be an implicit part of your creational work has gone a bit awry.' A pause. gGod wasn't sure what "implicit" meant and had to quickly look it up (after having first created an authoritative dictionary). 'When you started off I thought we were pretty clear about how anything you created should act or be—you know, whether it benefitted or harmed other parts of the creation, whether it was good or bad. You know, whether things acted morally against a sound ethical standard. Well, I had a few spare moments and I used them to look around at the sort of work you've been doing. I wasn't checking—just curious. And, I must say, there seems to have been, how should I put it, a bit of…moral slippage. Well, not so much "slippage" but more the lack of a proper standard to start with (from which then things could slip or not). I have the feeling that a solid ethical standard has not been laid down. So, time for a reappraisal, I thought. Maybe even some (re)adjustment. To start with, I've decided that the best way of doing it—the readjustment—would be to get you involved in some sort of project; one which teases out the good and the bad, the right and the wrong—one that challenges some of these ethical boundaries we talked about before. I thought it would be useful to allow you to see some good (and bad) examples of moral behaviour—lay things out against some basic standards and see what they looked like in their light. It'd make it easier for you to get a clearer picture, I thought, and so help you get the old creating thing running along the right lines—from the right station, you might say. What do you think?'

gGod knew God (himself) wasn't actually asking for his opinion so didn't say anything. This was a bit of a shock, though. He'd thought things had been going pretty well and was surprised (not to say a little hurt) to hear what God (himself) was now saying. Thinking this, he decided to reply.

'*I* thought things *were* pretty well on track,' he said rather unconvincingly, extending God (himself)'s "right lines" metaphor.

God (himself) wasted no time replying. He had no time for discussion on the subject.

'Well, I don't. And I should (all-)know—so I'm afraid, quite irrespective of what you may have been thinking, we're just going to have to do something about it.'

'Well, if you say so,' said gGod, now adding the feeling of being rather put out by God (himself)'s disciplining attitude to his initial feeling of being surprised and a little hurt.

'I do. And to get things off on the right *lines* (to continue my original metaphor) I've decided that you should use the "Jigsaw System". It's worked for other things—though you probably haven't heard about the kipper problem?' He raised his eyebrows to gGod. gGod looked blank—obviously he was familiar with jigsaws as they had been a long-standing and consuming interest of his, but he was not familiar with the "Jigsaw System" and the kipper problem was something that had completely passed him by.

'Yes,' said God (himself), passing over any possible query about the Jigsaw System to the other matter obviously still high in his mind. 'The kipper problem. On FX19!'

'No, I'm afraid not.'

'Exactly! See what I mean about slippage. Anyway, the Jigsaw System was very effective there, on FX19, and that was against all the odds. I can't begin to tell you how much the odds were weighted against a good outcome there! Kippers! Who'd have thought it! So, yes, the Jigsaw System, I've decided will provide the best foundation. It's a very adaptable system, so feel free to bond it onto whatever you want. As well as jigsaws, I've heard you're rather interested in the nature of time, so that might be something to cash in on. Always better to do things that interest us don't you think? We all need a hobby. But you'll need to stay on course, so there're a couple of things I'm going to insist on.' gGod threw his eyes up—though hardly noticeably. 'Yes, to start with you're going to have to include the impartial "IgnatiusM" programme to keep everything nicely balanced.' God (himself), having already noticed the hardly noticeable throwing up of the eyes, now detected a more easily noticeable suspicious look from gGod. He tackled it head on and with well-placed God (himself)-ly perception. 'That's not in any way to check up on what you're doing, you understand, but more just to ensure that circumstances don't cause you to stray off the main line. I'll take him (well "it" really) off his ("its") other duties for the duration of the project. I think you'll get on well together. And then, of course, you'll need a subject who deserves to be involved and will promote some telling discussion. And perhaps challenge your own views. It is, after all, those views which might have led me to detect the slight ethical waywardness that has brought us to this position in the first place. What do you think? Agreed?'

There was no option, of course. This was after all God (himself). Who could disagree!

gGod nodded unconvincingly but, strain to hold back as he did, he couldn't keep himself quiet.

‘Yes. Any *other* suggestions?’ he said with a somewhat biting edge to his emphasis.

God (himself) detected gGod’s sarcasm and responded curtly.

‘Apart from you doing a *good job* of things, no.’

‘Oh,’ replied gGod, bringing up his comb to his quiff and stroking that lovingly through its teeth.

‘So, gGod, using the Jigsaw System and keeping things nicely balanced with the IgnatiusM programme will provide the framework for the project. All you need now is the subject. And, as luck will have it, I’ve got just the right man. One of your own creations, a sound arguer, and someone I’ve only recently mentioned. Talk about coincidence! You’ve guessed haven’t you!’ gGod hadn’t. ‘I knew you would! Go on! Go on! It’s…’ gGod continued stroking his comb through his hair and smiled with a poorly executed look that said, “Of course! Of course!”. ‘Ah! I knew you’d get it! Socrates! Astonishing, eh? Only just mentioned and now he turns out to be the best for the job in hand. And more astonishing—yes, things can be more astonishing—is that it’s coming up to his last day of life. How fitting is that! Perhaps that’s another coincidence, that your “humans” have limited life-spans. It seems an odd way of going about things to me, but that’s how you’ve created it. So, on this last-day basis, I’m thinking how wonderful it would be if you could make the last day of this Socrates a very special one. Perhaps the most special one ever experienced by any of these life-span-limited humans. You’ll have to brief yourself well first—space and time in god-time and all that—and it will require quite a lot of additional creating. But you’re up to it—the challenge and so on—I know you are. And it’s all in a good cause—the moral straight and narrow and all that—tease it out, get it running right.’

There was a hair-combing pause then, with an unconsidered enthusiasm that brought him immediately into the swing of things, gGod came up with a question.

'What shall I call it, the project?'

'What about "Project Socrates"?'

'I like it!'

'Then go to it!'

'Yes…yes...I will,' said gGod, taken aback by God (himself)'s solid and supportive response, while at the same time realising that he didn't really have a clue what he was supposed to be taking on and wondering what had made him say that he was keen to get going on something he didn't for a second understand. 'Yes. Of course,' he said, now striking a *very* positive tone that almost convinced himself of the appropriateness of his certainty. 'I'll get at it directly.'

'Good,' said God (himself), keen as usual to make himself scarce. 'To it! Go to it! Give it your all!'

With that, and clutching his comb tightly in his hand, gGod disappeared!

God (himself) looked worried. He was thinking of gGod's sudden need to create and consult a dictionary (all-knowing), and then his unquestioning enthusiasm for being involved with Project Socrates. These features were now causing him to get the feeling that gGod had turned out a bit more rationally minded (and therefore philosophical) than he would have liked, as well as being a bit more incautiously taken up with enthusiasm than seemed prudent. There was nothing wrong with the philosophical bent in itself, nothing at all, not in itself, but it seemed that already (combined with his almost reckless enthusiasm) it might have gone to his head and started to influence him in the wrong ways. God (himself) knew that philosophy could do that. And that was the last thing he (himself) wanted to be muddled up with the aim of this particular project. During their meeting he had given these factors a great deal of thought and now found himself (himself) worried about how easily he had sold gGod on undertaking Project Socrates. It would be very involving for him, yes, and because of

for his comb, green tights and silver buckled shoes, though gGod's buttons were less shiny than God (himself)'s and the buckles on his shoes were not so large.

So, no longer embarrassed with his nakedness and feeling generally more comfortable, gGod, after a great period of "god-time" had passed, utilised his own freshly challenged powers, inserted his comb into its pocket, and with some judders, flashes and a few false starts, he disappeared.

With that, God (himself), who was still being omnipresent, brushed himself down, and without further ado and, completely forgetting to warn gGod about losing any jigsaw pieces (the important use of which he had not surprisingly missed out as he had completely forgotten to mention how the jigsaw system worked anyway), he too disappeared.

CHAPTER 3

gGod gets started

A few ("god-time") moments later, gGod wriggled down in His chair to make Himself comfortable. He had from the start acclimatised Himself to His role as (good, creative, philosophical and perceiving) gGod, and unknown to God (himself) on their subsequent meeting, elected for appropriately reverential capitalisation for all circumstances in which He was mentioned. But, as pointed out by God (himself) (at that subsequent meeting) (God (himself) according to his own edict, with no capitalisation), gGod had very quickly found the strain of keeping an eye on everything—the perceiving side of things—not only gruelling but quickly telling on...well, according to God (himself) His grip on the ethical side of things. He didn't mention it to God (himself) but He was also aware of His health having suffered. Right from the kick-off He had been made aware (and was aware) of the responsibility that He had for the oversight of any of His own creations—in fact even before he'd created anything He'd felt the weight of it. And from the same time He'd been suffering from nervous anxiety and incessant tension headaches. Even thinking about creating, tempting as it was, was itself very taxing. But once He actually started creating, the looking after of those things that He created was in a different league altogether; it left the exacting nature of creating looking like simplicity itself (which it was not). It was this keeping-an-eye-on-things that had taken its toll. To start with He hadn't realised that to keep His created things in existence they needed to be perceived. And, when He did tumble to this, He badly underrated the concentration and right-mindedness that constant perceiving demanded. And all this was undertaken under the influence of His philosophical bent that kept throwing him into a labyrinthine turmoil of questioning and re-questioning. So it was, He had to be honest, a God (himself)-send that God (himself) had recognised his failing here and emphasised the need not to duck the importance of perception. Yes, even though He'd felt (quite rightly, he thought) a little got at by God (himself) during their second meeting, he had to accept in all honesty that the project as outlined seemed the best thing to do; it would absorb Him, get Him on the right lines, and stop Him concentrating so much on his own anxieties.

He had certainly been been working very hard at the creating business lately—He called it a "business" though for Him it was really more a vocation; So far it had been His life's work, creating —"causing things to be"; bringing things into being with only an act of will. And, on the whole, problems aside, this vocational creating had proved altogether very pleasing. He had, along the way, come up with a couple of real gems. One of them, His favourite, He had called "Earth". He'd taken a special interest in Earth right from the start—when He created it from the firmament with a single word (He had come to find this an ideal and most economical method). Yes, creating was a real blast. But this one creation, this Earth had, no matter how much He liked it, been a bit troublesome. Nothing really *bad* obviously—it was after all part of His creation—but it manifested the sorts of thing that demand that extra bit of perceptive attention. And, He had to admit (particularly since God (himself) had pointed it out) that this had led to some neglected aspects. Good and bad, this ethical stuff, definitely needed keeping an eye on and He had failed to keep His focus there. You never know who is there setting the seeds of evil. Well, you should, if you're gGod, and if you've continually got your eye on the perceiving ball. But He just hadn't seemed to have had the time to give His attention to all of it all the while. In fact, sometimes He hadn't even been sure whether some of those things

He was supposed to be perceiving were there at all. No, being all-perceiving wasn't necessarily all it was cracked up to be. It only seemed to work if gGod was actually *doing* the perceiving thing. And if He wasn't *doing* "all-perceiving", then things seem to have a way of sort of well, disappearing, well, not being there at least, well, not so far as He could perceive anyway.

He created a small table upon which appeared a cup of hot tea. He looked at the other table that He'd created earlier and shook His head. He felt the movement of His quiff. He pulled His comb out and went to comb His hair but, suddenly distracted by a need to perceive, stopped Himself, placed it back in His pocket, forced a shrug, got up from His chair, brushed Himself down, created yet another table with a cup of hot tea, and left to press on with his (all-seeing) labours.

CHAPTER 4

gGod and creation

gGod created things—just by thinking. That was easy.

CHAPTER 5

gGod and philosophy

gGod thought about things—just by thinking. That was more difficult than creating but still fairly easy.

CHAPTER 6

gGod and anxiety

gGod was anxious about things. Because of His philosophical turn of mind, gGod worried about most things, and this caused Him to make mistakes. His biggest mistake was creating a woman for Himself. That was very easy.

CHAPTER 7

gGod and perception

gGod perceived things—just by perceiving things. Well, at least He thought He did. But even when He thought He perceived things He wasn't at all sure that there were not other things He'd missed perceiving. This aspect of gGodly work was far more difficult than either creating or thinking, and philosophising didn't help, and all of it only added to His already often overcoming feelings of anxiety. Perception wasn't straightforward. This was far from even approaching a hint of easy.

Perception had been a worry for gGod ever since He'd been created by God (himself) and had become involved in the creating business for Himself. Yes, perception was a difficulty that had pressed on Him continually. And even after considerable deliberation He had to admit that it was more than tricky to come up with a working framework that enabled Him to feel satisfied that things were properly known via perception and therefore really there (even though He'd created them).

The pressures soon proved too great a burden to shoulder alone, so He came up with the idea of creating Himself a companion who could share the load (at creating, yes, but most of all at perceiving). But straightaway it was a problem. He couldn't decide what form such a companion would take. He'd had enough trouble with matching the first man He'd created on Earth with a companion when the man had moaned about being alone. And, in that case, it wasn't as if He hadn't given the man plenty of choice —all those animals He'd paraded in front of him. Talk about fussy! gGod had almost lost His patience! Not a single one was right! Talk about too much choice! Anyway, in the end, He gave in and created something from part of the man himself. He couldn't possibly moan about that! But then the trouble really began! Trees! Apples! Serpents! Knowledge! Anyway, inspired by the more positive aspects of this business (at least the man and his new companion found out that it was a good idea to cover up their reproductive parts), and because He was not happy with His own isolation, He thought He'd use His previous experience as a template and have a go at creating a similar companion for Himself. And so He did. And there she was—naked! And He created a special relationship for her—His "wife", He called her. And, because of her nakedness, He gave her a wardrobe of clothes which she immediately delved into with enthusiasm. It had all seemed such a good idea at the time, but now He had to admit that His new wife was one of His worst mistakes. The clothing and the wardrobe set off in her a desire for things that He had not anticipated. And now He was stuck with her—gGladys.

So, with His new companion not sharing the difficulties of perceiving and with her proving to be a continually distracting force, He was even less well positioned to press on with the task that God (himself) had put before Him (well, "lumbered" Him with). And, being the natural worrier that He was, gGod's concerns about perception continued and very quickly over millennia progressively got worse. And this made Him worry more. And the more He worried about how much He was worrying about it, the more concerning the original worries about perception became. Every perceiving difficulty that presented itself seemed to spawn another. Quickly His worries multiplied and He found Himself burdened by an ever-increasing and regressive perceiving anxiety. And this was quite apart from the problems that gGladys now brought to Him: demands for more clothing, extra wardrobing, increasing domestic demands.

To begin with, having just literally burned His fingers trying to calm down a volcano that had gone off unexpectedly (this sort of thing happened quite often, and was He believed linked directly to lack of continual perceiving), He'd begun by wondering if it was actually possible to touch or reliably sense an object at all (such as a volcano, and indeed, even the burned fingers that supposedly touching it had produced). And, so the confusions piled in. And so He strained more with the difficulties of it all. His worries (in this case, though also typically) went like this: because He'd just burned His fingers, it seemed most likely that He *could* touch an object, and if He *could* touch an object, He thought, then that would mean in some way that *He* was the same thing as *His* sense experience. Now, He knew that didn't make sense because He had created things separate from Himself—that had been the whole motivation behind His creative thrust—and so straightaway He was trapped. The philosophical problem had left Him stuck. He had become epistemologically suspicious, and that had thrown Him into full-blown introspective scepticism—He was sceptical of His own place in His own creation. Things could surely not get worse.

And as He thought about it more, He came to realise that this rational scepticism caused Him to doubt much of what He perceived in the world (even though it was He who had created it). However, in the everyday, and to maintain some degree of sanity, He held a view—a "common-sense realism" He called it (He had quickly become keen on labelling things philosophical for convenience)—that, when it came down to it, the world seemed fairly reliably to consist in real objects that He sensed. This seemed unavoidable (vis the volcano and the burned fingers). And if He did *not* think this He could see that He would find it difficult to live with any sensible degree of reliance on the world around Him —and that He would probably go (to use another one of His philosophical labels) "bonkers". For example, He might decide to sit on a throne He did not think was there (though, never one for self-aggrandisement based on furniture; He actually always preferred a commonplace chair), and such a situation would soon cause Him to become psychologically unhinged—He would lose grip. And gGod without grip was a scary thought from any point of view—and especially for the gGod who had no grip. Nevertheless, if He asked Himself how He actually *knew* that these objects existed, the only answer that came back to Him was that He knew they existed via His *senses*. In other words, if there was an object in the world "He", as the "knower", even if He *was* gGod, did not "know" it directly; He only "knew" the *sensations* He *had* of it. If there was anything that was in "contact" with the object it was not Him but the sensing apparatus that sent Him the information (the "sense data" He decided to call it). For example, if He touched something hot (His recent encounter with the volcano was still fresh in His mind (wherever that was)) and felt a pain, the pain He was feeling would be caused by the sensation He was having. His only "contact" was therefore between the sense data and Himself and the sense data were a result of His sensing apparatus (not "Him") having contact with what they sensed. And, following this train of thought, He realised straight away (He was gGod, after all) that this was not so odd as it might at first seem; it would be unusual to imagine that the pain itself resided in the object He touched and that therefore He "touched" the pain that it held. But, even though this was largely convincing, He still felt the pricking horns of a dilemma. Did it make sense, He asked Himself, to think that "He" was somehow separate from the world around Him even though the "He" that He identified as "Himself" was part of that world of objects? And on top of that, this "He" that He so glibly thought of as "Himself" seemed to be able to think about what His mind was doing, as though *it* was a separate thing as well. The more He thought about it, (of course) the worse things got.

Indeed, at this point in His philosophical investigations, He even became uncertain about what had been going on with creation. He had even begun to wonder if the whole business of what He had created was all a dream. So, He decided to examine this idea by causing Himself to imagine that everything He thought He knew was in reality a (real) dream. The thought immediately grabbed hold of Him and trapped Him. Then, as if things weren't epistemologically bad enough, suddenly they got worse! What, He thought, if everything He was believing He knew might be the work of *another* god—one, created by God (himself) with just as much power as Himself (that is gGod himself, not God (himself)). He reeled with the thought. Then, impossible though it seemed, it got worse still! What if that (possible) god was one with a malicious agenda—an "evil demon" that simply made things *seem* as they seem even though they were *not* as they seemed at all. His reeling turned into a swoon. This was terrible! He was panicked by everything He was thinking, and in a state of rigidifying shock, He stared into the space that He had created for a long while.

After a few millennia of stagnation on this He finally got a grip on Himself and started again (more soberly this time) to address the problem of whether reality was in fact real (experienced as a first-hand directly-sensed reality) or a dream (real in itself but part of an imagined, secondary and not directly perceived sense-based experience). But during this stagnating interval, no matter how long, little had changed to affect the problem. He saw that sometimes He slept and dreamt and sometimes He was awake, and that the difference between the mental experience of His dreaming world and waking world was only slight. And His senses provided little conclusive or even mildly differentiating information to distinguish them—His dreams, sometimes vivid and realistic, could provide all the mental experiences He had in His waking world. However, He realised that in His waking world He used additional information from objects that were *not* Himself and that these had a continuity that His dreaming world did not. He realised that if He returned to the same dream every time He slept (at the point at which He had last left off) and "woke up" into an entirely different world each time (or perhaps sometimes did not "wake up" for long periods at a time) then He might tend to favour the dreaming world as the "real" world. But this was (almost certainly) not the case, and this continuity, this "almost certainty", gave Him the strongest guarantee of the distinction between the two. On realising this, He went to sleep happily, not concerned about His creation acting inconsistently in His conscious (waking) absence.

But His sleep was quickly broken. This "almost certainty", His scepticism told him, was no proof of what was actually the case—one side simply weighed more heavily in favour against the other. This then led Him to wonder if, instead of a dream, the whole thing—this amazing creation of His—could be just a hallucination. This He found to be an encouraging new starting point. He thought that because He had created them, He knew what hallucinations were. He had made a hallucination something that He saw or believed that was not seen or believed by the "public" world. But, as His experience was in both the "private" and the "public" world (indeed, He *was* both the "private" and the "public" world) He had to accept that this was difficult to make sense of. Obviously He was not in a position to check on the experiences of others directly as there were, strictly speaking, no others (except for God (himself)) that were not part of His creation. If it had been the case that there *were* other independent others it would have made things a whole lot easier. If this had been so, then He could have checked with these independent others as to whether they were sensing something that He could agree was more or less the same as that which *He* was sensing. Such a constant checking process would have allowed Him to be fairly sure that His world was not His personal hallucination. However, in the absence of such others and this sort of check, and, as if things weren't proving bad enough, the doubt remained. In the end, He decided that if He *was* hallucinating then the rest of His creation was hallucinating too, and as He was quite happy with the idea that He had (almost certainly) created the world, then there would be nothing lost if both He and the world He had (almost certainly) created were some kind of absolute illusion.

But, (more-or-less) satisfying as this conclusion seemed, still there was no escape. His scepticism dragged him down ever further; there seemed no end to it. Now, He began to doubt His memory of things—all things. And this caused Him to think that if He doubted His memories, His own memories, then, as the process of doubting and deduction required memory, no explanation of the world and His perception of it could be soundly deduced. And if His memories were a fiction then, He thought, it would be possible that all of His creation had come into existence, say, only a few minutes ago—or even a few seconds ago. Yes, He thought, there would be no way of telling if such a supposition were untrue as everything that spoke of the past—every apparent piece of evidence—could be part of the creation that had only just been created (a few minutes or even a few seconds ago). However, He did think that He couldn't remember creating such a world, and straightaway He realised that *that*, unbelievably, if not un-memorably, just made things worse (as if there could possibly be anything worse to be found). But, as He thought more about it, the likelihood of such an extreme case (even though difficult to dispute) seemed small. And because of the speed of His creational activities (only six days labour for Earth, for example, and only a fortnight for FX19), He couldn't think that He would have gone to the trouble of incorporating such a convoluted and deceiving system.

But maybe someone else could! As soon as He thought that, the idea of the evil demon came crashing back into His mind. What if the demon had created the whole world, including the earth, only a few minutes (or even a few seconds) ago? And this demon was making gGod think that the world had a long previous history before the present moment because he (or she) had also somehow created the (false) memories of such a history in gGod's mind. No matter how hard He thought about it, He couldn't get away from the suspicion that He might in this way be mistaken about His memory, though, as with all His other scepticism, He could find no evidence to disprove His misgiving. So again, as with dreams, He was left with no proof that whatever he suspected might be an alternative case was probably not the true case.

At this point He began to question whether creating was really His thing. He wondered whether He might have done better following a different path—maybe taking up an absorbing hobby, like landscape painting or perhaps something that involved Him in spotting things (like wild flowers) or collecting things (like stamps). So He tried them all. Of all the ones He tried He liked in particular making model planes. And He stuck at this for a long time, though even by the time that His interest waned and He gave it up to pursue something else, planes used by humans on Earth had still to be invented. But, model planes aside, His most consuming hobby was making jigsaws. From the first moment that He invented them He couldn't get enough of them. He invented a fretsaw that was easy to handle and began producing sheets of mahogany-faced plywood to use as his base. All of the images that He put on the sheets before tackling them with his fretsaw He prepared by hand, utilising skills learned from His landscape painting period, and using colours that he thought up as He went along. He added, as a piquant twist, a particularly exciting and most appropriate feature to be effected when the last piece was placed—the complete picture! Marvellously original and rewarding, He thought.

But such distractions and considerations aside, He still couldn't stop Himself worrying about the nature of existence. He realised that in whatever form the world as He existed in it was, He was stuck with it. No distraction brought about by doing jigsaws or spotting wild flowers or collecting stamps would provide a permanent resolution. And, because of its inescapability, He remained drawn to the common-sense idea that objects in the world were as real as they need be and more or less how He thought of them. He had, He kept reminding Himself, after all, as far as He could tell, created them. However, He knew that although somehow providing a consoling background, that apparent fact did nothing to support the case against scepticism.

But, drawn to this consolation as He might be, He had to be honest with Himself (He was, after all, gGod); the whole matter of other objects continued to confuse Him—caused Him unavoidable sceptical consternation—and He could not find it in Himself to be prepared simply to set it aside as "more or less" okay. No, "more-or-less-ness" did not sit comfortably with all-knowing, all-seeing omnipotence. The reality of objects as they represented themselves (He named this, for obvious reasons "representative realism") obviously forced an acceptance of objects of the world being separate from the objects of His senses. It forced Him to think that although the picture of the world that He had in His mind was a (divinely) mental one, it nevertheless represented something that was real inasmuch as it stimulated the sensations He had of what He thought it was. Surely *this* conclusion was unavoidable. What else could His creation be except, on these terms, real?

But still He was not satisfied—and He didn't like being forced into an empirically based corner like this. He had never had much time for science and its workings even though, of course, He had created both science and its workings. But scientific method (no matter what He thought of it) seemed, as far as He could tell, to make it incontrovertible that although many of His sensations were a product of sensing in-itself (for example, sensing a feeling of consternation), the objects that He sensed were (must be) themselves real. And the only outcome of thinking like this was that objects seemed undeniably to have some sort of "primary qualities"—qualities they had in themselves irrespective of them being perceived. And these qualities—"qualities qua qualities"—must be separate from any sensations He had that were derived from His contact with, but were not *part* of, these objects (like His consternation at trying to accept this). Yes, on this argument, these qualities (such as His current consternation) could not be "primary" but had to be "secondary" qualities. And by definition, these secondary qualities could not possibly be held by the object itself and could only be the subject of, or the result of, perception. But even though this separation of qualities seemed to make sense, He was still left (yet again) with a general scepticism. There was no directly known evidence that a smooth, round and blue object was in fact smooth, round and blue. There was not such a thing as direct evidence. There could be no evidence other than the sensations that He had via the sense data that He received—and this was unavoidably secondary.

So, even though the scientific approach used a useful distinction between categories of quality, and it had rational appeal, He was still left wondering if any such primary objects could *truly* be held to exist. His sceptically regressive considerations on the whole matter had time and again run Him to ground and trapped Him in a spiral of confused madness.

Perhaps, He thought, for the sake of His sanity, He should just accept that everything that He had created was simply there—in existence, all by itself: He was the cause of it, He was real (as far as He could tell), therefore what He had caused must be real. Yes, He thought, this (coining Himself another descriptive term) "causal realism" was definitely appealing and it could release Him from the trap of the sceptical regress. Using this principle He could hold that the primary fact was that the world existed and that He perceived it (more or less) accurately, and that His perceptual processes provided Him with information that bore a strong (if not complete) resemblance to the world of objects He created. On this view He could accept that the world existed in its entirety in the absence of His continual (or passing) perception and therefore it must (in some way) have a reality all its own. He sighed with relief. At last He had a satisfactory answer.

But His sigh quickly turned to a groan. He found himself wondering how some things that He experienced (such as consternation, pride, self-importance, confusion) could possibly have a place outside His mental self. Also, if the external world *was* real even without His mental self, what sort of reality could He attribute to the mental experiences that He was continually having? If He felt unhappy, was it the world that had caused this, His mental self, or a mixture of the two? If it was the world, then where was the object "happiness" that existed in the world in respect of which He could feel the opposite? If it was His mental self, then where had the emotion come from if not from the world? If it was a mixture of the two, then how was it that the world of objects and His mental self could correspond?

And His groan deepened into a heavy, moaning whimper. He just could not reconcile the correspondence between *thinking* about something and something actually *being* as an independent object. For all these "realism" arguments the problem remained that He did not have any direct contact with the objects He sensed. Even though He might be strongly encouraged (by Himself) to believe in "real" objects of the world (by common sense or for the sake of divine sanity), His experience gave Him no *certainty* of their existence. Because of this He was left floundering (and groaning, and moaning, and whimpering) in the grip of His continual and persistently regressive scepticism.

So, from all this, He came to thinking that the only sensible way of believing in the world that He had created, and the only way of preserving His divine sanity, was by accepting that the thinking or perceiving process that He found himself in was central and that indeed all objects relied upon it. This appealed to His sense of divine importance too. And when He realised this He pounced on it.

Yes, everything must be an "idea" in His mind! This was the only satisfactory conclusion—everything that He knew was mental. The world was unknowable unless it was perceived—its very being (which seemed unavailable by any rational means) was brought about by being perceived. He knew that on this thesis, though it might (in some unlikely circumstance) be the case that some objects remained in existence when He was not perceiving them, His scepticism (working in His positive favour this time) about this overruled the likelihood. And unperceived objects could not possibly have meaning. How could anything that was not known and therefore had no being have meaning? This could not be the case—perception meant being. And being demanded continuity of existence.

So, He concluded that in order to prevent things jumping in and out of existence according to whether He was there to perceive them or not, and to hold back the overbearing doubt of the independent existence of objects with primary qualities, things must be perceived all the time by a perceiver—they must be, and could *only* be "ideas" in a perceiver's mind. This sort of (another term came into His mind) "idealism" meant that at the time of His creating He was the only mind in existence and that all other things were part of His own mental processes—His own "ideas". He gave up on pursuing the problem back to His original creation by God (himself), or any thoughts about where God (himself) came from—He had to stop somewhere.

CHAPTER 8

Project Socrates (at last)

And so, with an upward flicking of His fingers, He tidied his ruff, and without further consideration got going on the project that God (himself) had charged Him to undertake.

God (himself)'s thinking had gone like this: gGod had lost his grip on the ethical side of things and had failed to keep up with the perceiving that was necessary to maintain the known being of things. To get things back on the straight and narrow, gGod was to focus on one of His creation (a "human", God (himself) had (quite correctly) ascertained they were called), and do something very special for it. The human that God (himself) had chosen to be the subject of this operation would be the Ancient Greek philosopher Socrates. God (himself) had appropriately (if somewhat dryly) entitled it "Project Socrates" and had charged gGod to "give it His all" as he put it (humouring gGod with a capital "H", which gGod, quick off the mark as always, straightaway picked up on as an entitlement and used from that point on). Project Socrates should, God (himself) had told gGod, involve giving something to Socrates that no other human had ever had before. It was to be the "best ever" day of his life and should involve not only plenty of thought-provoking activity, but the whole thing should be framed within novel and challenging (hopefully taxing) circumstances of enquiry. It was to be a day of great enlightenment, the like of which no human had ever known. A pretty clear brief he thought (even for the rather unpractical and easily distracted gGod).

So, working beneath the umbrella of God (himself)'s instruction, and bringing together His interests in philosophy, time, and always hoping to do something good, gGod got to it. He ascertained the whereabouts of Socrates and went straight to it with a readiness to, as God (himself) had instructed, "give it His all". Although He couldn't remember exactly what God (himself) had meant by that instruction, and was not quite sure exactly what the "all" involved meant, He nevertheless set about giving it.

CHAPTER 9

The Time Machine

When gGod had created earth, He had also created "man"—He referred to him as the first "human". In keeping with the general manner of His creative work and His tendency for the naming of things in catchy ways, He called him "human". This He did as, with a single word, He had brought him into being—*H*is *u*tterance of "man", led Him via His fondness for initial letters to the convenient and easy to remember "*h*(is) *u*(utterance)man"—"human". It was of course not the case that He had invented the word at all as it, in the form of "humanus" had already been coined and used by God (himself) to refer to the possibility of what it was that gGod would eventually come up with. Indeed, many of gGod's assumed originalities stemmed from the same source in a similarly confusing god-time sort of way. Anyway, irrespective of the etymology of the word "human" (and gGod's naive belief in the originality of much of His workings), He thought, as He reviewed the product of his creative work, that this one man, this human, would be enough. But He hadn't accounted for that man's powerful sexual desires (which He didn't think He'd created). So, to satisfy the man's need, He created another human (this time not from a single utterance but from part of the existing man) and made it possible (utilising the man's need) for them to produce more like themselves. This, on the "killing two birds with one stone" principle, would, because of this self-perpetuating system, also save Him much creative energy in the future. This meant that, by causal connectivity, all humans were part of His original "man"; "Man-ness", therefore was carried through the procreated generations.

Sometimes, as this process continued, there was an exceptional human and this emphasised the meaningful connection that could be traced back to gGod's (not exactly) original and exceptional creation: "H-u-man". gGod, who was of course outside the normal process of change over time, but always in some divinely mysterious way in god-time involved in perceiving all things (at any "time") perceivable, was always gratified by witnessing an exceptional human as it reminded Him of His (not exactly) original creative effort. One of these exceptional humans was the Ancient Greek philosopher Socrates. Another was a Saxon farrier called Tomkin Tompkins. Although Tomkin Tompkins easily drew gGod's attention, gGod's obligation to God (himself)'s edict meant that for the matter in hand it was Socrates who would be His main interest.

It was coming up to Socrates' last day of life on earth (as all humans were mortal their physical form stopped working after a fairly short span of time). So, now being driven by God (himself)'s proposed "Project Socrates", gGod was determined (and of course obliged) to make this last day of Socrates' the most special day that any human had experienced. He knew that this would place demands on areas of His conduct criticised by God (himself), so He quickly summoned all He could from His benevolent side—the "good" that He had been endowed with by God (himself), which since then had been indelibly, if somewhat erratically and unevenly, attached to His standard gGodly powers of omnipresence, omniscience, and omnipotence.

And, without further ado, and beginning to "give it His all" with a vengeance, in 399BC He turned up at the Athens State Prison, just outside the Agora, where Socrates had been imprisoned to await his execution (to be performed by the self-administered taking of a hemlock potion). gGod found His way inside without any trouble, though He did trip a couple of times as He descended some unlit steps—but for a god, the strictly human form He had adopted had many sensory disadvantages and, even with all His (creative) grounding, He still experienced the odd sensory hiccup.

As He was checking where to place His feet, He took the opportunity to look around. It was an unusual building, not a normal design for ancient Athens—less "composite" and more "stretched out", He thought. At the bottom of the steps, a central corridor flanked by five small rooms on one side and three slightly larger ones on the other, led to a walled courtyard at the far end. Still a bit unsure of His footing, gGod picked His way along the ill-lit corridor. He peered into one of the smaller rooms. It was packed! Socrates was sitting against the far wall surrounded by friends and admirers. There were certainly a lot of them, some of whom gGod suspected didn't even know Socrates. Squeezed up closest to him was Euryphro, a religious expert who held great certainty in his own opinions on "piety". Indeed, such were his convictions that he had decided only weeks before to charge his own father-in-law with manslaughter as he had bound a worker who had been responsible for the death of another in chains, and let him die of starvation in a ditch. Next to him was Crito and Crito's son Critobulus and next to him Phaedo. Then here was Xanthippe, Socrates' second wife, with one of their smaller children on her knee. She said something which Socrates clearly didn't like and he asked for her to be removed. Because of the crush, she was led out with difficulty. It made gGod think that Socrates might have been a trying husband, though from His own experience He suspected that Socrates might also have had a trying wife. And crammed into the room were other Athenians: Apollodorus, Hermogenes, Epigenes, Aeschines, Antisthenes, Ctesippus of Paeanis and Menexenus. And non-Athenians too. gGod recognised the young men Simmias and Cebes, both disciples of the Pythagorean Philolaus, Phaedondas of Thebes, and from Megara, there was Euclides and Terpsion. gGod noticed that Aristippus and Cleombrotus were not there, being in Aegina (an island that gGod had enjoyed some fine times in Himself). And there were some others whom (omnipotent or not) He did not recognise.

Plato (forty years Socrates' junior) couldn't be seen. gGod had expected him, then remembered that he had been feeling a little unwell and had kept away.

Crito, with tears in his eyes, stood up (with difficulty because of the lack of space) and spoke.

'Well, we are here at the end of it, my friend—life is closing for you. Let us honour you with a brief review of how it has been spent—a pause to picture it before it goes.' Everyone nodded in anticipation. 'Born into a world that valued beauty, courage and justice, you found yourself working with your father as a mason. A physical, dusty and exacting profession, eh, my friend?' Socrates smiled. 'As a boy, you say you started hearing a voice in your head that persisted throughout your life. It was a particular voice, one that taught you caution, one that, you said, "Always discourages me from doing what I'm about to do, never encourages me".When it came your time, you served the state as a soldier. Here, they say, you marched barefoot in the snow without concern, seemingly being impervious to extremes of heat, cold, hunger and thirst. After this you took on a life that embraced poverty and, noticeably continuing your disregard for bodily comfort, you were often to be found standing for hours in all manner of circumstances in a trancelike state. Then, for which we are all thankful, you embarked on what became your lifelong commitment—not to what we would generally call a "philosophy", but to a system of interaction with others based upon persistent, and dare I say it, sometimes incautious questioning.' Socrates tightened his lips and nodded. 'Your method of enquiry, often ironic, you described as "midwifery"; helping those with whom you spoke to reach conclusions of their own—to "give birth" to their ideas. Your later life coincided with an unstable time for Athens—indeed a time of crisis. Defeated by Sparta after many years of conflict, then taken over for a short while by the "Thirty Tyrants", Athens did not form a welcoming background for your insistently challenging nature. By the time the Tyrants were deposed and democracy was reinstalled, Athens had already fallen into its present decline. And during the period we now find ourselves in, after the Tyrants have lost power, you have been what some would call an irritant to the authorities. No, Socrates, you have made no friends there. Your single-minded preoccupation with what virtue is and your constantly challenging manner have made you a ready target for authorities unsure of their own grip on power. And so you found yourself up against those in power and ultimately you were brought to trial. There, before your judges, you insisted that your own wisdom lay in your admission that you knew nothing, "I know that I know nothing," you said. And your insistence that we have to die in order to attain wisdom finds itself well placed here, where life has brought you—to imprisonment and awaiting death at your own hand by drinking a mixture containing a fatal dose of hemlock. Such sadness. My dear friend Socrates, with your death we will all die in some part with you.'

They all sat, silently moved by Crito's summary of Socrates' life. Socrates laid his hand affectionately on Crito's arm. Tears glistened in the corners of Crito's eyes.

gGod nodded knowingly but did not intrude. Instead He carried on along the corridor to the walled courtyard at its end. He looked around, checking the space, peering into the corners and nodding His approval. Then, with a sudden burst of pleasure at what He saw, He clapped His hands together in a most satisfied way and set about His task.

After some diligent, and rather noisy creating, He stood back and allowed Himself to be gratified with the result—a hotchpotch assembly of many different types of material and style wrought into different shapes and roughly resembling a large four-poster bed with a chair at its centre. The whole assembly swayed from side to side. A few sparks and crackles emanated from it, but those subsided and settled and after that all was still and quiet.

gGod then went back and stood at the door where Socrates and the others were talking. Irrespective of the sheer numbers, and with the exception of Socrates, with an easy wave of one hand He put them all to sleep so that He could give His attention exclusively to the subject of His project.

He stepped into the room.

'Socrates! Soc! Σωκράτης! Σωκ! It's good to find you in such rude health,' said gGod cheerily. 'Two hundred and eighty one votes for; two hundred and twenty against, eh, Soc. Well,' He said, having moved quickly from His Ancient Greek salutation to something entirely more colloquial, 'you can't win 'em all!'

'And you are?' asked Socrates, standing, shoeless as usual and seemingly not too perturbed by the sudden sleeping of his friends and the entrance of this rather larger than life character dressed in a most unfamiliar manner.

'Oh, Soc! It's Me! Me! gGod! Come, come! Soc! gGod! Me!'

Socrates cocked his head to one side and looked at gGod with some degree of puzzlement—well, puzzlement bordering on disbelief; well, actually disbelief overtaken by complete incredulity. However, resisting Aristophanes' gibe in *The Clouds* about him disbelieving in God (even though his resistance in this case was to disbelieving in the wrong god), he decided to proceed by accepting the apparent reality and press on in his normal questioning mode.

'What have You done to my friends?' he asked as if their sudden somnambulism in his company was a fairly normal occurrence that needed only a simple answer.

gGod picked up unusually quickly on the simplicity and tailored His initial response accordingly.

'I've just let them rest a while. You and I have things to do, Soc. And I wanted it to be private.' Then, getting into His normal more thoughtfully involved stride, 'You see, as you know, it's your last day, Soc, and I'm determined to make it your best. It's lucky that I found you at all! I know I'm infallible and all that, but I was made late by following the signs and going up to those caves west of the Acropolis, the ones cut into the Hill of the Nymphs and the Hill of the Muses. Yes! Me! Making a mistake like that. Ancient Athenian Tourist Information! Anyway, are you ready?'

'gGod?' said Socrates, struggling to catch up.

'Yes, gGod. gGod the creator. Omnipresent, all knowing, all powerful, and infallible! And a bit philosophical!' He chuckled. 'Oh, and good! Mustn't forget that!'

'But you are—'

'Like a human? Well, it's humans that are like Me, actually. Made in My image, and so on. Do you like the ruff?' He flicked at it with His fingers. Socrates was lost for a reply. 'Here, take My hand, friend. I've something to show you. I think you'll find it very interesting.'

Socrates, still not caught-up but ever-trusting and always one for a new challenge, stretched out his hand. gGod took it and led him out of the cell and along the corridor to the walled courtyard. gGod caused some additional light (when He did this He wondered why He hadn't done it when He'd stumbled on the steps on the way in). There, in the centre of the chamber, was a strange contraption the like of which Socrates (nor anyone else, should they have had the opportunity) had never seen (obviously, because gGod had only just created it) or even imagined (four-poster beds certainly had not been invented in his time, so he couldn't even place it as similar to anything he knew).

'Wow!' exclaimed Socrates in an unusual demonstration of non-Ancient-Grecian awe.

‘Wow indeed, Soc! Get an eyeful of that. Your machine! This is your Machina ex Deo! It’s My gift for you, to celebrate your life, and make the very best of your last day.’

‘I don’t quite understand.’

‘Sorry, Soc. That’s Latin. Your “ἀπὸ μηχανῆς θεός” I should say. That probably makes more sense. Yes? All these different languages. Though I know I’ve only got Myself to blame. That Babel mob. They really got up My nose! The cheek of it! Trying to break into My “heaven”, they called it—My “haven” actually; just somewhere to go for a bit of peace and quiet. Really! And entry there is strictly limited—to Me actually. And, of course, the wife. Perhaps “peace and quiet” was an overstatement.’

‘Oh,’ said Socrates, unable to follow gGod’s connection of thoughts.

‘Anyway,’ continued gGod, getting back to the matter in hand. ‘It’s so good to see you. And for Me to meet the man himself. Socrates!’ He paused to absorb something of the moment. ‘There’ve not been many like you—outstanding reminders of the first man (*My* first man)—and I can assure you of that!’ Another pause for Him to absorb a little more of the thrill of the event. ‘It’ll be interesting to get to know you, even if we don’t have too much time (in your sense of the term, it being your last day and all that). And to find out which Socrates you truly are, eh?’ He chuckled in acknowledgement of a joke completely lost on Socrates.

Socrates managed another weak ‘Oh.’

gGod continued with some explanation.

‘Are you Xenophon’s figure of history? Are you Aristophanes’ character in a play? Are you Plato’s philosopher? Will the real Socrates please stand up! Eh Soc?’ Socrates stared. gGod did not wait for a response and moved on to the matter in hand. ‘So, Soc, what d’you think?’ He spread His arms out towards the strangely mixed up jumble of bits and pieces that formed, for Socrates certainly, just a confused heap of unfamiliar clutter. ‘So here it is, Soc. All for you. A specially created device. An engineering achievement that is…' He added with a forced yet still flourishing attempt at modesty, '…though I say it Myself, beyond compare! A machine to make your last day the very best of your life.'

At last, Socrates found it in himself to speak in a meaningful way.

'Can there be such good fortune?' he asked in his soft but well managed voice.

'I think there can, dear friend. I *can* call you "friend", can't I?' Socrates nodded. 'You must look for the best health even as it all ends. When the soul is at last released, only then will you have true being, and so the best of health.'

Socrates stood in wonder before the device—the "machine". He bent to a part of it seemingly inquisitively, though actually thinking about gGod's wise words on death.

'Better have that cock ready, eh?' he said.

'Yes, indeed, Soc. Don't worry, I won't forget. It's on My list. Yes, it'll be ready. A-doodle-doo! A-doodle-doo!'

Socrates did wonder for a moment why gGod should need a list if He was infallible, but he dismissed it as a concern not worth pursuing and instead, and ignoring gGod's cockerel impression (now being accompanied by lifting His elbows rhythmically in a cockerel-crowing sort of way), paced around the device, bending down and looking up at and poking into its various parts. He could see now that whatever a "machine" was, this, if it was that, was not just a random mixture of bits and pieces but a coherent whole (even though the coherence of the whole was at the moment completely outside his comprehension).

He started to take it in. The bits and pieces were held together by other bits and pieces inside a framework. A chair was worked into the middle of it. A canopy was supported by four marble columns together forming a square shape. Brightly painted figures adorned the ceiling that the canopy made: maidens with lyres, men lying back on grassy banks being fed grapes by nymphs, gods in clouds watching from above. In front of the chair was a chunk of perforated metal on a long arm hung out towards it. Just above that a shiny rectangular plate of some sort was supported by a light metal chassis. Against the chair seat a long and heavy-looking lever stood out from the floor. On top of the lever was a shiny knob. On top of the knob was a red glass bead (unknown to Socrates, a light, at the moment unlit).

'It looks…' Socrates stopped when he realised that he had no idea what it might be that it looked, and was lost for finishing his sentence.

'Magnificent?' asked gGod beaming with omniscient pride.

'Magnificent, yes. Puzzling too.' Socrates made a show of scrutinising it more closely though still nothing he saw added up to anything he could comprehend. 'Complicated as well.'

'It has to be. There're a lot of factors to take into account. And many modifications were necessary to bring it to its present stage. Creation isn't as straightforward as some people think, you know. Not at all!'

'Oh! Were there problems?'

gGod threw His head back and laughed.

'Problems! My dear Soc, you wouldn't believe the problems! Some of the early trials were, well, I have to say, decidedly life-threatening.'

'Life-threatening?'

'Well, if you're to travel in it, it needs to be safe. Everything must be checked rigorously. And, well, some of the checks revealed…' Socrates cocked his head in an enquiring sort of fashion. '…that some things needed a little extra thought. Still, everything's all ironed out now!'

Socrates, getting into the swing of things, felt concerned to pursue the safety angle.

'So you believe it's safe now?'

'Yes, without doubt. They were just teething problems. Nothing to worry about. Though, I have to admit it hasn't been what you would call *fully* tested, well…not…yet…but I'm pretty sure it'll do the job…when it has been.'

Socrates was getting increasingly involved, and increasingly concerned about the singular quality of safety.

'So it *is* safe?'

'Yes, as houses! Well, at least as far as I can tell. It's My first one, of course. And sometimes things seem to have a will of their own, don't you think.'

Socrates, really thinking that (an omnipotent) gGod should be able to do a bit better than "at least as far as I can tell" nevertheless pressed on.

'Did it take a long time to assemble?'

'Not really. I did it just before I came along to collect you.'

'But the trials. You said there had been early trials, and many modifications.'

'Well, what I meant was that I'd switched it on.'

'And the problems.'

'Well, I had trouble switching it off.'

Socrates' frowning face revealed a mixture of puzzlement, confusion and general lack of knowing what on earth gGod was talking about. However, his inquiring nature was foremost and he tried his best to suppress his scepticism. He smiled and nodded in a that-all-seems-to-be-in-order-then sort of way.

'Right,' said gGod, keen to move on and bolstered by Socrates' nodding approval. 'Let's get going. First, a general briefing.' He waved His arm proudly. 'This, my dear Soc, is a time machine—well, *the* time machine as it's the only one ever built. Yes, time machine. Hard to believe, I know. But it's a fully functional (as far as I can tell, and who needs an assurance more than that—from gGod, the creator), first ever machine for travelling in time. Well I say "in" time though of course it's more travelling "with" time, or really "outside" what you might generally, and incorrectly, think time is. But we'll get to that—later. First, let Me give you the run down. Here, please sit in it. You'll find it easier to become acquainted with the controls if you get into the driving seat from the word go—learning in practice is the motto here. It *is* a bit complicated, I admit that, and even *I* still find some of the controls a little difficult to understand. This lever here, for example, now, what was that for? Ah, yes! Of course! Holding onto!'

Socrates was not much reassured, but at gGod's invitation he crawled over the mass of pipes and wires and tried his best to settle down onto the chair. The seat and back were covered in a heavy brocade with figures sewn into it that looked like a representation of a battle between soldiers with bows and arrows. He imagined it depicting the Greeks battling year after year outside the walls of Troy. Socrates turned to gGod, but didn't get the chance to ask if his assumption was correct.

'It's a tapestry of the Norman Conquest of Britain. That was one in the eye for the English, eh, Soc?' He chuckled. 'Oh, I'm sorry, you're not familiar with things in what you call your future. *I*'ve got a different access to things in "time", of course. You'll get used to some of it as we go on. Well, that's part of our purpose, after all.'

'Oh,' said Socrates as he wriggled around to make himself as comfortable as possible. It was a struggle. Whichever way he turned there always seemed to be something sticking into one part of his body or another. It disappointed his natural bent for a comfortable place to sit or recline—an appropriately inclined grassy bank being his favourite.

'Sorry if it's a bit uncomfortable. I haven't had much chance to work on the ergonomics. It's been as much as I could do even to get it to work at all. Well, I say "work" but of course, as I've already said, it hasn't been *fully* tested yet. But it does turn on! And off!'

Socrates' hard won sense of (barely) moderate reassurance left him temporarily. He started to get up, thinking that he might prefer not to sit in the machine at all but, as he grabbed the lever to help himself get up, the whole thing shuddered and as his natural curiosity (and fear) took control, his body went rigid and kept him in place.

'Try not to touch anything! Not yet!' said gGod, hurriedly reaching forward to move Socrates' hand away from the now vibrating lever.

Socrates eased back and tried to settle himself.

'What's this for?' he asked, albeit rather tentatively as he pointed to the large, shiny red bead at the end of the lever.

gGod ignored the question. He looked at Socrates' position on the seat and nodded in a positive way.

'You look as if you and it were made for each other, Soc—man and machine, perfectly matched. Though, it *was* after all made for you, so that's not surprising. At least half the statement is correct, eh Soc? And as you can see you'll be well sheltered.' He pointed up to the canopy. 'It seemed to Me that the machine had to be something you could get inside—sense of security and all that. And I thought a well-decorated ceiling would go very well. I found out at an early stage that if we (though of course I mean *you*), are going to move *in* (or *with*, or *outside*) time, then we, that is, *you*, need to carry on going forwards into the 'after' in *B*-time. *B*-time, you ask?'

Socrates shook his head to affirm that he hadn't, and didn't intend to.

'I'm glad you did, ask that is.' Blank response. 'Oh, you didn't! Not to worry, I'm sure you were getting ready to,' He was wrong. 'Humans owe the definition of time in this way to the philosopher McTaggart—John McTaggart Ellis McTaggart, the last

British idealist they came to call him. Like yourself, Soc, he was an insightful and mystic philosopher. It's a pity you couldn't meet up. I think you could chew over a few knotty questions. Anyway, *B*-time refers to anything connected to the relation between "before" and "after". Unfortunately that brings with it the erroneous connotation of change. But that's a separate question. Anyway, the going forwards in *B*-time thing. Yes, you need to move together with your own life-rate even though you might be travelling at a different rate to what we (well, *I* really) might call "machine-rate". You wouldn't want to get unusually old if you travelled forward into the future (which is impossible anyway) or unusually young, if you travelled backwards into the past (which you can't do either) as you yourself travel. You wouldn't want that now, would you.'

Socrates was beginning to catch up.

'So I can't actually travel *in* time even though, if this is a sort of time travelling machine, one would assume it is built to allow me to do just that?'

'Yes, you can travel in time, but only in a "sort-of-way". As gGod, I can of course perceive all moments in time, forwards, backwards—whichever way I choose. And I can be *involved* in any of those temporal moments. But this will not be the case for you. The machine will take you to different parts of time, but you will not be able to interact with anything there in the normal sense. You will be a sort-of-watcher only. No one will see you (well not exactly) but you will be able to *feel* involved more than just listen in or watch what is going on. What's going on, you might ask?' Socrates didn't; he was still very much at the "sort-of" stage for all of what was going on. 'What…' said gGod readily picking up on Socrates' "sort-of" take on the subject. '…I've done is placed my man—*the* man, the *first* man—to feature in everything you sort-of-feel-involved-in-hear-see-well-not-exactly experience. He'll have different names and appear in different ways. But though he will be the same, he will always be an image of My first creation—My first man. In a way it'll be like a play—an audience-participation job. You'll be up close, as if you were in an audience, but you will in some way feel part of it. And in this play there will be quite a number of acts—more than Aristotle would suggest for proper tragic impact. Mind you, on that, sometimes I don't take some of Aristotle's thoughts too seriously—he was a bit of a know-it-all at times. Even so, a lot of what he said he knew he got right. Pity about his theory of emergence though. Things appearing from nowhere out of nothing! With just a thought! Really! Anyway, you'll be able to follow the "ways of the world", I think I'll call them, as you follow these "acts". But you've probably realised straightaway that this means we're faced with another problem.' Socrates hadn't realised anything of the kind, indeed anything at all, and certainly not straight away. In fact, he was practising his thesis of knowing nothing to perfection. 'If you go forward, say, half a day, and the journey has taken you, say, a minute, although you have only lived a further minute, everything outside the time machine might have moved on, say, half a day. With me?' Socrates looked glazed. 'This means that the earth has travelled quite a long way. To start with, it has made half a rotation. In addition, it has moved a long way in its circuit of the sun (that is, 1/365.25 times the number of miles it is to the sun. That is 1/365.25 times 93,000,000 miles—I prefer the imperial measure; twelve is a much more useful number than ten—so that's 254,620.123 miles). So this means, and not wishing to be too technical, in one minute the earth has rotated fifteen arc-minutes around the sun, meaning of course that every four minutes there is one degree of rotation. Now, the distance that the earth will travel in one year is, measuring this in metric (a measurement system, I must say I think inferior to most other methods, even so, here I'll use it for the sake of variety—and it's better than the cubit anyway) 940 million kilometres, which is approximately 6.7 times the average distance between the earth and the sun (whether it's imperial or metric or even cubits). On top of this, my friend, the solar system itself has moved, and also this galaxy has moved. Indeed I can tell you that within only a minute everything that there is (and in the world of things that is a lot more than just this galaxy) will have moved quite a long way! In fact, the red shift distance the universe travels each year is 7.26 billion kilometres. Yes, 7.26 billion kilometres! And that's in kilometres! Just imagine what it would be in cubits!'

'Miles? Kilometres? Cubits?'

'Yes, units of measurement. I created the cubits as a standard measurement to begin with—in the early days—and that worked very well. But after the trouble I had with that Babel lot I thought I'd extend the variety of languages I'd inflicted on them into a variety of measurement systems as well; thought it'd just add to the confusion—bit of a joke really.'

'I see,' said Socrates, just to show that he was involved, though it was obvious he didn't see anything of the sort. He thought of saying "miles?" and "kilometres?" again, even "cubits", but put the idea quickly aside.

'So, if our time machine is positioned here in this courtyard (as it is), and you travelled to another point in time, unless the machine moved it would within minutes be in say somewhere in Australia, or more probably would be adrift somewhere in space. It could easily have got as far as FX19! Yes, even that far.'

'Australia? FX19?'

'Yes, as far as that! So, Soc, our time machine has got to move. But it has not got to move fast. Indeed, if it moved fast we would have to get involved in Relativity Theory, and we don't want that, do we. So to avoid this I've made sure that it moves only at a *moderate* speed.'

'Relativity Theory?' Socrates asked, really just deploying his questioning mode rather than asking anything that might lead to any consequent enlightenment.

'Yes, Relativity Theory; sadly based on Newton's acceptance of time as real and regular. Not everybody realises that Einstein was a Newtonian. And of course that involves Minkowski and his none too considered coining of the term "space-time". As if space-time is either spacial or temporal! Really! He knew, of course, that it was neither, and he was just stuck for calling it anything else, but I think he could have done better than "space-time".'

Socrates screwed up his face in utter befuddlement.

'Newton? Einstein? Minkowski?'

He couldn't even think of pursuing the idea "space-time", and as for the apparently poor use of the terms of which it was composed, he was at a loss for any terms by which to express himself.

'Yes, remarkable, eh, Soc? Anyway, this need for the time machine to move (I emphasise, at a *moderate* speed), means that some of its competitor machines (real or imaginary) are quite literally, non-starters—they would never get off the ground.' gGod laughed at His joke. Socrates tried but failed. 'H. G. Wells might have thought it amusing to sit and watch the dresses on the manikin in the shop window changing with the seasons and the fashions, but in sitting there like that, George, Wells' time traveller, would soon have found himself wallowing in empty space.'

Socrates was getting increasingly confused. gGod was piling in with references that meant nothing to him. Just for a moment he thought of asking for clarification, but then decided against it—things were baffling enough as they were without the complication of answers. Something simply along the lines of being an affirmation, with maybe just a hint of enquiry, would be best.

'I'm sure,' he said instead. 'Perhaps even as far as FX19.'

'Yes, indeed. FX19. Yes. Good. Good. Nevertheless,' continued gGod. 'Wells was right about the *speed* of travel — it should not be *too* fast! However, not a caution shared by all experimenters, well actually fantasisers about time travel, I must say. But Dr Emmett Brown's machine in *Back to the Future* (that's a film, by the way), for example, is generally a bit better on this. The idea of a car moving is helpful. However, the de Lorean (that is the car with the time-travelling device on board) is moving for the wrong reasons. Dr Brown's idea was somehow to approach an optimum speed at which time travel would "suddenly" occur. But he was badly wrong on that front. *Badly* wrong, Soc. Time travel will not "suddenly" occur. Any movement our time machine makes must be carefully calculated to compensate for the earth's, the solar system's, this galaxy's as well as all other galaxies' movement (and the movement of every living or inanimate thing that exists in any of these places)—for the whole of creation, in other words. A small personal computer is sufficient for the job, but of course, you've guessed that already, I'm sure, Soc. Dr Brown was also incorrect in assuming that it did not matter in which direction his car moved. Of *course* it does. If you go the wrong way the compensation problems would be so much more complicated. *Our* personal computer has an inertial guidance system to work out the necessary compensations according to the direction we (that is, *you*) go (and anything else that's going on). In fact, here it is. And…' holding up the lump of perforated metal, '…or at least here's the microphone for contacting the computer, the voice activated interface.'

Socrates couldn't hold himself back any more, though only going for the last thing mentioned.

'The voice activated what?'

'Interface! The voice activated interface. I've spent a lot of time on this particular aspect (no pun intended—"time", "time"). I've made it as human as I can, Soc, knowing well your appreciation of the human style. And it's not just any old human voice, but something with a bit of personality—dare I say it, character even. He's been given a name too, well *him* a name. He's called "IgnatiusM". The "M" is silent—I think that adds even *more* character, don't you?. And I've embellished the machine itself in a way that I thought might make you feel at ease (if for any reason, unlikely as that is, that any of this time travelling business causes you a little concern). Yes, I've tried to engender something of those early days in Alopeke. I expect you recall them with some affection. All the dust from your father's workshop, eh, Soc? Brought up into the life of the stonemason. Got a good covering of it yourself, I expect—dust. So there'll be plenty of dust to help you feel at home. Well, anyway, on the time-travelling *experience*, I couldn't get everything exactly right—no time to test it that far—but I think there's enough there for you to pick up on what I would call the "scenic intention". It was a complicated part of the project, and I admit I had a bit of trouble with some of it. And, as I've said, there are some elements of it that still aren't exactly right. Nothing,' He added hastily in an over-reassuring way, 'that should affect the overall performance of the machine, though. And don't worry. I'll be working on sorting out anything I might have missed. IgnatiusM will be able to advise anyway. So, I think that's all angles covered—more or less.'

Socrates didn't look particularly or even generally reassured. 'What about—'

'The power source?' replied gGod, missing Socrates' intended but cut-short question by a mile. 'I'm glad you've asked, Soc. I hadn't forgotten. As if! Of course, if the time machine is to *do* something, well, anything really, then, as you point out, it must have energy to *do* it. The Victorians, of whom Wells was one, by the way, were fascinated by something called "electromagnetism". Good word that, eh? One of My best, I think. Well, anything that shone or whirred or caused a spark seemed to excite their belief that somewhere within things there was some amazing force. And such a force could only be released by friction, they thought—by rubbing the genie's lamp, so to speak. I've used a similar principle here. But don't expect to get results by a gentle caress of a magic bottle, Soc. I don't deal in magic! For Wells, having a "magic" crystal was all that was needed to get his machine going; push it into the right hole, spin something with numbers on and the magic force would propel you, well George anyway, into the distant reaches of time. It's never going to work like that in any respect, I'm afraid. Dr Brown was of course influenced by twentieth century Earth science. But this still involved belief in some sort of "magic" essence, and, I'm sure you'll agree that anyone standing next to a lump of plutonium would find it hard to dispute. Don't you think, Soc?'

Socrates widened his eyes without even being able to summon a nod. He was lost with everything: Victorians, Wells (he'd been mentioned already but that hadn't helped), electromagnetism, sparks, genies, Dr Brown, plutonium!

gGod, now caught up with the (for Socrates, future) history of it all, pressed on.

'But twentieth century Earth science had an affliction, yes, I call it an "affliction", that led them into much worse problems than the genie's lamp. They believed in (ever) smaller components of matter; in fact they were obsessed by them. And that's not just the atoms that you would be familiar with, Soc—the components of the theory of one of your predecessors, Democratus—but really, *really* small bits! For these scientists the smaller the bits, the better. Indeed if they were so small that they had no mass then they were the best smallest bits of all the smallest bits. But for these afflicted, scientist-mathematical investigators, the best components were the ones that didn't even *have* any bits. They really loved these: if their particles were without mass then they had what they called "spin", if they did not have spin then they had what they called "charm", and if they were totally bereft of any measurable quantity at all, and if when you tried to find them, they were never even where you looked for them they were called "quanta". This last category was the most fascinating of all to these scientists and because mass-less, un-spinning, charmless and unpredictable matter was impossible for humans to locate (even though their mathematical calculations said it must be there) then the reason for this must not be that it didn't exist, but that its sheer speed made it impossible to get to grips with. So, accordingly, these fundamental particles apparently (or not apparently) went very, very fast and scientists built a lot of very expensive experiments to make other things go very, very fast in the hope of catching some of these elusive very, very fast bits in the further hope that they might prove that they did, against all practically-based odds, in fact exist. This led people to believe that because space and time were blended in Einsteinian physics, if you made particles go very, *very* fast then you must somehow be affecting the speed of time. Thus Dr Brown's de Lorean car goes fast, catches time up and travels with it (or something like that). But, Soc, you must realise that this is no good either.'

'Oh, I see,' said Socrates, scratching his head—a fly had landed on it.

'A working time machine will not sit around like a lump of bits waiting for the next day to arrive. And it will not accelerate down a road in any direction we choose in the hope of squeezing through some sort of temporal porthole. Honestly! Some people!'

Socrates shook his head in agreement.

'Indeed.'

'Indeed, indeed. So, what will it be like, you ask?' He didn't. 'Well, my friend, you're sitting in it!'

'So, the energy source?' Socrates said, simply repeating the term gGod had started out trying to explain, while at the same time working hard to get into the swing of things.

'You are a card, Soc! Don't tease! The first thing is that, as I've said, you have got to travel *with* our machine. That may seem obvious, but is not as obvious as it *does* seem. More precisely the machine has got to do the travelling and somehow we, or *you*, have got to be taken along at the same time as it (no pun intended). So, it needs to be big enough to hold us, well *you*, and sufficiently enclosing to encapsulate us, or *you*. By the way, I hope you like the marble columns. For simplicity I've stuck to a standard Doric design. And the painted ceiling drape? Adds class don't you think? Hylas and those beautiful Naiads—he really was easy game, wasn't he! And he only wanted a drink! Anyway, you will need to be able to see the monitor of our, *your*, personal computer. That's the rectangular shiny thing in front of you. And you'll also need to be able to reach the microphone—that's the perforated metal chunk on the end of that arm—so that you can communicate with IgnatiusM, the interface. And when you want to start and stop the machine you'll need to pull on the big lever, here in front of the chair, Soc. I've made everything pretty intuitive. Couldn't be simpler.'

'This lever?' Socrates gingerly touched the end of the lever.

'Yes, quite right. And, yes, I can see that you're still thinking about the energy source. Well, I've equipped the machine with what they called at one time a "battery", and a "transformer" to transform the "voltage" to the right level to make the personal computer work. Everything else can run easily direct from the, what at the time, was called, the "battery". There aren't many things, just some general lighting and a bit of illumination for the instruments (few as they are). And that battery will also run the small light I've placed on the left hand side of the chair. That could come in very handy if, say, you dropped your sandwich (I have created a small box attached to the right hand side of the chair with ever-replenishing refreshments and supplies) on the floor and couldn't find it because for the moment the machine is stuck in solid rock! Only joking! That's not going to happen. Who drops their sandwich! "Ah, but surely the battery does not drive the machine into other parts of time!" you may say. And, no, you would be right. It does *not*. You are correct (and I repeat, there's absolutely no need to worry about being trapped in solid rock—as far as I can tell, anyway), the battery is *not* the power source that will allow you to move about in time. To enable this, we need something that isn't a magic crystal and something that isn't some sort of weird "warp drive" that simply makes us go fast. And to find this source of power we must recall what lies behind the illusion of time, what time really is—yes, you have it, *C*-time!'

'*C*-time,' repeated Socrates neither in the form of a question nor statement, but more in the manner of a bemused mimic.

'Yes, *C*-time is the term McTaggart used (well, he just called it the *C*-series) to describe the real nature of non-temporal "time". You see, people tend to use "time" to measure intervals between things, or, for example, to work out how long it is until the next train arrives. But this is "chronology", and chronology misleads us into thinking of time in ways that it is not. *C*-time explains time not in a past, present, future sort of way like some remorseless river (*A*-time, McTaggart called that, and showed correctly, even if not too convincingly, that its elements are self-contradictory), but by ascribing apparent moments in time to what in truth is really a perception. Yes, Soc, back to the old perception business. What we need in order to make our machine work is what I've called, rather originally I think, the "*C*-drive". The *C*-drive is something which will accelerate or decelerate the "flow" of perceptions. In some ways, this is a bit like the experience you have sometimes when going to sleep; that sensation you can have when things are rushing past or broken up in a way that doesn't equate with perception in your normal waking world. So, when you start the machine and the *C*-drive kicks in you will be able to perceive parts of My creation that are otherwise outside your time. You will see things happening, hear conversations and commentaries, come to know of things, Soc—really come to *know* them. Yes, Soc, this last day of your life will not only be the best for you, but the best that any person has ever known. It will be both completing and complete.'

Socrates eased back in the chair, for the first time looking a little bit relaxed. He patted the ever-replenishing refreshments box, hoping for some added reassurance. And got it, although he had no idea where it came from.

'I think I'm ready,' he said with an assured optimism the source of which was completely untraceable.

'Good,' said gGod. 'I'll just run briefly through the instructions for actually making the machine go. Then you can be on your way!'

Socrates, now, building upon his confidence and seized with keen-ness, grabbed the lever that stuck up in front of him.

'Ready when you are,' he said, patting the refreshment box again.

'Right. You turn it on by pulling the lever back.' gGod pointed to the lever. 'The microphone switches on automatically.' He pointed again to the lever. 'And that's how you speak to IgnatiusM.' He pointed again but still to the lever and not to the microphone. 'IgnatiusM will give you all the guidance you need. You can look at the screen here, to get the full flavour of things. I've added some extra touches on that score too.' He pointed, this time to large ceramic urns perforated with holes hanging on chains from the four corners of the canopy roof. 'And don't forget the navigation system.' He nodded towards a large, flat wooden board fixed to the left hand side of the chair. 'That's crucial!' That He pointed to the microphone as He said this did not really fill Socrates with time-travelling confidence, but he was too keen to get going now to worry about details. gGod continued with enthusiasm, still pointing to the microphone, 'Yes, pull the lever, the *C*-drive will kick in, and hey presto! Oh! And if you should need it, this is the emergency button.' He pointed to the microphone again. 'So, Soc, nothing more to think about. Give her a test run! I'll see you later! (No pun intended).'

Notwithstanding his ready keen-ness, Socrates' fragile confidence in some of the technical details took a downturn at the mention of the emergency button. But, not wishing to be seen in any way as a spoilsport, he grabbed the lever and, using all his strength (for the lever was very stiff), pulled it back towards him.

'Let the good times roll,' he said without the slightest detectable quaver in his voice.

There was a heavy grinding sound, a shuddering vibration and, with Socrates barely managing to hang onto the lever, the whole machine started shaking.

'Oh! I almost forgot!' shouted gGod as He hurriedly swept a small pile of strangely shaped wooden pieces from the wooden board attached to the chair into a poorly made cloth bag with a long carrying strap He had just created for the purpose. 'Here! You'll need these!'

He thrust the bag at Socrates, not noticing that one of the pieces had fallen under the chair, (and as God (himself) had failed to warn Him about this, He would not have bothered about it anyway). Socrates nearly fell from the chair as he let go of the lever with one hand so that gGod could drape the bag strap over his shoulder.

'What are they for?' he shouted over the noise of the machine, as with some trouble he regained his two-handed grip on the lever.

'You'll find out! IgnatiusM will brief you.'

With his teeth chattering along with the erratic, shuddering vibrations of the machine, Socrates could barely get the words out as he shouted, this time even louder than before.

'Then let the good times roll! Again!'

'May your God, that is Me, gGod, be with you!' gGod shouted back as He walked out of the room, not noticing the wooden jigsaw piece He had missed still lying under the chair.

CHAPTER 10

The test run—meeting IgnatiusM

The moment Socrates took hold of the lever everything around him began shaking in the most unsettling of ways. First he was thrown forward in the chair, then he was tossed to the left, then he was hurled to the right. Then he was vibrated all over, then he was deafened by booming noises that built to a crescendo before suddenly stopping then suddenly starting again. Then there was silence, which only served to confuse him more, for when it stopped it was replaced by a whirring noise that caused his innards to vibrate. And then the chair began jolting up and down and he was jolted up and down with it. It was as if the whole world had come loose, was determined to fall apart and so take him with it. But nevertheless, battling with his fears, and the general terror of it all, he hung onto the lever while at the same time trying not to be thrown free from the tapestry-covered chair. Then the whirring was replaced by low crashing noises and erratic flashes of light as the marble pillars rocked from side to side. But still, staring ahead, his whole body seized with tension, he hung on. Then, with a great, wrenching judder and a sudden and sickening thump, everything stopped. With glazed eyes staring ahead, he waited for it to resume, but it didn't.

Socrates was gasping for breath. He slumped forward. His hands, unable to hang on any longer, slowly slid down the lever. Sweat dripped from his forehead onto the microphone that swayed sideways on its mounting. The screen had become loose and wobbled and flickered. The marble columns swayed and the painted figures on the flapping ceiling drape moved about as if they were alive. There was a broken humming noise from every part of the machine and, although it had stopped bouncing up and down, the chair was still rocking from side to side.

He had no idea where he was. He wondered if he was dead. Suddenly something, a recollection, jumped back into his mind. Was he recalling a past life? No! He was riding gGod's time machine!

Socrates thought he heard someone speaking to him. He wondered if it was gGod. Then he realised it could not be gGod—it lacked the timbre of gGod's booming tone. So who was it? It kept telling him to speak into the microphone.

'Speak into the microphone,' it said. 'Speak into the microphone.'

Socrates couldn't remember what the microphone was. He looked hopefully at the lever, then the screen, and then he remembered that the microphone was the lump of perforated metal on the cantilevered arm that stuck out from behind the screen. It was still swaying. He tried to match its movement by moving his face in front of it. When he had (more or less) synchronised his movement with it, he spoke.

'Hello. Is there anybody there?'

He felt foolish. He shook his head.

A crackling pause. Then the machine started shaking again. Socrates looked up and saw the urns that were attached to the corners of the roof canopy spinning on their chains. Dust began flying out from the holes in them. It fell like a mist around him, covering everything in a grey film. He recalled what gGod had said about the dust, but he didn't in any way feel at home.

More crackling, then the voice again.

'Ah! At last we've made contact,' it said.

'Who are you? *Where* are you?' Socrates asked still moving his head in an effort to keep his mouth in front of the microphone.

More crackling and a fresh, heavier sprinkling of dust from the urns. Still he didn't feel at home.

‘I am here to guide you. Remember? gGod told you about the interface with the machine Well, I am it! I *am* the interface.’

‘You’re…’

‘Yes, I’m IgnatiusM. It’s good to meet you at last, Socrates. gGod has told me a lot about you. In fact, He’s been going on about you for ages—ever since He said *He* came up with the idea for your last day (Mm!). You really have got to be the luckiest human ever! You’ve got the pieces have you?’ Socrates looked blank. ‘The pieces! Socrates! The pieces!’ Socrates raised his eyebrows, but sill retained the blankness. ‘Here! Socrates! Look! They’re in your bag. All safe, I hope. We don’t want to lose any do we. Take one out and we can get started.’

Socrates had forgotten about the bag. In fact, he’d forgotten just about everything. But now he felt the weight of it on his shoulder and remembered gGod hanging it there just before he pulled the lever. He looked inside it. It was filled with large flat wooden pieces with oddly curved edges. He felt amongst them and this added complete mystification to his blankness.

‘Ignatius…’ said Socrates, not knowing how to take it any further.

‘Yes, as I’ve already said, my name is IgnatiusM. The “M” is silent.’

‘What “M”?’

There was a silence that spoke of puzzlement. Had IgnatiusM been visible he would have been scratching his head. A few moments for consideration passed, then a reply.

‘Strange, don’t you think, Socrates, that you didn’t pick up on that when I said my name?’

‘On what?’

‘That the “M” is silent.’

‘If you did not speak it then I don’t believe I could have heard it. I could not have heard the absence of something. And surely, if it is silent, then by the definition of “silent” I wouldn’t have heard it.'

Socrates recognised the kindly yet disputative tone in his reply; it refreshed him and straightaway he felt more at home with himself and what was going on.

'You have me there, Socrates. I know there'll be no pulling the wool over your eyes—gGod told me that. Anyway, as I said, I, Ignatius(silent)M, am your interface with the machine: give me instructions and I will do my best to carry them out, ask me questions and I will do my best to furnish answers, feel the need to analyse or discuss something and I am here to take part.'

'What instructions?'

'On the time travelling front. Anything you wish.'

'What questions?'

'Well, you may occasionally be puzzled by some things and they will need answers: references, names and so on, and I will try to fill you in with facts or details.

'And what might I want to analyse or discuss?'

'Socrates, you will be seeing many things that will cause you to think again about previous assumptions you may have made, or things which simply make you feel you must talk about them with another. gGod wants this last day of yours to be your best ever. And I'm here to ensure that's what you get.'

'Ah, my last day. Of course. I'd quite forgotten. I'm happy to die, IgnatiusM, but I feel there is still so much to learn. Will this one day be enough?'

'Recall the garlanding of the stern of the ship that was sent forth to Delos on its yearly trip to keep the Athenians' covenant with Zeus.'

'Yes.'

'That is what delayed the day for your execution. It could not take place until the ship returned—the city had to remain pure and that meant that executions could not take place.'

'Yes, of course.'

'Then remember, we are indebted to the virtuous nature of Athens for the time that we are shaping now. Even though it is your last day, it is beyond the previous time when, without the virtuous conduct of the Athenians, your death would have taken place.'

'That is very wise, IgnatiusM. You are saying that it is a bonus day.'

'Yes, and with the creation of this machine, gGod has made this day even more than it could ever otherwise have been. Now, let us get on with things, let us get on with this "shaping" and begin our travels in time, sorry, *with* time—gGod keeps reminding me to get the terminology right. So, you have got here, to this position *with* time, talking to me your interface, IgnatiusM, because gGod, keen to get you started, sent you on a test run in order to familiarise yourself with the controls (mainly the big lever), and get used to any disorientation that may occur. And I hope this first experience has proved useful and informative and not too unsettling. Somewhat undirected, I know—no destination given—and you had to go through it alone. The test run was needed to switch me on, so there was no alternative to it. But from now on, Socrates, it's you and me together, and, with the aid of what you've got in your bag, your last day should ultimately turn out to be the fullest and the best imaginable. Bonus City! Talking of what you've got in your bag, perhaps you'd like to take out one of the pieces from inside it. Yes, show it to me and let's get things underway.'

Unquestioningly, Socrates delved into the bag that had become twisted around on its strap and was now hanging against his chest. With something of a struggle he took hold of one of the strangely shaped pieces.

'Any one in particular?' he asked, not really knowing the purpose of what he was doing anyway.

'No! No! Any one will do. The first you can get hold of. We will get to all of them in the end. Oh, you *have* got all of them, haven't you?'

'Yes, yes, as far as I know, yes.'

Socrates removed the piece and held it out to IgnatiusM. Then he realised that IgnatiusM was not there in the normal sense. He pursed his lips in mild embarrassment. IgnatiusM giggled.

'Yes, it's all new. I know. Now, turn it over. Good. This is how your navigation system will work.' Socrates didn't bother to ask what a "navigation system" was. 'You select a jigsaw piece—that's what these pieces are called: "jigsaw pieces"—turn it picture-side upwards and look into what is depicted there. You will see an image form—sort of around you. You will start to feel absorbed into it, indeed you will *become* absorbed into it. But you won't *go* anywhere. As gGod told you, as a traveller *with* time you will always be a sort of observer, yes, but more than that, and most importantly, you will be a *perceiver*. Yes, a *perceiver*—perception, the bringing of all things into being. You may witness things sometimes that puzzle you. If so, as I've already said, you are free to ask questions of me and I will do my best to answer them. If there is an emergency, though gGod forbid, then straight away you should press the emergency button on top of the lever. If you see the red light flashing on the emergency button at any time—it will be an incoming message—press it and answer. Try not to get the emergency-call pressing and the answering-a-call pressing mixed up.'

'Is there likely to be an emergency?' asked Socrates rather anxiously.

'Don't be concerned about that. The emergency button is more a health and safety requirement than a necessity. Now, to continue—'

'I have a question for you,' Socrates said.

'Yes, go ahead.'

'What do the—'

'Letters mean?'

'Yes, there's a picture on one side, and you've just told me about that, but on the other side there are letters, I think. They're not Greek but I'm pretty sure they're letters.'

'It's going to be a job to keep up with you, Socrates, I can see. Sharp as a razor! These letters that you so quickly observed, are sort of co-ordinates—they provide a way of locating things.'

'Did I really observe that?'

'I think so, yes,'

'Oh! So they're not "co-ordinates" (whatever *they* are), these letters, they're only "sort of co-ordinates". A bit like the "sort of images".'

'If that were a nail, Socrates, then you've hit it right on the head. Yes, they're sort-of-ways of finding a location. And that location will be here! They are the letters that will navigate you from where you "are" with the images back to where you started out from—here. As you've already so quickly noticed—observed, well, perceived—this is a jigsaw, and jigsaws only make sense if and when their pieces are joined up correctly. These letters, these "sort of co-ordinates" will hardly make sense, even partially, as the jigsaw is formed from its pieces. Ultimately though, when all its pieces are in place, the jigsaw will be complete—in *all* ways. Then we can stand back and gasp!'

'"Jigsaw"? I observed it was a "jigsaw", you say. I'm afraid you still have me at a bit of a loss there. A "jigsaw"?'

'Yes, a puzzle consisting of images of some sort, in this case pictures printed on wood, and (rather roughly, I must say) cut into various pieces of different shapes that have to be fitted together in order to reveal "the whole".'

'So, altogether these images will form some sort of picture that is greater in some way than each individual picture. And that will be the completed jigsaw.'

'Exactly! The images on each piece will allow you to find your way with time. You'll need to keep hold of it and have the picture side facing you all the time. The letters on the other side are for finding your way back.'

'The letters on the other side.'

'Yes.'

'To find my way back.'

'Yes, when you are ready to return, just turn the piece over, place it on the wooden board—the one attached to the left of the chair—with the letters facing upwards. And hey presto! Back to base!'

'What do I do then, with the piece?'

'Nothing. Leave it where it is on the board. When you are ready for another journey, choose another piece and keep your eye on it. When you're ready to come back, turn it over and fit it alongside any others (except for the first one when there won't be any others) that are on the board. Obviously you'll just have to use the shapes to do that because the letters won't make much sense.'

'Oh,' said Socrates rather hopelessly.

'Until the end!'

'Then the letters will mean something?' said Socrates just as hopelessly as before.

'Got it in one! Yes, in the end, the proper fitting together of the shapes themselves will allow all the letters to be read and so for the puzzle to be completed.

'Oh,' said Socrates again.

'You must make sure that before, during and returning from a journey, you keep the pieces safe. I cannot emphasise that enough. Whatever you do, do not drop any!'

As if what IgnatiusM said was a cue, Socrates dropped the piece he was holding. It clattered down the side of the chair and disappeared beneath the self-replenishing refreshment box. He reached down in a panic, feeling all around the box and the feet of the chair until, with a gasp of relief he found a piece, clenched his hand around it and returned, relieved, to his sitting position.

'Sorry…sorry…butterfingers…'

'No need to apologise, Socrates. Early stages. Anyway, when you have completed all your journeys, each time having placed the jigsaw piece you used, letter side up, in its proper position on the board, then the jigsaw itself will be complete and we will have the answer to the puzzle—whatever that may be. And that's it, Socrates. Apart from that, it's a sort of suck-it-and-see job. And after we've sucked it all up, then we'll see what we've got. So, hold the piece you've got in your hand up to the screen, let me have sight of it, then turn it towards yourself and get looking. Get looking and let's get sucking.'

Socrates did as he was asked.

'Is that right?' he asked uncertainly.

The interface screen flashed and there was a rumbling sound beneath the chair. He took that as a "yes", and so turned the image side towards himself.

After a few more flashes, IgnatiusM spoke.

'Well selected, Socrates. This piece gives us a fine starting point. A subject close to your heart, I think—"knowledge", and how it does not always bring about good. The "penalty of knowledge", you might call it. Your first proper trip will provide an example of, indeed, a close acquaintance with this penalty of knowledge. gGod said He hoped you would pick this for your first trip. How does He do it! All-knowing or what? Anyway, in addition to it being a good choice, it will also be a chance for you to become completely familiar with the controls as well as the whole experience of the time-travelling business (which might almost certainly be a little unnerving until you get used to it). And it'll give *me* a chance to get used to the interfacing business. It's all new to me as well, of course. We're both time-travelling virgins! What do you think, Socrates? Are you ready?' He didn't allow for a reply—the wait for it would have been too long. 'Good. Then hold on to that piece. Whatever you do, hold onto that piece!'

Socrates turned the jigsaw piece over and to himself scrutinised the letters on the back. They were inscribed in different colours, with different styles and shapes, so that when viewed from different angles they could sometimes be seen and at other times they were invisible. Altogether they appeared as a moving tapestry that gave no idea of meaning or coherence. He nodded as if they conveyed something meaningful, even though they didn't. He scrutinised them again but they meant no more to him than they did the first time. He turned the piece over and stared at the other side. Straightaway he saw an image—greater somehow that the simple mixture of colours on the jigsaw piece itself.

'Look, Socrates. Look! Look into the image!' Socrates stared hard. He could see what looked like a landscape—a bare landscape. 'Are you ready?'

There was no hesitation. Socrates was seized with a compelling and overpowering enthusiasm.

'Yes, friend IgnatiusM. Fire her up! And let's get going!'

'Then grab hold of the lever, pull it back and hang on! Tight! Tight! The end is not yet nigh!' shouted IgnatiusM in a rather unconnected way but, drawing inspiration from Socrates' eagerness and getting fully into the interfacing swing of things, he continued. 'Pull back the lever! Pull back the lever! And hold on to that piece!'

Grasping the piece in both hands Socrates somehow wrapped them around the lever as well. He grabbed tightly onto it, pulled it back and, as the urns attached to the roof corners started spraying a mist of dust and the whole machine went into a shuddering, rumbling turmoil of noise and vibration, the image became clearer, and he was lost into it. He was travelling with time, and on this, his last day, by the will of gGod, his fret-sawing skills, and the interfacing expertise of IgnatiusM, true perception had begun.

CHAPTER 11

Underway

Socrates could not entirely agree about the end being not yet nigh. As a coldness spread up through his body, he thought something at least approaching the end was definitely nigh—if not already nighed. He could barely keep a grip on any of his senses let alone the control lever and the jigsaw piece. As his senses reeled in overstimulated shock, he was only vaguely aware of the shaking marble columns and the grape-eating figures painted on the flapping cloth of the ceiling. He realised he was gripping the lever between his legs as well now, yes, but he had no sense of controlling anything. Then the shuddering and shaking increased, and soon after that everything became a blur—a complete blur. At first he felt as if he was dislocated from everything solid—as if he was floating in a warm sea. Then, as the clamour increased, he could not tell what he was thinking and who was the "he" that was unsure whether or not he was thinking it. Then there was a purgatorial period of unknowing until, from beyond the confused veil, his senses returned to order and were again his. Now, in the known, living world, he was fighting for breath, struggling to regain himself. Then, with the same sickening jolt he'd felt on the test trip, everything suddenly stopped and there was silence.

He gasped and slumped forward against the lever. The microphone swayed in front of his face. He felt the sensation of warmth again but he still needed to locate himself—to know where he was in whatever world he was in. He moved his mouth silently, gapingly, until finally he spoke.

'Is…there…anyone…there?' he asked weakly.

There was no reply. He hung more heavily on the lever. Some flashing lines appeared on the screen. The thought of a name came into his mind—"IgnatiusM". IgnatiusM! His "interface"! Yes! IgnatiusM! His interface!

Still holding the lever between his knees, he let go of it with one hand and used it shakily to grab hold of the microphone.

'IgnatiusM! Are you there? IgnatiusM!' There was a faint crackling sound then a broken, fizzing whine. 'IgnatiusM! Is that you?' Silence. Socrates was more confused than ever and in desperation broke out into uncharacteristic screeching. 'IgnatiusM! IgnatiusM! Help! Help!'

Another period of silence was replaced by more crackling. Then, through a blizzard of spluttering static, the voice of IgnatiusM broke through.

'Socrates! Well done! You really are quite a pilot. You've just about arrived at your first destination. Congratulations! Everything went smoothly, I assume?'

'Well, it was a bit bumpy.'

'Don't worry about that—for the moment anyway. I'll look into it for you later. I'm sure it's nothing to worry about.'

And with IgnatiusM's reassuring words, Socrates, as forecast, felt himself absorbed within the image brought about by the jigsaw piece that he still held in his hand. He had been taken beyond his normally experienced world and was now within another.

CHAPTER 12

Blackwood—the penalty of knowledge

There were five of them to start with: Marfa, Ulric, Edric, Hilda and Tata. Of course, as Ulric was prone to say when they sat together on warm evenings, there was actually only one to begin with when things truly began—their primal ancestor, the first man. "What a start he'd had," Ulric would say. "No need to labour, yes, but not knowing how to occupy his time, companionless, and alone. What can a man do unless he has an aim—unless he can act? What can a man think unless he can think it with another? And when he, this first man, asked gGod for a companion, all gGod could think of offering was one of the animals he'd already created.".They would all laugh when Ulric reached his arms up as if appealing to gGod and proclaimed, "All those animals! No wonder he complained! Who wants to share their sleeping time with a hyena!" Though, he would continue to say, gGod was, of course, very busy at this time creating many and diverse things, and His man's welfare might not have been top of His agenda. However, when He *did* get around to it gGod obviously tried what He considered His best offer—a pick of any of the animals. What else had He got to work on! But the man wouldn't have anything to do with them. He was choosey, that first man. For him, it had got to be something like himself or nothing at all. And if it was nothing at all then he was going to be a very miserable and dissatisfied first man. So gGod gave in and that's what the man got, "Except for a few details", Ulric would say, and the girls especially always giggled when he said this. "You know, the bits!" he would add to make them giggle more. Then, to calm them down, he would spread his arms wide and say in a divinely-sober-sort-of-way, "And so it began! Our ancestors were in place: the first man and his companion the first woman."

Marfa, Ulric, Edric, Hilda and Tata had all been friends since they were speechless children—almost for their whole lives. When they were small children, and all their parents were asleep, they would sneak out of their huts at night, steal past the few left on guard against wild animals and other tribes, and meet and hatch plans for their next day's adventures. Every day was filled with the excitement and the carrying out of these mutually laid plans. As they grew up, they began to think more seriously about their futures and, fixed as they had become on the idea of always sticking together, they made an agreement that when they were able they would leave their village and become a group in their own right. They were, they thought, surrounded by too many old people, and they believed that this would hold them back from doing what they wanted to do—though they were unsure at the time what that was except that it would be different to the things done by the old people.

So, one night as they sat together, they saw in each others' eyes that the time to act was right. They clasped each other's hands in silent agreement and the next day, after a hunt, they left—just like that. They decided to walk towards the setting sun—"west" it was called by their parents. They were full of joy and optimism as they set off. They laughed together, and held hands, and pushed and bunted each other playfully as they walked and ran and skipped along an increasingly less trodden path. After a few days travelling along what by then had become a barely worn and dusty track, they were joined by two more, both females: Agga and Willa, wanderers by choice. These two proved invaluable as they were very good at catching food—something the others had only ever done under the direction of their elders—and they were quickly adopted as part of the group.

And so their new life began, and things went well. At night they camped alongside the dusty track, sleeping wrapped in what bits of fur and skins they'd brought with them, eating food caught or collected by Agga and Willa, and talking always about the hopes they had for their future. And each day they carried on, walking towards where the sun had set the day before. After rounding many hills and descending into many valleys, they found a beautiful grassy glade with a stream flowing through it. They stood together and stared at it, as if caught by the magic of it, and with nods and smiles they all agreed that this would be the place for them to stop.

So here they built their shelters and formed a little village. They used the black wood found there, the fruit of which stained their fingers black, and because of this they called their village "Blackwood". The seasons passed and they continued as a close-knit band working always towards the benefit of the group. Children were born and these grew up believing in the same ideas as their fathers and mothers: that, based on the beneficial grace of the repeated seasons, they had been able to work to fulfil and enhance their lives. The first children were called after their fathers: Ulricson, Marfason, and Edricson.

Ulric had been a firm believer in the story of descent from the first man—he believed in it implicitly. His child, born to him by Agga, Ulricson, was taught that over a long period of time they had all descended from the first man, and when he had children he passed that name together with his skills and knowledge and the story of lineage onto them.

Marfa had taken a different view, however. He always doubted the story of the original man created by God from nothing who then remained the model for all life that followed. Marfa believed that things changed. He realised that their small group had changed as they'd come to terms with living in their new environment: adapting to each other's ways, learning new skills, modifying what they did to fit in with their future plans. For Marfa it was illogical that there had been no evolving progress since the start of things—for Marfa, the world was constructed of change. He talked with Willa about his ideas and she agreed—even the act of their discussion was an evolved change, she said. So the two met together and firmed up their thoughts. They became a pair and when they had children they brought them up to think as they did. Their first child, Marfason was brought up in the way of Marfa, believing in the unavoidability and benefits of change. When he grew up he took to breeding the small herd of cattle that the group had put together, and he showed that he could breed better milk producers from ones that he selected on the basis of their previous record of milk production. Marfason's son took things further—from practical application to concept. He found bones in the ground, hardened to stone, that seemed to be from different creatures than anyone in the group had ever seen. He took this as evidence of animals that had lived before them and had died out because better versions of themselves had been more successful.

Generations after the original group had settled in Blackwood, a child was born whose father was unknown. Because he had no known father he was named simply Herac. He grew up to be a cowherd. By this time things had altered a great deal. The village, now a small town, had become split by belief: one side adhering to the thoughts passed down by the Ulricsons that everyone was descended from gGod's first man, the other holding the Marfason's view that everything had evolved from more primitive (unknown) beginnings and still continued to modify and change. But Herac, being uncertain that either argument weighed more heavily than the other, straddled both opinions. When he was in the company of the Ulricsons he was swayed by their ways and shared beliefs. Indeed, when they came together to talk of how their lineage could be traced back to the first man and so to the word of gGod, he was fulsome in his supportive crying out and chorusing. However, at night, he would walk out onto the nearby hillside and listen to a Marfason explaining the ideas of the changing and evolving patterns of life, of its antecedence in primitive things and forms that had through continual change brought things to the way they were now. And he would nod in determined agreement and see the sense and rationality of it all.

Then, one day, as usual, Herac took his milk pail into one of the nearby fields, dug an impression in the earth to secure it and began milking his favourite cow called Methabell. He was her favourite too—she welcomed his touch and always pushed herself to the front of the waiting herd when he arrived at milking time. He stared into the sky above—blue, vast and never-ending. He felt Methabell's slow breathing against his face. In unison with her, he breathed in deeply. He worked rhythmically at his chore when, as if it arose from the pace of his breaths and the measured tempo of his labour, he sensed something he had never sensed before. It was a feeling of the "closeness" of things. He looked at the pale red sun slowly emerging over the horizon and felt the wave of his perception reaching out to it. It stretched from him and linked him to it, and in so doing, in some strange way, his perception brought it into being. Yes, he felt the power of his perception—he felt through it the power to cause becoming. He stopped milking. He was transfixed. Methabell turned her head and looked at him expectantly—she was not yet empty. The sun grew brighter. Still he stared, still he felt its closeness, still he experienced its directness and the knowing of it that surged into him as he gained more understanding of the link between them. And as he stared and thrilled at the thoughts that were coursing through him, he realised that things did not accord to either of the opinions represented by the Ulricsons and the Marfasons. He realised in that one, beautiful, combining moment that although the world might have been created by gGod, its present existence was not reliant on existing forever frozen in the image of the first man, nor dependent upon the consequence of evolving change for improvement.

He continued to stare. There were only two objects in the world: him and the sun. And the sun was reliant upon him perceiving it—it existed *because* of him. In the end he broke away, the intensity of the experience was too great for him to bear. He had to find distraction. He patted Methabell and in that touching realised that she too was a creation of his perception.

He lay back on the grass, trying to absorb the impact of his experience. The realisation filled his mind—that without his perception of it an object could have no meaningful claim to exist. The object might well be there, but there would never be any way of proving it unless a perceiver perceived it—to be was to be perceived. And as he imagined himself as the perceiver he imagined that if he had only just come into existence himself, and had only just started perceiving, then there would be no way of proving that anything truly existed before he perceived it. He could see no way around it. He subjected it to sceptical attack—he had to be sure. He thought it through. He imagined that the world might have been created only a short time before he was born. He challenged himself to find any proof that this was not so. He imagined every possible outcome but he could find nothing that could convincingly dismiss his scepticism.

And so he was faced with a stark conclusion: if he believed that he had a history either remembered or recorded, and he believed that every event has a preceding cause, then he must conclude that the universe and its living inhabitants had some sort of antecedence—a previous history of causes. On the face if it this seemed common sense. On this basis there were two choices: either gGod created him, or he evolved from lesser beings whose origins are no longer evident. gGod's creation, if it was in His image, would have been pretty well perfect to start with (inasmuch as it was created by Him in His image, and so "perfection" would be measured against gGod's criteria for perfection) and therefore could not be subject to much improving change. If life had evolved

—even if gGod had created it in the first place—by definition it must have stemmed from something much less than perfect, something much more basic. It may even have arrived independent of gGod from the stars or arisen from the basic fabric of the earth. The problem was deeply puzzling.

Herac suspected the reality of gGod anyway. And if gGod had the moral and psychological welfare of those He had created uppermost, then why did He not give them certain knowledge of their antecedents? If Herac had such knowledge then he would not be troubled by any sceptical doubt. But he was! And if gGod did *not* create humans, then why did some people suspect that He *did*? Such a god would have limited power because he would have failed to make himself or his intentions at all clear. Or maybe gGod was *unable* to make Himself clear. Of course! That was it! This god, this creator, was not only fallible but had limited power!

This transported Herac into a quiet, calm and reflective realisation. He realised that the evolutionary story had some strength—Methabell, for example, *was* the product of progressive, selective breeding in a search for better milk production and an easy temperament—but the theory relied on there being living things from which more living things could be generated. It was illogical and unknown that living things arose if there had been no preceding living things. And there was no evidence as far as Herac could see that living things or indeed *anything* else could emerge from nothing. After all, if the universe were created out of nothing then surely spontaneous generation would be its fundamental principle, and much evidenced—and that was not the case. More reasonable to Herac was the idea that individuals and groups could change according to their more pressing or close-at-hand needs. On this basis there could be evolutionary change over time—Methabell's high-yielding milk production was the result of breeding over time. But Herac also knew that things were *always* changing, smoothly or catastrophically, because there was time in which they *could* change—change defines time (without change time cannot be inferred) and time exists (however it is produced), so change must happen in some form. Implicit change in time has no direction for improvement—it simply happens.

Neither of the arguments in whatever guise stood up against Herac's newfound scepticism. None of it produced any sort of replacement for his fundamental realisation that the reason for the world was unknown and, whatever form it took, if he were not perceiving it then there was no way of proving that it existed.

Still staring, Herac slumped sideways against Methabell. He closed his eyes, now dry and stinging from the glare of the risen sun. He felt at one with this creature and her existence. He realised that evolution, if it was from a primitive start, required more time than there had been. And if organic change was to be meaningful, it must involve some knowledge of the future—it must have foresight. And this was ridiculous. And if this was not the case, every change would be entirely random and would involve so many failures that again there would not be enough time for it to happen. And yet the idea of no change since the first man did not sit comfortably with obvious changes and modifications that were everywhere to be seen. Any considerations on this were quickly lost in a confusion that demanded a different answer.

Without thinking any more, Herac jumped up and ran from the field. Methabell was suddenly confused by his departure—she too had felt the closeness of another and now its sudden loss. Ill at ease, she kicked a hind leg and knocked over the milking pail, which spilled its hard-won contents onto the grass. Herac ran back to the village, filled with his thoughts and his revelation. He ran between the huts and houses, waving his arms and proclaiming.

'I have seen the truth! I have seen the truth! Come! Gather together! You must receive my news!'

The others began gathering around him but, at the same time, such was his frantic dashing and screeching that they found themselves holding onto each other, filled with the fear that they had a madman in their midst.

Herac climbed up onto a large boulder that stood in an open space between all the dwellings, and when everyone was there, he addressed them.

'I have seen the truth!' he started. 'All of you, listen to my words. We cannot rely on anything we think we know. We cannot be certain of our history. We cannot be certain of any change for the better. We cannot…' He paused and looked around at all who were staring up at him. '…we cannot be certain of there being any god! And if there is a god, it is not the kindly all-knowing one we wish for. No, it is more likely to be a demon—an evil demon with godly powers!'

Everyone gasped as if they were part of one massive breathing self. Then there was silence.

From the crowd a Marfason pushed his way forward. He stood in front of Herac who remained standing on the boulder.

'What nonsense this is! Herac, you have suffered some sort of fit. You must have caught something from one of your cows. Of course we have evolved. Look around you. Haven't we all become better? Hasn't our living world improved since our forefathers created our village in the now distant past?'

Someone else ran to the front. It was an Ulricson.

'No! We have "become", as Marfason puts it, because of the will and benevolent hand of gGod. We are simply part of His perfect creation. We are like his children.'

'Nonsense!' shouted Marfason.

'But your idea cannot work. It rests on almost inconceivable odds,' responded Ulricson 'The odds of life arising from something originally un-lifelike are so small as to be unbelievable.'

'Small they might be,' cried out Marfason. 'But the possibility of gGod creating it out of His mind and then leaving it to remain largely unchanged would also seem inconceivably small, if not smaller because, presumably, the creative act was an original thought on the part of gGod with no preceding model from which to work. And the evolutionary theory, no matter how improbable, can at least be tested (if not proved) whereas your creation theory cannot. And if gGod wanted to create life why should He want to create the appearance of previously evolved life? Surely He wouldn't have to create in us the suspicion of a falsehood.'

'But,' retorted Ulricson. 'You will find it difficult to account for certain human traits; for example, a sense of beauty or moral purpose, neither of which seem to have any evolutionary meaning. And indeed belief in gGod would seem to have no evolutionary purpose at all. And I think you still hold, even on your view, that gGod started it all.'

Herac raised his arms.

'What Ulricson could have referred to as the unfolding "drama of life", Marfason might have called the "struggle for survival". And there is a commonality in both these ways of thinking. Indeed, it is possible to hold both views as neither mutually excludes the other. But, I have to tell you this. They're both wrong!' Another gasp went up from all around. Herac continued. 'One theory might appeal more to common sense or may be more comforting than the other. But should we be guided by such simple election? I think not. The answer lies beyond this fragile context. Although it may appear so, this division is not two sides arguing to prove themselves right. It is a rift between two masses—a chasm between cliffs if you like—where the truth lies in the emptiness created by the crags on each side. Perhaps the two sides can be brought together? I used to think so. I believed that it could be the case that gGod had laid a trail of evolutionary artefacts simply to comfort us with a sense of history and belonging. Indeed, it is hard to argue that this is impossible. But it is more convincing to argue that it is unprovable. And these two unprovable ideas that we have had put before us have to some extent supported each other. But both ideas remain theories—they are not products of, nor do they respond to the impact of perceptual knowing. What do I mean by that? Answer me this. What if the earth, although appearing old, is actually young, and its apparent history has been put there by gGod in order to provide us with a secure sense of pastness. Can you say that this is untrue? I think not. If gGod created the earth and all its creatures (including humans) in six days, then why should He complicate the situation, and confuse us all, by laying a false evolutionary trail? Can you answer that? And what about the idea that evolutionary trends follow successful adaptation to the demands of the environment being in itself a justification for the evolutionary process. What reasons do we have for believing that animal and plant species *want* to succeed when faced with an adverse environment? None! And can anything look into its own future like this? No! Of course not! Logically, in the evolution theory, in the absence of environmental change and with sufficient time, a species must evolve to perfection. Is there any evidence that this has been, is, or might be foreseeably the case? No, there is not! What would a fully evolved, perfect state for human beings be anyway? And how would we judge that evolutionary change is a change for the better as opposed to a change for the worse? That something survives does not mean it has a purpose. And unless something has a purpose there is no reason why it should survive at all. Are these two propositions reconcilable? For humans, the act of creation is usually something to be proud of and we invariably claim our own creations if they are merit-worthy. If gGod created us, and our desire to claim worthy achievements, then why does gGod not make an obvious claim on His creation? Does this mean He is not proud of it? Does it mean that? Questions! Questions! All unanswerable questions!' He stared out at them. 'So, I offer this—a final challenge. The world is the work of an evil demon! It started ten seconds ago. Yes, just ten seconds ago! Show me that this is not the case.'

Herac looked around the faces in the crowd; everyone was clinging to each other, gasping with confusion, silenced by bewilderment. Then someone moved. Then another. Fear spread amongst them. Several of them ran from the crowd into their huts. Some began yelling and screaming. Ulricson and Marfason shouted to them to stop being fearful, that there was no need, but by then the panic had spread and no one was even able to listen. One of the huts caught fire. A woman ran screaming across the empty space as a man chased her with a blood-stained spear. Everything was disintegrating—the community, started all those generations ago by the small group of friends, was falling apart as the bases for their guiding principles were thrown into doubt, undermined and left in tatters.

Suddenly there was a great rumbling noise. The panicking inhabitants of Blackwood tripped and stumbled as screaming and crying filled the smoke-laden air. The rumbling noise increased—there was a sense of a presence.

'You called Me! Is there an emergency!'

It was gGod.

'No, sorry, gGod. It was an accident—'

'An accident! What's happened! Is anyone hurt? Has anything broken? It's not the refreshment box, is it?'

'No, it was an accident that I pressed the emergency button. I was gripping the lever too tightly, I think. And struggling to hang onto the jigsaw piece. It was an accident.'

'Oh, well, anyway…' gGod was clearly annoyed but making the effort to be helpful. '…I'm here now anyway, so is there anything I can help with?'

'Well,' said Socrates, not only disturbed by the contents of his journey, but now feeling very much on the defensive because of gGod's barely disguised annoyance and lack of solicitousness. 'As You ask, yes, there is.'

'Very well. Go on!' said gGod moodily.

Socrates continued keenly.

'My journey ended so quickly. I was on edge with it all. What happened? Was there an outcome?'

'Ah, a premature evacuation, eh!' chuckled gGod, now clearly softening His rather sulky humour. 'Well, Soc…' gGod was obviously warming and pretty well back to His normal, more cheery Self. '…At first, chaos ensued,' He started. 'Then there was a time of reconciliation. A new leader came to power and everyone swore allegiance to him. Then he was dethroned and chaos came back. And throughout all this turmoil, the names of the original group who founded Blackwood remained. There still were Ulricsons and Marfasons and Herac too had bequeathed his name, and the Heracsons were known for their questioning and challenging of the order of things. And from the times of stability and the times of havoc there arose a nation and all those that were part of it were born and died. And their births and deaths were like thread sewn into the weave of a great cloth. And the cloth persisted. And when the threads were worn out and broken they were replaced by fresh thread. And even though all the threads were replaced still the cloth persisted. And the cloth was the silent witness to the growth of the nation and the lives of those that took their part in it. And then there was a plague and the sickness afflicted all in turn—the young and the old, the just-born and the dying—and the nation was no more for there were no more members to play their part in it. Now the cloth lay exposed to the burning of the sun, the drying heat, and the ravages of the wind. And there was no one to sew in any new thread. And so nature reclaimed all the endeavours of the men and women that had formed the nation. And there were no more sons and daughters, no more conflicts of views, no more questioning, and the earth was quiet—as it was when it was first created. Oh, and I can see that you missed all this because you inadvertently turned the jigsaw piece over with the home-navigation letters uppermost. Watch out for that in the future, Soc. You can't afford to miss anything. Turn the piece over only when you're ready to return.'

CHAPTER 13

Thinking about...the way to live

Socrates stared—devastated. He had been part of the growth, the change and the ultimate conflicts within Blackwood, and now he had felt its destruction. He felt the loss of hope, the resignation to despair that all its people must have known. For a moment he was cast back into it. He thought he saw some children playing amongst the ruins of buildings. He reached his hands towards them thinking that he could offer some consolation, but they disappeared; they were figments of his own projected hope—they could make no plans for a future now spoiled by the wreckage of their past.

'Socrates!' It was gGod again. There was no mistaking His divinely booming voice. 'Socrates!' He continued, rather less boomingly. 'It's over. This part of your journey had come to an end—a little sooner than it should have, but still an end. Hopefully My summary of the latter parts have sufficed to fill in the picture. On this journey you have been perceiving matters regarding the nature of perception itself. I hope you have been rewarded by it. But, slightly aside, it has come to My attention that in doing this an evil demon was mentioned. Socrates! Is that true?'

'Yes, I think so.' Socrates felt somewhat exposed: to what he had witnessed, to gGod, to the premature exposure of the letter side of the jigsaw piece, and to the disturbing flashing light still pulsing on top of the lever.

'Let us be certain about this. There is no such thing as a deceiving, evil demon.'

'No,' said Socrates, keen to respond but still suffering from the experience of the journey and unable to disguise his abundant uncertainty.

gGod, picking up on Socrates' demeanour, continued in a divinely sympathetic way.

'Are you *sure* everything is all right?'

Socrates didn't know what to say.

'Yes, I think so,' he said meaninglessly.

'Are you sure?' said gGod, His booming now overshadowing his sympathetic tone. 'Put IgnatiusM on. I need to have a word.'

'IgnatiusM here, gGod.'

'How has this talk of the evil demon cropped up again?'

'It was there, Sir. Bold as you like. Socrates perceived it. There was no doubt about it.'

'When was it?'

'Just now.'

'No! I mean when in the history of things was it!'

'It was…' IgnatiusM couldn't really understand gGod asking him such a question; his own understanding of the workings of time hardly held a candle to gGod's knowledge on this front. And anyway, gGod was supposed to be all-knowing.' It was…er...near the beginning, when people were still finding their feet.'

'Oh, My…' gGod hesitated. 'Oh, My...Self!' He played for a while with his ruff, then turned back to Socrates, realising that He'd rather cut in on allowing him to recover from the after-effects of his journey. 'Anyway, Socrates, sorry if I worried you. You're still on course. Everything will be fine, I'm sure. You just carry on. Remember this is your special day. A day of healing. I'll be contacting Aesclipius later. Oh, sorry, you haven't got to that part yet, have you. Yes, sorry. This talk of the evil demon muddles up the old perceptual wherewithal a bit. Just a bit of paranoia. Well, anyway, I'll pass you back to IgnatiusM now. You're in good hands there. Must get on now. Always things to do: creating, perceiving, fretsaw work…counselling. Oh! That reminds Me, I've got an appointment later. See you soon, though. Have a good day,' He tittered in a slightly embarrassed way as He realised what He'd just said. 'Yes, have a good *last* day!' Then, with a flash, some thundering noises, and a brief twinkle of the emergency button light before it finally went out, He was gone.

Socrates put his hand to his forehead and breathed in deeply.

'Anyway, all that aside, you're back now, Socrates,' said IgnatiusM seemingly untroubled by gGod's sudden appearance, His state of edginess, His concerns about the evil demon, and then in what to IgnatiusM seemed a rather misplaced and whimsical way, His equally abrupt disappearance. 'Well, you've never actually *been* anywhere, to come *back* from, of course, but you know what I mean. How was it? At least before that last bit. Everything go well?'

Socrates looked dazed and worried. He tried to put the troubling appearance of gGod, and the very thought of the extremely sensitive emergency button to one side and concentrate on the journey that he'd been on. What he had seen had knocked him sideways—it had somehow got inside him and put him into an unusually sceptical mood. His normal feeling for seeking the truth by questioning had never led him to the sort of destructive scepticism that he'd been witness to, and the experience had somehow lowered him. And it *had* been an experience. He might have been "watching" in part, but everything about what he'd seen he'd felt in just the same way as if he'd been there. Yes, as far as he could make sense of the experience, he *had* been there. And now, knowing the fate of the sons and daughters of those children who had started out on their lives together, what he'd been through had taken his optimism and smashed it to pieces. A pessimism folded around him. What if *his* enquiring method should lead him to the same destructive scepticism? The thought was unbearable. He knew he must retrieve his optimism, but at the moment he could not think how. He had been left with so much that needed resolving and surely now he hardly had the time to tackle it. This was not what he'd been expecting from his promised, best last day.

He stared at the flickering screen.

'IgnatiusM, what I have seen has created a sense of despair in me. Does continual enquiry lead to scepticism that in turn leads necessarily to ruin and hopelessness? Am I to face my death realising that my life's journey has been a road to virtuous ruin? Suddenly my death, instead of a shining door, seems like a black cloud. What is life worth, IgnatiusM? Is anything we achieve of any worth, I wonder? Are all our aims valueless?'

He closed his eyes. He couldn't believe he was talking like this. He had never heard himself say such things. Life had always been of the greatest value to him, even if it was only as a substandard precursor to death. Wonderful death. Death that held the promise of what followed—immortality. How could he have lost his grip on his hope for the future beyond this life. On this, his last day, how could he be sinking into the darkness of hopelessness. To talk like this! To think like this!

The screen flickered some more.

'In three hundred years time we (I say "we" but obviously I mean "you") will be dead, my friend,' said IgnatiusM as if offering some consolation and straightaway realising that in Socrates' current mood this was not helping. He quickly thought of something to counteract what he'd just said. 'Though, I must say, there were some in the time of the Patriarchs, that lived longer. Yes. Much longer.'

'Were there?' asked Socrates, finding some optimism in the mention of something unknown to him. 'In the time of the—'

'Patriarchs, Socrates,' said IgnatiusM, realising that he had struck an optimistic vein. And even though in itself it didn't address Socrates' current negative thoughts he considered it worth following for the sake of pursuing a less dark trend. 'Yes, Noah, for example. He was six hundred years old at the time of the great flood, and afterwards lived another three hundred and fifty years. He was the last of the long-lived of this ancient era.'

Socrates brushed a thick coating of dust from his face and hair—the urns were still revolving slightly. Relieved by the action that brought back a sudden remembrance of his time as a boy, he felt a sense of his more familiar self. He bent forward enquiringly to the screen.

'That's some age,' he said coughing suddenly as some of the dust, still trickling from the urns, caught in his throat.

'And this fact—our (again, by which I mean "your") passing nature, our impermanence—might in itself be enough to make us (and for the sake of convenience and companionability I'll stick to the first person plural) think that nothing we achieve in our lives that satisfies us is worthwhile.'

With a sense of relief, at last Socrates felt some of his usual thinking processes coming back.The scepticism of Herac and the hopelessness of his cause had made a deep impact on him, but he was now finding a place for it within his own scheme of things. Questioning could lead to doubt, yes, but this was invalidated if the process was halted. Closing the process of enquiry brought about fixed and immovable opinions. If continued, the activity of enquiry could lead to more answers being supposed and in so doing expose more of the contents of any question. And this did not lead to despair and the darkness of unanswerable pessimism. No, this brought nearer the wisdom that could recognise the nature of virtuous reality. And IgnatiusM's words had again fired up his natural instinct for seeking the truth—the truth contained within hope and happiness, and the attainment of wisdom in life from continual questioning.

Invigorated by this refreshing surge of his natural flair, he pressed on.

'So, IgnatiusM, where is any worth in life to be found?'

‘If there is any meaning to our…’ he paused for clarification. ‘Again I include myself more (using the term “our”) as a companionable comfort for yourself. And anyway, I like being included in the human model too—it’s tough-going being a machine sometimes. So I’ll continue if you don’t mind?’

‘I think of you as my companion, IgnatiusM, and a very human one too. Yes, please continue in this way.’

‘Well, if there is to be any meaning to our personal experience of life we must find it in the context of our *transitory* life, for it is here, and only here that we have conscious experience of selfhood.’

‘Yes, indeed. I agree. Please tell me of some of these transitory values.’

‘Gladly. Many of our functions have meaning, for example, eating when we are hungry, or resting when we are tired. But, on the face of it, our whole life, as a thing-in-itself, does not. It is true that life may have meaning in the mortal world beyond the confines of our own life—for example, we may do something that benefits others in ways that we have no knowledge of. But benefits like this could bring no sense of personal satisfaction and even if we came to know them, any benefits would not extend beyond the confines of our transitory mortal existence.’

‘You are right, IgnatiusM. Though I believe you underrate the importance of the spiritual life after our mortal death.’

‘That is important too, of course. But surely we must estimate the value of our mortal life before we can consider what follows? It is after all, perhaps not only a precursor to any post-mortal existence, but what dictates the *quality* of what is to follow.’

‘Yes, again you’re right. So, tell me what you think of the values you mention. I’m keen and ready to know more.’

‘I think we need to get gGod in on this, Socrates. He’ll be able to fill you in much more proficiently than I can. He can put

His finger on the fuller picture more easily—"god-time" and all that. Let's see if we can rouse Him. Use the emergency button.'

'Is that quite the right thing to do?' asked Socrates reminding himself of gGod's recent irritability regarding misuse of the emergency button.

'Don't worry,' said IgnatiusM. 'When He turns up we'll tell Him it wasn't an emergency but that we didn't know any other way of contacting Him; that a button seemed to be the right thing, and it was the only button available. He'll never know it's a bit of a try-on. He's not as sharp as you might think. Really. Go on! Give it a good hard press!'

Socrates was more than a little unsure but, after reaching forward and holding back twice, he finally summoned up the courage to give it a go. He brought his thumb down and pressed the button. The lever shivered a couple of times then, looking a little flustered, gGod appeared.

'Where's the emergency?' he asked, looking around for clues. 'The emergency! Where is it?'

'No emergency. It was the only button,' said IgnatiusM unable to disguise the fact that he was lying. 'We're just after a bit of Your wisdom. Hope You don't mind.'

gGod saw through the simple deceit straight away even though He was a little vexed at this misuse of the emergency button again so early in the whole time travelling proceedings. So, taking it in good heart, He created Himself a chair, a small table and a cup of tea, eased His gaiters slightly, and sat down with a heavy though nevertheless relaxing wheeze.

'It's been all go since I was last here, I can tell you,' He said, trawling for sympathy and not taking into account that for Socrates and IgnatiusM it had only been minutes since He'd left. 'Nothing but trouble. There's something going on that I can't quite put my finger on at the moment. I know! Me! All-knowing and all that, and I can't put My finger on it! Sometimes there're just too many things to deal with: creating a counsellor, gGladys going on about a new…' He stopped. 'Where the next problem is going to crop up gGod only knows.' He thought about what He'd just said for a moment, smirked at the inadvertent joke, took a sip of tea and continued. 'Anyway, what can I do for you? I hope there're no more problems?'

He threw His eyes up as He focused a message-sending stare at the emergency button.

'No! No! We just need a bit of information to help Socrates on his next trip.'

'The first proper trip went well, I think? Except for the bit at the end.'

'Yes, so far, so good,' said IgnatiusM.

'Very well. How can I help?'

gGod sounded a little less preoccupied with His other problems so IgnatiusM pressed on.

'Socrates could do with some updating on the matter of the worth of life. Particularly, may I say, (seeing as this *is* his last day), in respect of the question of length of life.'

gGod smiled.

'That's an old chestnut, I have to say. But, as you point out, not a matter to be dealt with lightly under the present circumstances. Yes, a matter of the greatest importance, I agree. Length of life.' He turned to Socrates. 'Feelings, Socrates? On the subject?'

Socrates hesitated for a moment, but now, having pretty well shaken off the darkly sceptical feeling altogether, and having seemingly got away with his inappropriate use of the emergency button, he was keen to move on.

'I believe our mortal lives are merely introductions to what is to follow. And I believe our mortal life is best led when it extends beyond the closer concerns of world-bound self—when it looks to its worthiness in the life beyond.'

'Yes, Socrates, it's worth considering your ultimate destiny. But even if you extend the meaning of your life beyond your own life (and its relationship to parents, other relatives, and friends… and wives…and so on) and take part in large scale enterprises (for example, economic, political or religious movements and suchlike), you must still face the fact that, if you put your life into the context of the broadest possible whole, it will seem minuscule and meaningless. For example, and not wishing to let the cat out of the bag, I can tell you that the earth will ultimately cool down and be destroyed in a massive explosion. How can your life seem in any way important when you think of that?'

Socrates looked somewhat shocked by the forecast of the earth's end, but carried on undaunted.

'But surely spiritual existence goes beyond even the end of the earth. *All* material things end, but that cannot be the same for the spirit which has no material form.'

'Let me introduce you to some of the thoughts of others—I don't want you to feel I'm hogging it all when it comes to opinions, even though I think I do have plenty to offer here. Yes, you're right, this might be your last day on earth, but, as you point out, this may not be your last *day* (I use the term "day" in its temporally parochial sense just to make it easier to understand). Your "life" may, I stress *may*, reach far beyond your earthly life. However (and I can see now that IgnatiusM was right to call Me in —by whatever means), wisdom gained in mortal life will help shape the life that is to come. And the components of wisdom are, Socrates? Are?' Socrates just stared. 'Of course, our *ideas*. Plato, one of your young disciples (though, because of a chill, not with the others who are still sleeping in your cell), comes to believe that the meaning of life is a recurring system of re-birth ultimately leading to perfection. On that, though, I don't think he took the trouble to count up the total number of available life forms. If he had, he might have found some problems with supply and demand.

Nevertheless, two thousand years after Plato, someone with a very difficult-to-spell name, Nietzsche, on the other hand (if we can properly use the term "on the other hand" after such a long span of time), did not accept *any* objective reality in human life. On this account, if we take such a human life and allow it to live eternally it would have no objective reality to take forward. Though it must be added, that Nietzsche did not accept the reality of Myself either! And he did have a huge moustache! How vast the gulf between such ideas, eh, Soc? But it is this very breadth that we must take into account if we, that is "you", are to find any wisdom.'

'Perhaps we are here to fulfil Your purpose?' proposed Socrates.

'If an individual believes that his life has meaning because he is fulfilling the purpose of gGod—Myself, that is—we are still entitled to ask what is the point of gGod's, that is *My* purpose. Answering that it is "gGod's purpose" and leaving it at that, does not, in itself, bring the questioning process to an end (by that I mean that gGod's purpose, or *My* purpose, is not immune from such a question or further questioning). There is nothing in the nature of gGod, Myself, to stop you asking what is the point of gGod or how gGod can be explained. If gGod, or Myself, really can give purpose to your lives then it seems reasonable to suppose that gGod, Myself, must have His own, that is *My* own, purpose beyond giving purpose to your lives. And you would be right. I do!'

Rather foolishly ignoring asking what that purpose might be, Socrates continued.

'But if You provide ultimate justification for our existence and we cannot understand Your purpose, can such a justification provide us with a personal sense of purpose?'

gGod, not wishing to see mention of His purpose passed over so lightly, answered as if Socrates had asked about it.

'And, you would be right. I *do* have a purpose of My own!'

Socrates, again sidestepping enquiring into the nature of gGod's purpose, reiterated.

'But, again, even if You do have a purpose, and we cannot understand it, how can it provide any purpose in *our* lives?'

gGod looked a little disappointed, but not wishing to appear ungGodly (self-importance wise) in any way, allowed the lack of interest in His own life and purpose to pass.

'It may be, as Nietzsche thought, that if your lives have no meaning beyond yourself (that is, your relationship with yourself and others) you are mistaken in looking for one. Around the same time as Nietzsche, a man called Sidgwick (he was the teacher of McTaggart, who, if you remember gave us the "*C*" in *C*-drive) believed that the only things of value were conscious states (after all, conscious states are ideas that formulate values). And perhaps it'd be worth wondering if conscious states provide the material for continued existence? Who knows? "*C*"-existence? Worth thinking about? But this whole business of purpose can be misleading. In looking for a sense of purpose in your life you may be regarding yourself too self-importantly—you are taking life (and your possible purpose beyond what you can see) too seriously. A man called (himself son of a man called Nagel) Nagel, believed that if you cannot accept that you take life too seriously then you have to put up with your lives being ridiculous, meaningless and absurd. In other words, take life with a light heart,' He added with strong self-interest. 'If no one expresses interest in your own purpose, or My own purpose, then ride with it.'

No one did.

He rode with it and continued. .

'Aristotle, a student of your own student Plato, and in My view the greatest (human) thinker ever, said that life is never about ends but always about means, and that the process of reshaping the ultimate meaning of life (as an end) is pointless. A person may feel that his or her own developed philosophy of life may be more than any theory of meaning (for example: Buddhism, Marxism, Existentialism and so on) could ever encompass. That is, that your own view of your own particular life and its spontaneous living is the most important thing. This view would mean focusing upon the major benefits of life (that is, being alive, being human, being reasonably competent). In this way of thinking, even if ultimately you enter some spiritual realm (which may contain many things beyond what you presently know), you would, because of your need to explore and investigate, still end up in the (pointless) spiralling search for meaning.'

'You are indeed very wise, gGod.'

gGod smiled, nodded with agreement, took another sip of tea, flicked His ruff, and continued.

'Let your doubts lead to enquiry, and your further doubts to further enquiry—this is the process of wisdom and the significance of the lived life. The only place to live out your philosophy of life is the here and now. Love of life and love of the world is your fullest response to being alive (itself the most important benefit of life). Acceptance of your place in nature, and the debt you owe to the nature that sustains you, is the fullest recognition of meaning. And recognising yourself as a small part in a vast whole, and identifying with being part of it, can bring a sense of calm to your life. This, together with an acceptance of the unavoidability of your spiralling search for your own reality can be satisfaction enough for your living. Life is what you make it, Socrates. And the meaning of life is spiritual meaning—the meaning of the soul. Yes, the meaning of your life extends beyond these functional, bodily confines which can often seem so pressing yet be so misleading.'

'You've mentioned a lot of names there, gGod, names and terms that I've never come across. And some wonderful ideas. I like the sound of this Aristotle.'

gGod smiled, got up from His chair, cocked His head to one side as if listening to something, downed the remnants of His cup of tea, pointed at something that apparently only He could see, then with a slow rumble and a single flash of light, He was gone.

Filled with a fresh sense of keenness and optimism, Socrates bent forward to the screen.

'I'm ready for another trip, IgnatiusM—ready and keen as mustard!'

'Then shake the dust from your hair, Socrates, put your hand in the bag and draw out the next piece of our jigsaw. Let us see what chance is holding in store for us.'

Socrates did as IgnatiusM suggested. Dust billowed up around him as he dug his hand deeply into the bag that still hung from his neck. He smiled as he withdrew the next roughly sawn piece. He turned it over and looked at the letters on the back—they still meant nothing to him. He turned it back over and shrugged.

IgnatiusM spoke.

'Let me see what you have chosen.' Socrates held the piece up to the screen. 'Not the letter side, the other, please.' He did as he was asked. 'Mm, another good choice. And right along the lines of our current conversation. How do you do it, Socrates! How do you do it!'

Socrates smiled with a look of someone who feels satisfied with a worthwhile day's labour even though he might have forgotten what he'd laboured on.

'It's nothing,' he said unable to disguise a look of un-targeted pride.

'Well by the strangest coincidence, you've chosen to find out more about what it's like to live a very long time. Inapplicable in your case, I'm afraid, though I must say seventy years is a pretty fine record. Still, nothing like what we're going to be dealing with here—nine hundred and fifty! Now that *is* a lot of years! So, let's get on. Every piece brings completion of the jigsaw closer and every piece placed reveals a little more of where ultimately it leads us! And remember what gGod told us about the thoughts of

Aristotle: don't take life too seriously. I understand that people can sometimes worry themselves to death if they're not too careful. Yes, to death! Here, leave any worries you may have, Socrates, grab hold of the lever, pull it back and enjoy being alive! You still have your life! Use it!'

Without hesitation, Socrates took hold of the lever, gritted his teeth, and yanked it back.

'I'm on my way,' he shouted. 'Wherever it is I'm going, I'm on my way to it! And I'm going to enjoy it! Every second of it!'

As the dust started to pour from the urns, and the marble pillars began to shake, and the canopy flapped, and everything attached to the machine began heaving and groaning, and gGod's chair disappeared, Socrates was absorbed into its jigsaw-controlled workings as the *C*-Drive again kicked into action.

'See you soon!' shouted IgnatiusM, his voice already faint against the general rumble and clatter.

'Yes, see you soon,' shouted Socrates, somewhat unsettled at the idea that IgnatiusM wouldn't be with him and available, but nevertheless caught up with the enthusiasm of the moment.

A shaking turmoil rose to a crescendo, then, with what was becoming a familiar transition, a sudden jolt brought the machine to rest.

There was even more dust than before issuing from the urns as they twisted crazily on their chains. Socrates was still hanging onto the lever, covered in the even-more-dust, and gasping for breath. It took a few minutes for him to recover, but, still enthused by gGod's encouragement to enjoy and value every moment of his life, he soon got a grip on things and, easing his hold on the lever, sat back and straight away became absorbed in another journey with time.

CHAPTER 14

The Ark—what was lost is found

He was already old, very old, but he was still agile, alert and fertile. His three sons, born when he was already over five hundred years old, were Shem, Ham and Japheth. Noah, although he didn't know it during his life, was the last of a line of men of great age: Adam, gGod's first man, lived until he was nine hundred and thirty years. Adam had a son Seth, conceived to replace Abel who had been killed by Cain, who lived for nine hundred and twelve years. Seth's son Enoch, lived for nine hundred and five years. Enoch's son Kenan was nine hundred and ten years when he died. Kenan's son Mahalalel lived until he was eight hundred and ninety five years. Mahalalel's son Jared was nine hundred and sixty two years, and Jared's son, another Enoch, lived until he was three hundred and sixty five years. Enoch's son Methuselah was the longest lived of them all, reaching nine hundred and sixty nine years. His son Lamech lived until he was seven hundred and seventy seven years. Lamech's son, born when Lamech was one hundred and eighty two years old, was Noah who was to become crucially important to the future of all things.

These were all great men in age and wisdom, but at the time of Noah their progeny had become wilful and taken up by pleasure. gGod was angered by this. He had, after all, gone to a lot of trouble to create them in the first place, and it was more than He could do to keep them perceived let alone ensuring that they followed an, according to Him, appropriate ethical path. So, believing that striking them out at this point would mean they wouldn't have time to fall into moral debauchery, He decided that no one would live any longer than one hundred and twenty years (He found this number a calming combination of the metric ten and the imperial twelve, and splendidly far removed from the often confusing cubit).

But this did not correct things as much as gGod would have wished. From His (sometimes erratically applied) highly moral point of view, too many people were still acting in evil and generally disagreeable ways, evidencing little moral restraint and showing high levels of perversity and wilful fornication. He felt very low about the whole business, even wishing that He'd never created people in the first place. This wish took hold of Him and so, on the spur of the moment He decided to blot them all out by destroying the whole of His living creation.

But He stopped Himself. He knew this was a drastic step and He held back for a moment to reconsider. As He thought through the idea more carefully, He realised that He could not bring Himself to wipe it *all* out, and He searched His mind to think of any parts of it He *could* save. This was a great task that led Him down many blind alleys. He thought about creating a fresh first man, perhaps of assembling him as a woman. Then He thought of making humans capable of reproducing themselves without the physical intimacy which seemed so readily to lead them into such moral difficulties. He wondered about addressing the hierarchy of living forms and putting a different species in the prime position. He wondered about kippers. But no matter what He thought about, there were still problems. He couldn't find a solution. He was going to have to act. To help Him justify the action that He intended to take He wandered amongst His creation, reminding Himself of the moral depths that it had fallen into.

Then He saw Noah playing with his children—laughing and lifting them up and tickling them. And He realised that He rather liked Noah, and He looked at him more closely. He thought him righteous and liked in particular the way he prayed. And the sight of Noah lightened gGod's heart—and it had been a while since gGod had felt much of an inkling of this. And He felt many kindly and generous thoughts. So He decided to make Noah and his children an exception to the mass extermination that He was planning. Yes, this was the right thing to do, He concluded: eradicate the bad and save something of the good.

After further due consideration, gGod decided that the best way of wiping out life was to bring about a huge flood. He knew that this would mean fish and other aquatic life forms would remain, but He had been pretty sure when He created them that their mental abilities implied that they would never stray into difficult moral territory. And, as far as He understood, they didn't feel pain either. So, unseen, He communicated with Noah and suggested that he build an ark large enough to accommodate himself, his wife, his sons and their wives together with a (breeding) pair of every land-born living thing that He had created (though on this He was a little confused—leaving some creatures out and missing the fact that many birds didn't need land, and some life forms did not need pairs to replicate themselves anyway). After He was satisfied that the message had got through, He then appeared to Noah and in a booming voice gave him precise instructions on the size and design of the ark.

'It should be three hundred cubits long,' He proclaimed, 'fifty cubits wide, thirty cubits high, with a roof extending above the main deck to a height of one cubit. It should have a door in the side leading to a lower, second and third deck all below the exposed upper deck.'

Noah had no idea what a cubit was. This was not surprising as gGod, although He had entertained it as a possible answer to various measuring problems, had only just invented it. Even so, Noah did his best to make sense of the sort of size required to accommodate himself, his family, all the animals and enough food to last them for the duration (though he didn't know how long that would be either). So, as well as he could, Noah did as gGod had requested and knocked up the ark as instructed. It then took seven days to get all (barring those missed out on airborne or reproductive grounds) the pairs of non-aquatic living things inside. gGod then brought on the flood which, when He appeared again briefly, He predicted would last for forty days and forty nights (starting the day *after* the rain began).

And so it rained for forty days and forty nights (after the first day). And everything on Earth was covered with water. Even the highest mountains were covered to a depth of fifteen cubits and all (excepting the flying, web-footed and self-reproducing hermaphroditic) land-based life forms were killed. Actually, gGod was so involved in the flooding process and His time-consuming perceptual responsibilities that He entirely forgot He'd set Noah afloat in the ark. When, finally, He brought him back to mind He realised that He'd under-estimated how difficult it was going to be to get things back to normal—everywhere was so wet! He was stuck for thinking of a way to get rid of the water so, unable to think of anything else, He made a wind blow in the hope that it would dry things out. Eventually, after a further one hundred and fifty five days the ark came to rest on the top of Mount Ararat. But even then it took another three months for the water to abate fully, and even more time for the earth to dry out sufficiently for Noah and his family and the animals to leave the ark. It had been a long haul.

But even after all this, Noah was very pleased, and so was gGod: Noah because he'd been saved, gGod because He'd got rid of a lot of troublemakers. So, feeling on top of things, gGod commanded Noah and his family and all the surviving animals to be happy and free. But gGod found it difficult to concentrate on His regular tasks. He was caught up with a sense of guilt about the whole thing, thinking that He might have overreacted a bit. There must, He thought, have been some good people amongst those he so cursorily drowned. At first He thought of bringing them back, but that seemed very complicated so He took the more apologetic line and agreed with Himself that never again would He flood the Earth. To consolidate on this He provided a visual reminder, announcing that every time a rainbow appeared it was a sign of this guarantee, or "covenant" as He called it, and should be a reminder to all (few that there were) that the Earth was safe from any future deluge. And, as well as that, returning to His post-flood feeling of happiness, that it should be seen as a large-scale and brilliant sign of the simple joys of living.

And Noah was very happy with everything and, because he had become attached to it, decided to remain living in the ark and utilising the ground that surrounded it, to become a "man of the soil". Ararat was about five hundred and eighty-eight cubits (using the Hebrew "Long Cubit" that gGod had invented as a refinement of the original cubit, and Noah unknowingly had just happened to use for his construction of the ark) above the settled sea level after the flood, and its general climate was warm and temperate. The rainfall, however (to some extent an after-effect of the downpour that caused the flood) was significant, even during the driest months. So, in view of the prevailing westerly winds, he had to be selective about where he farmed. Sensibly, he chose the south-facing slopes and, hoping always for the best, he planted a vineyard which, after a few years, amazingly led him to producing some fine quality wines.

One day Noah lay back on a south facing grassy bank near to the ark, tasting his latest vintage. He had become very keen on the products of his harvests. This year had been a particularly good one—long sunny days with gentle fanning breezes in the evening—and although the wine was not at all matured it had the sort of airy fruitiness that Noah particularly enjoyed. On the south-facing slopes that he had chosen for his vineyards the מרלו (Malbec) and קברנה סוביניון (Cabernet Sauvignon) varieties (as he called them) did particularly well, and this year had been his best yet.

But his agrarian pursuits, good as they were, were not sufficient to make him feel fully content with his life. Indeed, over the years since the flood had subsided, his sense of initial happiness had progressively reduced. When gGod asked him to build the ark, collect the animals and then set forth to sail out the deluge, Noah had felt he had a purpose in life. And it was tough going, organising things and getting prepared on time, so he had been fully occupied. But since the rain had stopped and the waters had fallen back, and the ark had come to rest, things had been different: psychologically, he felt unmotivated (the incentives that he'd had previously were gone), and practically, the ark itself was a continual problem. It had been built in a hurry from unseasoned cypress wood, and though serviceable for its main gGod-prescribed purpose, it had not proved itself too good as a permanent, long term land-based dwelling. Much of the caulking, constructed from wound-together reeds, had started to come away during the first week or so afloat, but at this time the general dampness of everything made it fairly easy to keep stuffing up the gaps between the roughly hewn wood planks. However, since the vessel became marooned on the top of Mount Ararat, the long hot summers and seasonal lack of rain meant that the whole structure had dried out considerably and the reed caulking had disintegrated; and that meant gaping fissures along most of the joints. The roof had split too which meant the novel freshwater collection system that Noah had rigged up was ineffective. As well as that there seemed no way of preventing returning migrant birds nesting in its low beams. Recently, the second floor had completely given way and had proved impossible to get back to anything like level.

And his wife, Trixie (her sons and their wives referred to her as Naamah, but Noah always thought that incestuously inappropriate as Naamah was the sister of Tubal-cain, himself a direct descendant of Adam through Cain and so a close relative) was always nagging him. She had been very supportive when gGod gave his original instructions for the ark, but by the time they set sail she was already becoming more than a little tiresome. Caught up with the initial enthusiasm of the project, she had ignored the influences of her natural tendencies, but that distraction was now passed. Trixie was of an acquisitive nature and, since she and Noah had been together, no matter what items they had in the household, she always wanted a newer or better version. This had led to her continually pressuring Noah to fulfil her desires. But because of the task of building the ark and then collecting all the animals and looking after things during the flood, Noah had no time for, nor the means of fulfilling, these demands. But, driven by her freshly released avaricious ways, Trixie wouldn't accept that being the only people left alive on earth, and being marooned in a huge, leaking craft full of all the wildlife the earth had to offer (except for fish, airborne species, other aquatic life forms and those capable of reproducing themselves), made satisfying consumeristic demands not at all easy—well, impossible. On top of this she didn't like animals, hated sailing, never enjoyed a glass of wine, and she wasn't too keen on her daughters-in-law either.

So, enjoying his moments away from the ark and the constant pestering that went with its proximity, Noah lay back on the comfortably-angled slope of the ground and took another draught of his fresh though eminently drinkable Malbec. He turned his face to the sun and reflected on his life—questioning its worth and whether he felt satisfied with what he had accomplished. He liked the feeling of the sun on his face and he tried to find enough pleasure in just that to cause him to smile. But it wouldn't work. His self-analysis had brought on a background feeling of depression and all he sensed was the singularly brutal existential awareness that it was hot. He took another drink. He slackened his robe. But he was still too hot so he pulled it off completely and threw it aside. He felt the warmth of the sun on his naked body. He could hear Trixie ranting about something inside the ark—

something about needing the kitchen re-decorated and having some new tiling in the bathroom. She'd been going on about both things since before the end of the flood, but he still hadn't got around to doing anything about either of them.

The stark awareness of his existence turned to a darkness and within moments he found himself caught in a swirling depression.

It had been easier when the animals were about—he was readily distracted by giving them attention—but since they'd all gone out of the ark and left he'd felt very alone. He saw his sons and their wives occasionally, but they too had been busy with their own growing families. If it wasn't for his vineyard he didn't know what he would do. And he never heard from gGod any more. And his life just seem to go on and on! He'd lived so many years now that he didn't even celebrate his birthday. In fact he'd forgotten when his birthday *was*—and even how *old* he was!

'Life is so miserable!' he exclaimed out loud. "Utterly, utterly miserable!'

He finished off the Malbec then went on to the Sauvignon. After a few swigs, although things still felt miserable they seemed to have a softer, less jarring edge. He took a few more gulps and, enjoying the only other things in his life worth anything, the grassy slope and the warming sun, he lay back and fell into a comfortable, naked and broad-spread stupor.

As the afternoon went on, one of his sons, Shem, father of Canaan, came walking past. He was used to seeing his father the worse for wine but had never seen him naked before. He was very shocked. This was not a sight a parent's child should witness. Shem grabbed hold of the discarded robe and, trying all the time to look the other way, pulled it over Noah's naked body. Later in the afternoon he met up with his brothers, Ham and Japheth and told them what had happened. They too were very shocked even at the report that their father had been seen naked, and they were all very troubled by the thought. Isolated as they were on the top of Mount

Ararat they didn't get to see much of life and this much they really didn't want to see!

Later in the afternoon, when Noah woke up, he realised that someone had pulled his robe up over him. It was an odd thought to imagine some unknown person seeing him naked while he lay asleep; but, considering how things were going in his life in general, he really didn't care.

As he sat there, the sky darkened and within a short while it started to rain. He felt spots of it on his face and his mood fell even further as he imagined another deluge—just the thought of more months adrift on another flood in the leaking ark with the relentlessly moaning Trixie filled him with a heavy, ever-darkening spiral of despair.

Inside the ark Trixie was standing beneath the leaking roof. She looked up at the drips coming down from the splits in the boards. She shook her fist at them. But it wasn't enough to ease her annoyance. She stamped her feet in frustration, grabbed hold of a broom and poked the end at the bowed ceiling. A gush of water suddenly broke through, then straightaway several of the boards fell down and released a great flood of water. Trixie was drenched. She threw the broom down and, soaked, bedraggled and very angry, she ran to the door and began shouting.

'Noah! Noah! The roof's fallen in now! I've had enough! Wherever you are, get back up here! If you don't do something about this, then I'm off!'

He heard her shouting and shook his head in resigned despair. Now he felt overcome by a wave of complete hopelessness. All he could think of was running away, but when he thought of actually doing it he realised that he couldn't even work up the effort to make a start. Again he looked up into the sunless sky and, accompanied by the screeching of Trixie, fell back again onto the grassy slope and let the rain fall onto his face. He reached over to the goatskin bags that he used for storing his wine, but they were both empty. It just felt as though anything that he had done was worthless and where he found himself now was insufferably pointless.

Then he heard another voice. The voice of a child!

'Grandpa Noah! Grandpa Noah!' it shouted excitedly. 'Grandpa Noah! Look what I've found!'

Noah, arrested by the child's joyful shouting, turned his head and looked towards its origin. A young boy was running from the ark towards him. He'd pushed past Trixie who, bedraggled and soaked with water from the collapsed roof, was still waving her arms and screaming.

As the boy approached, Noah could not recognise him though he knew, of course, that he must be one of his many great-great (or greater still) grandchildren.

'Ah! It's...' he said offering the questioning pause to be filled with a name.

The child responded appropriately.

'Bill! Grandpa Noah. It's me, Bill!'

'Of course, Bill,' affirmed Noah, used to falling in with names given like this by his unrecognisable progeny.

The young boy ran up to him. He was bursting with excitement.

'Look, Grandpa Noah! Look! Look what I've found!' He held a leather bowl out. 'Look! Look!'

Noah got up onto his knees and peered into the bowl. It was half filled with water and in the water two goldfish swam in frantic circles.

'It's the goldfish! he shouted joyfully. 'I thought they were lost! Wherever did you find them...er…Bill?'

'Their bowl was hidden in a dark corner on the second floor of the ark—where the level has sunk. Father says they must have fed on insects falling down from the disintegrating floor above them. Look! They're alive! And well!'

'Well, I can hardly believe it,' said Noah, staring down at the fish.

When the ark had been emptied of its cargo Noah had checked off all the animals against a list he'd made when they went in. The only creatures missing were two goldfish. He had won them years before at a fair—throwing quoits over pegs—and had treasured them ever since. They were always there for him when he became despaired with Trixie. When gGod had announced the flood He made it clear to Noah that only land-based animals should be taken into the ark—that fish and so forth could look after themselves: "There'll be no room for passengers!" He'd proclaimed after what seemed a very summary calculation of numbers of species and ark-volume available. But Noah couldn't bear the idea of being parted from his goldfish so, although knowing that he was acting on his own behalf and not towards the gGod's greater good, he sneaked them inside the ark and hid them where they would be safe and where he could every now and again visit them. However, the responsibility for the ark, and all the animals, and the constant bickering from Trixie took its toll on him, and one day he realised that he'd completely forgotten where the goldfish were. He had thought briefly of asking gGod for help (Him being all-seeing and so on) but straight away realised that by doing this he would be exposing his deceit. So thereafter he had lived without seeing them. And now here they were! After all these years they'd survived! They had been lost and now they were found. Noah was overjoyed. His previous misery fell away. The simple pleasure of the discovery of the lost goldfish had reminded him of the joy to be found in the simple things and he welcomed it and was filled with it.

He patted the smiling Bill on the head.

'Well done, Bill. You have brought me great joy.'

'Then I am happy as well, Grandpa Noah. I smile because you smile. And both of us are happy. And look! I think the goldfish are happy too, because they knew they were lost and now they know that at last they have been found.'

'Yes, you're right, Bill. You are very wise. You will go on to great things. And you've shown an old man how it is the simple things that make life worthwhile. Thank you, Bill. You are my inspiration.'

Noah got up, pulled his robe around him and, with Bill skipping behind, walked towards Trixie, smiling and holding out his arms to her. She stopped shouting, and began to smile as he got closer. They looked at each other and remembered the love they had found together all those years ago, and were both overjoyed at feeling it again.

Noah looked up into the sky. The rain had stopped, the clouds were moving away, and it was becoming lighter. A rainbow was forming. It became intense. Noah looked up at it and, as he watched, the bow of it slowly turned upside down. Then two light clouds positioned themselves as if they were eyes above a broadly smiling, spectral mouth—gGod was smiling!

Noah thought of the covenant that gGod had made with him all those years ago, telling him that whenever he saw a rainbow he should be reminded of gGod's guarantee never to bring harm to living things again. He stopped to stare at it. He felt absorbed by its beauty. He thought of gGod smiling. He rested his hand on Bill's shoulder.

'Never take life too seriously, Bill,' he said. 'Be happy. There is always time enough for joy. Look! Even gGod has time to smile.'

CHAPTER 15

Thinking about...the nature of virtue and the place of action

With an increasingly familiar heavy and jolting shudder the machine came to a bone-crunching stop. Socrates almost lost grip of the control lever but, with the experience gained so far, and tightening his fingers as much as he could, he managed quickly to reassert what passed as a firm grasp on it.

After staring ahead and gasping for breath for a few minutes in what now had become an accustomed manner, he was sufficiently recovered to speak.

'IgnatiusM! Are you there?'

'Yes, of course, Socrates. I'm here.'

'That was some trip!'

'It was indeed, Socrates. I hope you feel rewarded by it.'

'Rewarded by it! I'm exhilarated! That gGod can emanate happiness like that is just amazing. Yes, IgnatiusM, I'm truly exhilarated! I feel an overwhelming sense of good. I feel as if I've been somewhere over the rainbow!'

IgnatiusM conceded a sort-of-laugh at Socrates' witticism, though it was obvious that such an expression of levity did not come naturally to him.

'So, Socrates, you're going along with the idea that happiness is linked closely to the good, if not synonymous with it.'

'Going along with it? I'm its keenest supporter! Noah found delight in the finding of the goldfish, the joy of the young boy in bringing them to him and, writ large in the sky, the sign of happiness from gGod. All that evidence of the good. And I was much moved by witnessing it. So, yes, IgnatiusM, I am the greatest enthusiast of combining happiness with the good.'

'Then you are indeed an Aristotelian, Socrates, for Aristotle was the paramount proponent of the idea that good is a state of happiness. And what better goal. Indeed, even though ethical goals will vary according to how or to whom they are applied, they almost all rest upon the foundation of the goal of happiness.'

'So, you are saying that there is a difference according to whether you apply your goal to yourself or to others.'

'Yes, and taking them in that order, in this regard you could classify yourself as either an egoist or an altruist.'

'Egoist?'

'The term comes from the psychoanalytic theory of Sigmund Freud. He had a beard, you know—quite an impressive one; a long goatee I think you'd call it. The "ego", he says is that part of the human personality which is experienced as the "self" or the "I". It is that part of the human experience that sees itself as contacting the world via perception. This "self", this "I", is the aspect of the human that remembers, evaluates and plans what actions it will take. For example, you might say: "*I* remember that", "*I* think that's the better course of action", "*I* think *I*'ll set about achieving it like this". In all these instances the "I" is the experience of the "ego" as the "self". According to the Freudian theory, the ego coexists with the "id" which is founded on primitive driving forces, and the superego which is—'

'Too much! IgnatiusM! Too much, my friend!'

'I'm sorry, Socrates. It's so easy sometimes just to dig this stuff out without thinking. I know you only need to know what is necessary to inform you and guide you on your travels—to help see you through this, your last day.'

'No, don't apologise. You are my fount of knowledge, IgnatiusM. And I need to know as much as I can if, as you point out, I am to face all that this day, this, my final day on earth, has to offer. Please, please carry on.'

'Well, if you apply your ethical goals to others you should consider yourself an "altruist"—an all round "good egg" you might say, that always puts others before himself. Though it is difficult to see altruistic goals as not containing some egotistic reward—the "good egg" will often, if not usually, feel pleased at the good deed done for others. But that's enough for the moment, Socrates, we must push on.'

'Yes, you are right about not having too much information at any one time. Though some updating on the problems of how we should act in a virtuous way will never be out of place. And the Freudian system as you've explained it is most helpful. Let it be that through the story of Noah I have found the root cause, the foundation if you like, of virtue to be happiness. But I know there is more, because I feel the weight of pieces in the bag that hangs from my neck. So let us press on, and, as you say, find out what our next destination is to be. Shall we look at the next piece now?'

'Yes, Socrates, let's see what's on offer.'

Socrates dug into his bag keenly and taking hold of the first jigsaw piece he touched, removed it and held it up to the screen.

'Well! Would you believe—'

IgnatiusM was suddenly cut off as the machine started shaking for no apparent reason. Then there was a down-pouring of dust from the urns, and the flapping of the canopy sent the nymphs reeling as though they had been caught in a sudden storm.

'What's happening, IgnatiusM! What's going on!' shouted a panicky Socrates.

'I don't know! I don't know! Unless it's gGod again! For your own safety, I think it's best if you let go of the jigsaw piece!'

Socrates dropped the jigsaw piece onto the board. It landed picture side up. He gripped the lever as tightly as he could in both hands. The emergency button flashed a few times. He gasped for breath. The chair shook so much it nearly tipped him off. Then he heard IgnatiusM telling him that now the best thing to do might be to make an emergency return, so he should turn over the piece he'd just dropped and fit it against the other two.

He reached a shaking hand down towards the board. For a moment, he stopped, confused and wide-eyed, but drawing on the primitive driving forces of his id, he forced his hand to move. He touched the piece, then turned it over, then pushed it towards the other two. However, before he could match them he was thrown back roughly in the chair as the marble columns wobbled and the whole machine lurched and swayed.

Confusion reigned.

Then, with a final shudder everything stopped.

There were some crackling sounds then the reassuringly familiar voice of IgnatiusM.

'I think we need to get gGod back on this, Socrates,' said IgnatiusM anxiously. 'Let's hope He's got the time!'

Without anything like an invitation, there was a bright flash and gGod's chair appeared. The next moment He was sitting on it, looking up at an angle with a fixed smile as if posing for a portrait. He brushed back His hair with both hands.

'Ah, gGod!' said IgnatiusM, apparently recovered from his previous anxiety and now, seemingly unsurprised by gGod's sudden appearance, continuing as if nothing unusual had occurred. 'Socrates and I have been discussing the link between happiness and the good. I've just been talking about the ego, but feel you could throw a lot more light on the whole subject.'

As if seeking a better, more flattering light, gGod tipped His head to one side and gave His hair an attentive flick.

'I've been trying out a new style lately—the James Dean look—but I must say I've been having trouble with the free flowing textured quiff. I just can't get the front to look as natural and wavy as it should be. And it's a style that needs a certain facial expression, and I'm not at all sure I've got the hang of that. What do you think?' He threw His head back and struck an undirected, rebellious expression. Neither Socrates nor IgnatiusM responded. gGod resumed a less affected look. 'Sorry. Ego, you say? How can I help?'

He gave His hair a final stroke and settled back.

'Well, it's like this—'

'Just let me get comfortable,' He said wriggling down into His chair. 'Then, as they say, We'll begin.' He giggled at His weak "creation" joke but its levity was completely lost on both Socrates and IgnatiusM. 'I just need a cup of tea before we start.' His small table appeared with a cup of tea already sitting at its centre—there was not the slightest ripple on its surface. The label of a teabag dangled over the edge—"English Breakfast". Then, picking up on their concerns, He started. 'I agree that happiness is the goal, and I also agree that virtue is crucial to any plans we may make in order to bring about happiness. Shall I expound?'

Socrates nodded keenly.

'Of course. Please. Expound away!'

gGod, took a sip of tea then, still not having shaken off His attempts at the James Dean look, turned His head from side to side a few times as if He were looking into a mirror. Unsatisfied, He continued.

'Very well. Morality is at the root of all this—that is, how you conduct yourself according to what's right and what's wrong. But it's when humans are involved in morality that dilemmas arise. It's complicated. Even for Me! Moral judgement is bound up with proportionality, and it is the desire to attain some sort of moral symmetry between competing views that guides moral thinking. Moral doubts occur when the negative aspects of the means seem greater than the positive aspects of the ends. When this occurs the essentially physical aspects of a situation take on a moral character. Following Me? Good. For example, someone may wish to help a friend die because the friend is suffering great pain. In this case, the end would seem justified—the cessation of pain. However, it is a fundamental and well established rule with humans that life is sacred and the taking of it by another is an ethical wrong. If the latter case is made strongly (as it usually is—it was after all Me that set it up to deal with the problems I had with the first man's sons) then the simple situation becomes a moral dilemma.'

'I see,' said Socrates. 'So are there ways of solving dilemmas like this?'

'I'm glad you've asked,' said gGod, again troubled with His hair and pawing at it fussily. 'Over time, humans have developed three major theories that describe how they should act or behave. Shall I elucidate?'

'Please. Please.'

'These are: duty-based, consequence-based and virtue-based. Though the different theories have separate starting points (different bases); when you get involved in considering how they can be applied, their distinctions tend to blur.'

'So, the duty-based theories?' prompted Socrates noticing that gGod was still fiddling with an irritating curl on the right hand side of His troublesome quiff.

'Yes,' He said, though obviously with His mind more on matters tonsorial. 'Duty-based theories propose that some things are right or wrong irrespective of their consequences. According to duty-based theories, the most important thing about moral action is that it is applied according to a deeper inner sense of responsibility to such things as, though I say it Myself, *My* wishes, or other (though clearly not so important) ethical standards that have been developed over time to become deemed unassailably right. If moral action is based upon *My* wishes then the rules do not have to prove themselves—they, like Me, just *are*. Obviously, any wishes that I have must by necessity be perfect and so are unassailable. My existence is crucial to this, but I think we can take that as a given. Can we not?'

'Of course,' said Socrates.

'Of course,' agreed IgnatiusM.

gGod continued in an unassailably existent way.

'Even if My existence couldn't be accepted (which certainly at the moment would be somewhat perverse as I'm sitting here telling you it would be perverse), there is the question of whether or not humans actually *know* what My will is. And I know that sometimes I haven't helped this to be as clear as perhaps it should be. It's tough going, you know, sometimes, being gGod. But, to be fair, I didn't have anything to work from when I created the rules. It's easy to underrate the difficulties of working from scratch as I had to. Just imagine! Thinking up all that never-thought-of-stuff from nothing! I know that My rules might seem to have some underlying universal quality, but they actually just arose from My will. And, I say again, I had nothing to go on. It's a bit of a conundrum, I can tell you. Think of this: if I had declared killing praiseworthy would it have been good because I willed it and because I am good, or only because I willed it and it is good just because it is My will?'

'Questions, questions. So many questions,' said IgnatiusM thoughtfully.

'Yes. Lots of pressure. If I'd only had someone I could depend on…well, I won't say anything about that at the moment… yes, that would have taken a lot of the pressure off. Oh well.'

'But the questions,' repeated IgnatiusM, not wanting to see gGod wallow too much in self-pity. 'So many of them!'

'You're right. Yes. The application of duty-based theory raises many questions. Let alone the others that we haven't even looked at yet. And before we do, I must point out that they all rely on establishing what are "wants".'

'"Wants"?' asked Socrates.

'Yes, "wants". Let me explain. For example, who (at the risk of being a little Biblical) is your neighbour? Is it someone you know because they live next door or is it everyone in the world? If you are a masochist or a liar should you do unto others as you would wish them to do unto you, that is, do others harm and always tell lies? You cannot do unto others as you would have them do unto you without your "want" to be treated in a certain way. Because of the variation in individual "wants" this view is notoriously difficult to apply.'

There was a reflective pause. gGod seemed to be straying from the main line of His argument.

'I feel we're cornered here,' said Socrates wisely, not being in any way critical of gGod's approach, but hopefully nudging Him in the right direction for better understanding.

'Aha!' exclaimed gGod. 'Not necessarily. Let Me move onto consequence-based theory and bring back Immanuel Kant.'

'Yes, good,' said a now rather self-satisfied Socrates.

'Kant believed that people should be treated as ends in themselves, never as means to ends. In other words, in your dealings with people you must always recognise their humanity. In this context, Kant believed that you should be responsible for your actions but not for the *consequences* of your actions which may be out of your control. This is based on the idea that although you may think you can know many of the consequences of how you act at any one time, you only have to imagine a future time beyond that time to realise that this connection (of action to consequence) soon becomes impossible to plot. Clever man, Kant! Though, of course, he didn't understand time in any proper sense. Even so, because of the problem of not being able to work out all consequences, Kant believed that the only way to govern human actions was by the use of what he called a "categorical imperative". This categorical imperative is an instruction to be carried out as an absolute and unconditional duty. This is how he framed it: "Act only on maxims which you can at the same time want to be universal laws". In other words, you should only do something if you would be happy that everyone else did it too. Oh, and I should have asked. Do you want a cup of tea?'

'This is most interesting,' said Socrates ignoring gGod's question about tea. 'I wonder if I could raise a few points here?'

'Of course,' conceded gGod. 'Please. Just give Me a moment.' He sat forward in His chair and created a second cup of hot tea. Again a small label hung from the string that stretched over the side of the cup from the bag. Then, ignoring the fact that the offer of tea had been declined, He pushed the cup towards Socrates. 'I prefer a tea bag over leaf tea every time—much easier to handle. Oh, and he didn't have a beard, by the way.'

'Who didn't have a beard?'

'Kant.'

Socrates continued.

'I can see that within this system it may not be too difficult to work out moral rules for ourselves, though it is clearly more difficult to work out acceptable rules that can be applied to everyone. We might think that such imperatives as "always tell the truth", "always keep promises" or "never kill another human being" are reasonable moral duties, but even these would be difficult to apply universally. Should we tell the truth if it means that our friend would be unfairly punished? Should we keep a promise when this means that others will suffer? Should we hold back from killing anyone even though killing them is the only way of saving our friend?'

'Very wise, Socrates. Overall, categorical imperatives do lack both a regard for human emotions as well as an absolute measure against which to test the imperatives themselves. There are always categorical rules by which humans are expected to abide, but the strongest influence on how they should act morally is more usually based upon the prospective consequences of actions. This view is called “Utilitarianism”. It was a view formulated in different ways by Jeremy Bentham and John Stuart Mill. You won't have heard of them.’

‘No, not until now, of course,’ said Socrates nodding encouragement for gGod to continue and hoping that He didn’t mention beards.

‘For Bentham and Mill (both lovers of tea, might I add),’ He said, pushing the second cup closer to Socrates, ‘the ultimate aim of moral action is hedonistic (that is, motivated by an increase in happiness). However, even though they had different views about what happiness is—Bentham thought it a blissful state, whereas Mill believed it is founded on an ascending scale of lower to higher pleasures (according to him, the more refined pleasures such as music or art being higher on the scale)—they both believed that “amounts” or “degrees” of happiness could be calculated. For example (on both their views), happiness is the absence of pain. So, if action X will bring about “+4” amount of happiness and “-3” amount of pain then the potential net gain in happiness of “+1” means that action X is the correct moral path to follow. You have to be good at arithmetic to make this add up!’

Again the joke was lost.

gGod gave a rather throwaway flick of His quiff, as though a little disdain would be enough to give tribute to His (He thought) rather clever play on words.

‘Please go on,’ said Socrates.

Another sip of tea and gGod continued.

‘Not only is it hard to know if such calculations are using equivalent qualities (for example, does one unit of happiness equal one unit of pain and so on) but calculating probable consequences is notoriously difficult. How would you know that an action you take will lead to particular consequences (especially in the long or very long-term)? In normally-experienced time (as opposed to god-time), you cannot see fully into the future so you can only extrapolate outcomes from known circumstances. This means that you do not know future events that influence later future events and so on. For example, who could have imagined in the time of Adam (My first man, you will recall) how important Noah (My favoured man) would be in the future? Or who would have thought how important the two goldfish would turn out to be to Noah's state of mind when they were first placed into their leather bowl? Their names were Geoffrey and Maybeline by the way; the prize-won parents of all goldfish that followed (goldfish being a bowl-bound breed and not suited to the wilder aquatic environment). Indeed, the question of whether your moral actions should also be applied to non-human species further complicates the issue. For example, you do not know at present (and I'm not going to tell you) whether or not the human race will be superseded by a species of creatures that currently are victimised by humans and who may remember this in their future regard for human beings.'

'Such as cocks,' observed Socrates, nodding in a self-congratulating way to IgnatiusM's screen. 'Or,' turning to gGod, 'a species that might favour the human race because of its previous good treatment—like goldfish!'

'Exactly,' replied gGod, moving on quickly. 'Utilitarianism also suffers from the same ethical vacuity as the categorical imperative. It can readily be used to justify actions that seem intuitively immoral, for example killing someone as a punishment or in the cause of a just war. Or it can produce results that vindicate the happiness of the individual as more important than the happiness of the many. For example (again), a large gain for one rich person at the barely noticed expense of many small losses for many individuals. Ah! This tea is wonderful! English Breakfast! Such a blend! If it has to be a teabag (and it does), then this is the only one for Me (and it is). I don't mean the *only* one, of course, it's fresh every time, but the only *variety*.'

gGod then squeezed the teabag dry to get the last few drops of moisture from it, lifted the cup to His lips and drained it.

'But what about the negative effects of an action,' asked Socrates.

'Are you absolutely sure you wouldn't like a cup?'

Socrates shook his head, at the same time deciding not to take up gGod's seeming misuse of the term "absolutely" when He obviously really only meant "sure" in its necessarily confining case.

Another cup of tea appeared on the small table replacing gGod's empty cup which, on the arrival of its replacement, just disappeared.

'Whereas positive utilitarianism tries to achieve an increase in happiness, negative utilitarianism only wants to reduce the amount of pain or suffering. For example, in order to achieve the greatest net gain in happiness, the positive utilitarian would share a fixed amount of money between, say, a thousand people (each of whom would gain a very small but calculable amount) against giving it all to one sick one (with great personal needs). On the other hand, to reduce the total amount of suffering, the negative utilitarian would give all the money to the sick one (whose suffering would be reduced) and ignore the others (whose well-being would be relatively unaffected).'

'So, is it possible to apply either negative utilitarianism or positive utilitarianism as separate principles irrespective of circumstances, or do circumstances always dictate which one we should choose?'

'Soc, it all comes down to the third theory—the virtue-based one. Aristotle believed that your actions should be dictated by inner reflection on the question "how should I live?" He thought that if you encourage your virtuous self then it would lead you to a virtuous life and cause you to act morally to the highest ethical standards. But, I'm afraid, it's not necessarily that easy. As well as being culturally influenced over time, your personal estimation of what is virtuous and good tends naturally to be different from the estimations of others. Few of you get pleasure from exactly the same things as others. Aristotle's theory assumes that there is such a thing as an absolute standard of virtue but, I have to say, it is hard to see where this comes from. The application of such a principle could easily become (as Nietzsche—who, I should remind you, had a huge moustache—points out) simply an extrapolation of your own wishes.'

'So can You tell us of something that is a true virtue? And if there is such a thing, could it be applied universally?'

With a flick of the hair and a tight-lipped smile brought on by the feeling that His James Dean quiff was at last responding appropriately to the attention He had been affording it, gGod avoided the question and carried on.

'It really all boils down to how you *do* it—how you *apply* it. No matter how appealing utilitarianism or virtue ethics are, when it comes down to it, and I know this goes against My will (that is always in the background), you are forced to question the meaning of "right" in human behavioural or evolutionary contexts. This is a "naturalistic" view (drawing often on scientific or inductive evidence) based simply on the way that most human beings behave or have behaved—you act the way you do because that is what you are (or have been). Exceptions to this, for example, someone who kills human beings for their own reasons, is considered aberrant from the "norm" because to kill someone is considered psychologically destructive. Though, there is a view called "existentialism" which is a form of individual naturalism that considers psychological destruction part of the innate nature of self. Jean-Paul Sartre, a big noise in this field, explained that human nature, in the way it is interpreted by science, is a self-deception and that you alone, as an individual, can make value judgements about how you act. The test for how you act is your response to an inner sense of what he called "good faith"; and your conduct should be guided by this alone.'

'I'm beginning to wonder…' said Socrates, resisting asking if Jean Paul Sartre had a beard or a moustache '…if there is anything in the nature of life that is absolutely right or absolutely wrong (excepting what might be going on in the background).'

'So it seems, Socrates. It may be that your views about right and wrong are entirely human, that is, human beings invent them to deal with human problems. It may be that there are no truly right or wrong acts, in other words that there is nothing absolutely right or wrong. Rational thinking would dictate that it is more likely to be conditions or beliefs at any one time that dictate them; that everything is ethically relative. It may be that I, all-knowing and all-seeing, and ever-present, am not (amazing as that thought might be) the only producer of ethical standards (albeit in the background)!'

Socrates was bowled over with it all. His mind was brimming with ideas, overflowing with questions, and he couldn't hold back the flow.

'I can see how moral standards rely on so many things. If I was the only person in the world I doubt I would need any such standards? Or if there were no conscious beings in the universe I wonder if it would still be possible to imagine that there could be a concept of right and wrong? And the questions keep coming! Other forms of life on earth do not seem to have any ethical standards. So if we are part of an evolutionary process, and have evolved from species with no ethical standards, why should we believe that our human standards have ethical meaning? I cannot even define "good" and "bad" without referring to human beings. On the negative utilitarian view the best way to reduce all suffering would be to eliminate all sentient life. Does this make sense in any way? gGod! Does this make sense? Of course not! And if I ask myself whether we are means to some greater end, or whether we are ends in ourselves, I am tossed even further into the stormy sea of confusion!'

Socrates drew breath.

'Then have a cup of tea? And when you've finished it, take action, pull on that lever and see what happens! Anyway, you'll have to excuse Me now. I've just perceived something that I think needs My attention. Again!'

'I'll do my best,' said Socrates trying to calm himself down.

'Good. I'll leave the tea. Help yourself. I'll make it self-filling so you'll never go short—much more efficient.'

And with only a barely noticeable shudder, He was gone.

The screen flickered. Socrates, seized with gGod's directive to take action, ensured that the jigsaw piece was picture side up, held it towards the screen for IgnatiusM to give it the nod, then looked at it fixedly, grabbed hold of the lever and pulled it back.

Immediately he was engulfed in a cloud of dust as the urns spun wildly in time with the bone-shaking vibrations of the *C*-drive that heralded another port of call in the jumble of changing events that is time.

CHAPTER 16

War—action and mercy

Since Noah's death, gGod's patience with His creation had been tested many times but, often struggling with His need to act positively and remain in accordance with His will, He had always kept His word and stayed His hand. The rainbow had appeared in the sky many times, though sometimes, it has to be said, it was ill-defined and broken. And sometimes it was more to remind gGod Himself of His covenant than anyone else. But, for all His efforts, the evil side of human nature had been impossible to suppress, and the desire it nurtured to harm others had always been easy to promote. Enmity or possession were the common driving forces—hatred of another race or society, or the wish to take over their land had never failed to galvanise one group against another. Yes, the rainbow often appeared in the sky, but gGod's covenant against destruction did not extend to holding back the desire for war within the descendants of His first man.

And the current war, like so many others before or after, had gone on for many years. On each side fathers passed down to their children the same hostile feelings towards the same enemy, and so the justification of bitter hatred was sown in the very seed of their progeny. Militancy brought about the development and production of ever more effective weapons and the training in their use. Walls had been built, ditches dug, and fortifications strewn across contested borderlands. It did not matter that the founding reasons for the war were by now lost; the need to continue with it remained deeply embedded in the minds of all those on both sides. The acquisition of territory had distilled out as a crucial aspect, but again whether this was an initial cause was lost in history. By its measure the warring factions could easily prove their progress by any gaining and holding of even the smallest amount of ground. And so now, in the present day, with nothing else as a measure, that was all that mattered.

Religious belief also played a part (and could indeed be an original cause), and different (imagined) gods were called upon to support the different armies. Sometimes it was the case that the same (imagined) gods were supporting the opposing sides, but this did nothing to negate each side's belief in its own divinely ordained authority for war.

In order to wage the war effectively, allegiance of the individual was paramount. The nature and form of the state and its laws provided the underlying structure for the fealty that individuals felt for their society. And it was the developed beliefs in which laws should govern each society that were more convincing even than religious beliefs as a motivation for the loyalty of individuals involved—the state looked after its people whereas religious beliefs held out what was sometimes only an uncomfortable mixture of obligation and hope. Destroying the enemy and taking over its land fed back into the ultimate aim—the right to be part of a certain legalised state. And each state promoted itself forcibly to its members. When individuals lost their comrades or their families were killed as by-products of the conflict, claims made by leaders of each state about the evil-doing of members of the opposing state provided each group with an enhanced desire to eradicate their enemy.

But whatever the reason for starting the conflict and for continuing it, in order to motivate individuals to take part, the war had to be shown to be, and acknowledged as, just. It was believed by all states that only the just war had right on its side and the acknowledgement of that right brought about unquestioning commitment to its cause.

The state sanctioned the "just war" as the only acceptable form of war. The just war had to take place within the context of certain carefully prescribed rules: before it began it had to be shown to be right (*"jus ad bellum"* was the common phrase used by the more ancient states and had been passed on through the ages), and once it had started, it had to be conducted in a proper and established manner (*"jus in bello"* this was called), and when it ended (if indeed it ever ended), the opposing sides had to promise that proper agreements would be made involving all future aspects (*"jus post bellum"* was the phrase here).

Once underway, irrespective of the reasons, the hatreds, the claims and justifications and the progress into the other's territory, the fundamental and inalienable purpose of the just war was glaringly exposed—the killing of the enemy and the taking of their lives in greater numbers than the lives lost to the enemy in achieving this. It was acknowledged that there were many different kinds of killing that take place during a war, and each of them posed different moral questions. Killing could come in the form of self-defence. It could be done in cold blood. Sometimes it was face to face, sometimes it was impersonally or remotely done. It might involve the killing of someone good or someone evil. It could be the killing of a member of a professional army, perhaps the killing of a willing conscript or an unwilling conscript; often it was the killing of an innocent civilian. Some were killed simply for being different. Some were assassinated. Killing within any of these categories could involve combatants in personal conflict, or en masse perhaps in a siege attack. All types of killing had a different character and attracted various levels of human approval or condemnation. Each of these different ways of killing involved everyone concerned in a world far removed from anything that they would otherwise consider in any way normal or acceptable.

This present war, with all the preceding ingredients and resultant conflicts, had pitted two equally balanced states against each other for many years. Time after time newly trained recruits were paraded through the streets on their way to the battle lines. Each side saw its heroes off with great enthusiasm, awe and respect. Resplendent in their armour, they marched through the streets, their ears filled with the din of cheering encouragement and support that issued like a storm from the clamouring crowds. Wives and girlfriends, lovers current and estranged, women who had given succour to the lonely soldier out of sympathy or as their profession, lined the streets. The arms of these women reached out as they showered flowers or parting gifts on these their men. The men merely turned and met their gaze, unable to show the emotion that would have caused them to run so eagerly to the arms that would have welcomed them so readily. Some of the women clutched garlands, some waved brightly coloured cloth.

One, Rosanna, held bunches of shiny ribbons that she twirled in the air. She was beautiful. When her husband Praxis marched into view, she stood up on her toes, screeching her love for him. She pressed herself forward, prising herself up on the shoulders of others, waving her ribbons, pleading for his valour on the field of combat and praying to gGod for his safe return. He turned briefly. He almost smiled. His friend and comrade Mychos pressed his hand on Praxis' shoulder. They could hear nothing but the shrieking of the women. Mychos looked at Rosanna and nodded as if he was promising to look after his friend. Tears streamed down Rosanna's face, and she bit her lips as Mychos turned away, and he and Praxis were both lost in the milling, screaming crowd. And so they passed and marched on to meet the others marshalled outside the town who had left in the same way.

Now, their war had gone on so long that the killing itself had become the only feature that any of the combatants could understand—reasons and justifications for their actions had long since been forgotten. Each battle held only a loosely understood future hope, a veiled promise that heralded an outcome—perhaps the achievement of an end to it all, and the promise of a peaceful life. But no, such a thought was fleeting and misplaced. The outcome was always the same—the achievement of more killing and the promise of more to come.

And this latest battle had been the fiercest of all battles—the fiercest of the war so far. The losses had been great and the suffering on both sides more than even the most hardened amongst them could bear without tears. Warriors—heroes every one—lay sobbing like frightened children amongst the bloody debris of it all. That humanity had come to this. That the progeny of the first man could bring this level of degradation upon itself. It should have been impossible to imagine. And yet the bare fact of it was undeniable—it was so.

Some that were able to sites held their heads in their hands, shivering. Others lay on their backs staring hopelessly into the sky with unfocused eyes. They wondered if there was a heaven waiting to rescue them from their living, bloodied agony, whether there was a life to come after their death, and if they could bear the time that it would be before they had to know. Those that had fallen face down tasted the earth in their mouths and, in its blood-soaked flavour, were reminded of the base ingredients of human life and the unavoidable fatality of existence. All around them, the air was infected with the cries of pain, the murmurings of regret, and the mumbled recitation of pointless devotions and unheard prayers.

Mychos knelt by Praxis' side, cradling the wounded man's head in his own bloodstained hands. How distant they were now in every way from their festive send-off—how far away from Rosanna's twirling ribbons and cries of love.

Blood bubbled noisily from the corners of Praxis' mouth. He tried to speak but failed.

It had been early in the day when they had entered the field; the sun was barely showing itself and light was only just creeping out of the shadows of night. It was the magical time, the time of newness to come and of clarity to be discovered. Then, as the sun broke through, it brought with it the reward for anticipation. The finery and the sparkle of it all could be seen in its light. Shields shone as they were turned on muscular forearms, helmets glittered as heads tipped towards the sun, sword edges cut the air with practised swings, and keen, bright eyes looked ahead only to the destruction of the hated enemy in the battle that was so eagerly awaited. No, no one could bring to mind the reason why they were there. No one even considered asking for it. There was no need. All they knew was that they had an enemy that they had to kill. And that was their only motive—to bring death to the adversary through conflict. A warrior has only one function, and that resides in the wish for the death of his enemy through battle.

Again Praxis tried to speak. His words were muddied by blood and confused by his struggle with pain.

Mychos bent his head down to listen.

Praxis' words were faint.

'I'm finished,' he said.

Mychos smiled and shook his head. He did not hear a serious statement.

Mychos and Praxis had been together for what now seemed all their lives. They had trained together as young men drawn to arms. They had served on many campaigns together. They had looked after each other when they had been in danger. They had congratulated each other on each other's fighting prowess. They had celebrated with each other when they had won victory. They were as close to each other as it was possible to be. Each held the other's interests as highly as his own—whatever one wanted for himself, he also wanted for the other. Their comradeship was for each an ongoing participation in love—each was beyond himself and within the other; each was touched by a shard of love that emanated from the loving whole.

'Don't say that, my friend,' said Mychos, suddenly hit by a stab of selfishness as the possible horror of being left alone if Praxis should die struck home.

'It is too late for me, Mychos. All you can do for me now is put me out of my misery.'

'Don't be foolish!' said Mychos returning to his state of disbelief, refusing to accept that anything could happen to sever their being together. 'Our comrades will be along soon. They have not yet collected the bounty of our battle. Think of all the armour and the riches that our victory today will bring.'

'I fear there are not enough of them left to take any bounty, my friend. Look around you. What do you see?'

Mychos looked around. The battlefield was strewn with the debris of the day's combat. Blood, exposed bones and torn flesh now lay spread upon the shining armour that had only a few hours before been proudly carried forward by the resplendent heroes that it clothed. Swords lay in tangles, their edges broken and stained red with the injuries they had wrought. Red-streaked mud was spattered over everything. The grime of battle soiled it all. There was hardly any movement—just choking or the clink of steel as a body strained one last time to move against its all-involving pain.

Mychos saw figures moving between the fallen heroes—women. They walked amongst them, staring down at them, touching them sometimes, moving them sometimes in order to see their faces. Some were in rags. They all looked weary and hungry. A tiredness seeped from them that testified to the length of time they had been abandoned by the men who would otherwise have provided for them.

One of them came closer. She stumbled as she stepped over the bodies at her feet. Her black hair lay across her bare shoulders in unkempt and sticky tangles. Worn and faded ribbons dangled from its ends. She reached down and briefly touched each man she stepped over before drawing back and moving on to the next. She was looking for someone in particular, perhaps the lover she had waved off, perhaps the husband she needed to provide for her, perhaps the father of her growing children. But her touch brought with it not only disappointment but a shadow of darkness. It was as if in carrying out her search she was sealing the fate of those she did not recognise, closing their last moments with a touch that imprinted on them the failure to be recognised and the foretelling of an eternity of unacknowledged unknowing. She looked up. Her face spoke only of exhaustion and lost hope. It was as if her task was draining away her own life-force and now there was barely any of it left. She stood motionless, unable for the moment to salvage the strength to carry on.

'Is the battle lost?' asked Praxis weakly, his stare now becoming blank and unfocused.

Mychos paused, caught between the obvious truth and his wish for something better. He bit onto his lips and nodded slowly as he fought to make the admission.

'Yes, it is so. The evidence lies around us, my friend. We are certainly lost. It has gone against us. We must face it. All things end. And this is *our* end. We are defeated.' His attention was suddenly caught be a different thread of thought—a spark of optimism. 'But, my dear friend, this is only today. We must prepare ourselves to fight again tomorrow.'

'Whatever you decide for yourself I cannot argue with. But I have decided what is to happen to me. You must help me be released for I have no taste for any more of it. For me, it is too much to suffer.'

'I cannot do that, friend. I cannot. It is my duty to care for you, not to take away your life.'

'But you will be saving me the humiliation of being dragged away by our enemies and, still struggling for breath—for death would not be kind enough to take me—being stripped and hurled onto a pile of bodies to be burnt. Surely there could be nothing worse than ending my life like that; to be defiled in that way. And you would not want me to suffer that. Surely, my dear Mychos, you would not want that for me?'

Mychos brought his stare closer. He peered into his friend's face.

'You are right, my dear Praxis. I have a duty to save you from such humiliation. But I also have a duty to preserve your life. And within myself I cannot bring those two things together. Whichever one I favour, the other pulls against it.'

'Please, my friend. I implore you. I am overcome with pain. And I dread the humiliation I could receive if I am left to live. The thought of my body being degraded is too much for me to bear. To have such things in my mind as my last living images fills me with terror.'

'But we can fight again, my dear comrade. This day will end and we will come to battle once more.'

'No! You deceive yourself! Again, look around you. Do you see any hope of recovery from this? No! We are finished. This is the end of it all. The battle is lost. But *you* can still leave the field with your life. Have pity on me. Do as I ask. Have pity on yourself. Seize the rest of your life.'

Mychos hung his head. He had never felt the weight of the world like this before. He had trained himself to face an opposition that was always outside his own fraternity—to face and destroy an enemy in a justified conflict. But the idea of bringing his own dear friend's life to an end was beyond him. How could he consider such a thing?

He looked up again. The women were still moving amongst the fallen men. The one with ribbons in her hair was again checking the faces, shaking her head and moving on. Another woman carried a book in one hand. She was dressed in the black robe of a woman of the priesthood. She touched a screaming man and he fell silent. It was either that her touch was more than he could bear, or it was a touch of peace—a cure for the pain of injury. But if it was a cure, whether it took away the pain endured with more life or whether it brought it to an end with death, Mychos could not tell. She looked across and saw him and Praxis. She stared at them. Mychos watched her. He wasn't sure what he was seeing: a bringer of death or a saving grace.

He turned back to Praxis.

'Hold fast, my friend. Do not despair.'

'Please. Please,' urged Praxis, now fearing being abandoned with not even the hope of being saved from the misery of his pain.

Mychos got up and, stepping over groaning bodies, walked towards the woman in black.

'Can you help me? I am lost for a way forward. How should I act?'

The woman looked at him fixedly, waited, then spoke.

'So, you are unable to decide on what action to take. You know you must act, but you don't know how to do that virtuously. Perhaps you should get up and run away like a coward, or like a child fleeing from the thought of something in the dark that does not exist? Have you no code that leads you in what you do?'

Mychos responded angrily.

'Of course I do! I could act in accordance with the will of gGod. I can respect the sanctity of life.'

The woman laughed.

'Which god is that? The same one that tells you to kill as well?'

'It is the god I give libation to. The god that visits my place of worship and takes whatever I offer in allegiance or sacrifice.'

The woman in black threw her head back and laughed again.

'Oh, you have indeed become lost.'

'My god tells me that it is right only to kill an enemy, and here, my dear friend Praxis is asking me to take his life. How can I go against the will and command of my god. It is a terrible and ridiculous thought.'

'Do you ask your god to guide you with every decision that you make?'

'No.'

The woman strode over and bent to Praxis. She reached out to touch him. Mychos rushed to her and pushed her back.

'Ah! You fear my touch. Even when it is directed at another. A gallant warrior fears the touch of an unarmed woman! You are indeed lost!'

Mychos dropped his head into his hands. When he looked up, the woman was gone. He ran after her, but there was no trail to follow—she had vanished. The mire of dead and injured was now even more difficult to cross. He stepped on someone's face and jumped back as the mouth whimpered in pain. He turned, having gone in a circle. Praxis still lay as he had been left.

Mychos bent down to him.

'Praxis! Have you come to your senses yet?' he said.

'My sense still needs me to ask for your mercy, my friend.'

'But we agreed. Do you remember all those years ago? We agreed that no matter what befell us, we would always act in the other's best interest. And helping you lose your life is not acting in your best interest. Your best interest is to live.'

'But,' continued Praxis weakly, 'we agreed always to keep any promises we made between one another. And one of those promises was to act on the other's wishes. How can you say you are acting in my best interest while at the same time breaking your promise to support my deeply held wishes?'

'But I could not live with myself if I knew that I had taken the life of my dearest, most treasured friend and comrade.'

'But my wishes surely must press hard against that.'

'Who knows, my friend, what could be the value of your saved life to the future. You may become a great leader and help save our nation and benefit all the members of it.'

'You cannot know that, Mychos. I could just as easily become an evil despot. And you would have been responsible for helping me to power by preserving my life at this crucial juncture. Act virtuously, Mychos! Please, act virtuously!'

'But it is wrong, Praxis. It is wrong.'

'There is no such thing, Mychos. Wrong cannot be separated from the moment, from the way that you see yourself acting, from the way that you know you are acting and how that fits with your view of rightness at the time.'

Praxis fell back.

Mychos dropped his face into his hands. He suddenly realised the truth.

'I have deceived myself. I see it now. There is no absolute wrong. I can only act in such a way that my actions fit with what I, and I alone, believe to be right at the time. If I act in this way then I will know that I am acting truthfully because the only test of truth is whether my actions fit with what I sincerely believe to be the case. I must hold myself to be the measure of right for all of my actions. I must know that I am acting in accordance with my most closely and truthfully held belief. I must act in accordance with what the moment is demanding.'

Mychos stared down at Praxis. He felt a stream of love flowing between them. He realised that death, although the end of life, was not the end of all things. He felt a wave of compassion for his friend. He realised that their comradeship was drawn from a loving understanding of each other, and that that extended beyond the simply mortal.

Then he felt someone touch his arm. It was the young woman with the ribbons in her hair—it was Rosanna!

He gasped. She found a smile and fought with her weary face to let it show. Mychos stared into her eyes. They saw each other for what they were. Amid this scene of horror they found again what had passed between them—the recognition that only lovers have. Their eyes could not break free. They became within each other as for so many years they had in secret been. And Praxis lay between them, Rosanna's husband and provider, and comrade of Mychos, and obstacle to their love.

Mychos drew a knife from his belt, held it for only a second against his friend's throat before drawing it slowly, lovingly and carefully across it. Praxis made no sound. Mychos knelt for a while, watching the blood flow from the deep gash he had made. Tears welled up in his eyes. He felt a wave of love and rightfulness sweep over him. But he knew that he had acted from a different motive than Praxis had desired; he had removed the obstacle that stood between him and Rosanna—he had acted with overwhelming and cruel self-interest.

He stood and turned. The woman in black was again now standing before him.

She spoke.

'Reflect! Look what you have done, look at the result of your selfish action.'

Mychos turned back and stared down at the now lifeless body of his friend. He bent his head and wept. In that one act, he had lost something of himself that was irretrievable.

And so again, another battle lay ahead—another summons to kill or be killed. And Mychos paraded with the rest—heroes every one. And the women swirled garlands and tossed flowers as they passed. And Mychos caught sight of Rosanna. And she leapt towards him, thrusting her hands out and excitedly shaking the bunches of brightly coloured ribbons that she held. And he felt a hand on his shoulder—another comrade using him to pull himself up on. And Mychos saw Rosanna's eyes move away from his. And he knew that now they fixed on the one behind him—the one levering himself up behind him, following in his footsteps. And now it was he, Mychos, who was marching to his own abandonment and death.

And so it was. And the thrusting sword of an enemy brought him down.

Suddenly, there was great crash and the machine came to a sickening stop. Barely able to hold into the control lever with one hand, Socrates fell sideways on the chair. Dust was falling in thick clouds from the urns. The marble pillars swayed giddily. Everything was in confusion around him. Everything was in confusion within him. He took a deep breath but choked as his lungs filled with dust from the urns. He tried again. All he could see was the image of the battlefield and the woman in black!

'IgnatiusM! IgnatiusM!' he spluttered desperately. 'Are you there? What happened! I don't remember how we started this trip. And I don't understand how it ended, or what ended it. It all seemed to happen of its own accord! IgnatiusM! Are you there? Please! Please be there!'

There was some heavy grumbling as the machine settled.

'Yes, I'm here, Socrates.' said IgnatiusM uncertainly. 'I don't know what happened either. I don't think the piece was placed properly, so I can't understand how things were set in motion. And as far as I can see you haven't turned it over, so your return has been a bit uncertain. I think this is definitely a time for the emergency button!'

Socrates didn't waste a moment in thought. Unsure about how he was controlling his hand, he made a grab for the emergency button and squeezed his thumb down on it as hard as he could.

CHAPTER 17

Thinking about...the unexamined life is not worth living

gGod wasn't slow in reacting; the emergency button light had barely flashed once and His chair appeared alongside the machine. The small table came next and within moments of the cup of tea appearing on the table gGod was sitting comfortably and preparing to take a sip.

'Nothing serious, I hope,' He said, not apparently reacting in a determinedly-emergency-sort-of-way. He lifted the steaming cup of English Breakfast to His lips in what seemed a more convincingly casual-sort-of-way. 'Mmm,' He declared with satisfaction. 'I have to say it. Leaf tea! Really! I don't know what all the fuss is about! And so inconvenient! All that messing about with strainers. And the holes are never the right size. And the tea leaves! They're never the right size either! And the blocked up drains! I can't begin to tell you the trouble I've had with *them*! Sometimes I think gGladys is obsessed with blockages! Although, I have to say, there's a strange sort of pleasure to be found in unblocking them—drains, that is. Pass the rods! Eh, Socrates? Anyway,' He said, refreshed and, now obviously, having got some of His more pressing problems off His chest, getting more into the swing of the emergency mode. 'There's a problem I see—something of an emergency, I suspect.' That it had been the emergency button that had brought Him here made this statement seem glaringly obvious if not superfluous.

For a moment, Socrates, influenced by gGod's divine nonchalance and concerns about drains, felt he might have summoned Him with less than just cause. Was this really an emergency? He hesitated. Perhaps not. He was greatly confused, yes. But did that add up to an emergency?

gGod looked up, His lips still glued to his cup. He raised His eyebrows encouragingly. He tipped His head slightly to show off the freshly pomaded quiff of His James Dean hairstyle. It was enough. Socrates submitted to His will—He was after all gGod and His hairstyle was just about perfect.

'I have witnessed...' Socrates dithered a little then, getting a grip on himself, pursing his lips and nodding in a sort-of-private-confidence-giving-self-agreement-way, found the pluck to continue. 'In seeing the working out of moral dilemmas I have witnessed some of the horrors that can be exposed by self-examination. Even though I served as a soldier myself for many years, I have still been affected by the sights I have just witnessed, and the conflict brought about by such things as allegiance and duty, and the drive for personal gain or satisfaction. Yes, I have seen how the ethical value of an action can change from right to wrong during the very progress of its undertaking. I have seen how the motivation for doing right as the hand is lifted may be doing wrong by the time it falls. Oh, how easily mistaken is the true quality of wisdom. How capricious the nature of virtue. And this has driven me to the very edge of my certainty. And so I have been caused to question much of what I have dedicated my life to—seeking out wisdom as the route to virtue. Have I been wrong in devoting my life in this way?'

gGod stared ahead obliquely.

'So is this the nature of the emergency? That you wish to talk about the nature of wisdom and virtue?'

Socrates ignored or did not notice gGod's obvious irritation.

'Yes, indeed,' he continued. 'That virtue is the goal and that wisdom is the only route to finding it has been the rule of my life. And I have been reminded, as if it was necessary, that this life of mine too is soon to end. Yes, wisdom, I believe, is *necessary* for virtue. Yes,' he said (hoping that repeating his affirmative "yes" would somehow reinforce his point). No sign that gGod took the bait. Socrates pressed on, offering yet another (wasted, though now decidedly emphatic) "yes". '*Yes*, it is my view that all virtue depends upon or arises from wisdom. And wisdom can only be gained through diligent and persistent self-examination. I have always advocated that without self-examination life is worthless. Further, I have always held that without examination nothing in life can rightfully be believed in, or in any way usefully used as a guide. But now, I am torn with the horror of what self-examination can unearth when faced with resolving critical and practical issues. My lust for genuine understanding has been knocked sideways by seeing stark evidence of the awful results arising from the most difficult-to-make decisions. I say again, have I spent my life deceiving myself? Can I have been so wrong? Have I wasted my years living in cloud cuckoo land? Please, gGod. Have I become lost in the clouds?'

gGod, placed His teacup down on the table and smiled broadly; His brief irritation now passed as, with a brief caress of His quiff, He got into the swing of things.

'That is indeed where Aristophanes puts the inquiring human—and you are truly one of those, Socrates—in cloud cuckoo land. It is true that if you drift too far away from the here-and-now, you may end up in the land of the birds! Yes, there in the clouds, in the "Thinkery", measuring the distance a flea can jump, detached from the more pressing and relevant matters of life (assuming, of course, that the distance a flea can jump is neither pressing nor relevant). Maybe this latest journey has quite properly brought you down to earth. Perhaps this trip has shown you that the only place for mortal life is standing firmly, no, forcibly on the ground which bears it. Perhaps, importantly, it is telling you, reminding you that true wisdom can only be attained with death, for it is death that releases the soul from the body and all its distractions. It is only when this happens—when the body is separated and the misleading nature of time and change, and sensual physicality are eradicated—that wisdom and virtue can be seen in their pure form. It is the harmony of death with the release of the unencumbered soul that unifies true worth with wisdom and releases pure virtue.'

There were no "maybes" here. Socrates only heard certainty. And it carried much weight, and was convincing. Yes, indeed, he was struck by gGod's wisdom and lifted by it. And his optimism started returning.

Socrates looked down at the ground for a moment. It helped him picture himself coming down to earth—leaving the cloud cuckoo land and any problems with fleas—and gave him a chance to take a deep breath and the ability to provide an at least seemingly confident reply. But not quite yet.

'Good,' said gGod, slightly guardedly, but clearly returning to His thoughts about drains and, thinking of gGladys' recent nagging on that front, feeling the need to do some practical work to assuage her. 'So, if that is all, I'll be moving on—things to do, things to clear up, things to unblock. Emergency over, I think. I don't think I can add anything to our conversation.'

'Well, actually—'

'Good,' gGod interrupted. 'I'm pleased to have been of help. Stick at the questioning! Think of it as just another day!'

And with that He was gone. The small table stayed behind, as did the half drunk cup of tea which was still warm. Then suddenly the table shook and He, together with another cup of tea, was back.

gGod looked as if He was going to speak. He hesitated.

'There was something about beards I wanted to ask you. Or was it moustaches. Oh, I've completely forgotten. Omniscience, eh? Who'd credit it!'

Then again, leaving the still shaking table and His tea behind, He was gone for a second time.

Socrates felt very confused. He slumped forward against the control lever, almost pressing the emergency button by mistake. He jumped back as he realised what he might be doing—he'd had enough of emergencies for the moment. Confusion turned to dismay. He pictured again the images of the battlefield. Was this really what gGod planned to be his very best of all his days?

There was a crackling sound, a minor judder and the voice of IgnatiusM broke in.

'Are we ready for our next excursion?' he asked keenly, and seemingly unaware of gGod's visit.

Socrates tried to pull himself together.

'Ready? I'm not sure. *You* seem to be. But am *I*?'

'Well, ready or not, you don't want to waste any time—last day and all that.'

This time Socrates shivered at the reminder.

'I suppose not. IgnatiusM?

'Yes?'

'What's all this about beards and moustaches and gGod?'

'Oh, it's just His thing. It's a lot to do with…you know who.' Socrates didn't. He has to put up with a lot there. And the beards thing is because of His in-laws, maybe. I think a bit of counselling would help, and I have tried to sow the seeds of interest there. Get him started on a few sessions. In fact, He did give it a go. But no sooner does He get going on one thing than He's off on something else. And anyway, who am I!'

'Oh.'

'Anyway, come along, get the next piece and let's see where it takes us.'

Socrates, though still with something of a heavy heart, and still somewhat confused that the all-powerful, all-seeing, and ever-present gGod should, for whatever reason, be obsessively interested in beards and moustaches, dug into the bag and brought out a piece. He held it up to the screen, one side at a time.

'What does it look like?' he asked rather wearily.

'Interesting,' replied IgnatiusM. 'Very interesting. Hold it up so that you can see the image and let's get under way. Let's get examining! You know what you say: "the unexamined life..." and all that.'

Socrates, slowly regaining some enthusiasm, held the piece up and stared at the partial image that was on it. He sat back, took hold of the control lever with his other hand and pulled it back. Nothing happened. He looked from side to side, re-asserted his grip on the lever, sat forward in his chair to get extra leverage, stared ahead, and pulled again. Still nothing happened.

'IgnatiusM! Is there a problem?'

The screen flickered, the marble pillars swayed, the urns began to rotate and dust started falling.

'No! It was just the *C*-drive playing up—one of its anti-temporal valves had blown. All fixed now! Good as new.' Then, with a sudden jerk, Socrates was thrown back in the chair as IgnatiusM's voice cried out with a barely discernible, 'Hang on tight, Socrates! We're on the way!'

CHAPTER 18

The Pool—how evil lies behind the good

The sun shone.

He took her hand and led her into the warm water. She looked down at the surface as if fearful that it might break as the ripples spread out from around her shapely waist. She swished her spare hand amongst them. Fresh ripples caressed the others and they danced and played in response to her touch.

The sun shone.

'Come, Bella,' he said, recognising her concerns, smiling encouragement and drawing her on. 'It's delicious.'

They were both naked. The reflections from the water outlined the curves and shapes of their forms: the beautiful young Bella, her long blonde hair falling across her shoulders, her full lips parting slightly as her excitement was released, her wide and beckoning eyes drawing in everything around her; and her caring and handsome lover Cyrus, studying her with devoted attentiveness.

Even though Cyrus was reassuring, Bella still felt excitedly anxious. She took a cautious step forward. She held her free hand out to steady herself. The water responded—rippling some more in broad circles around her. She wanted to look up at Cyrus and smile. She wanted to show him how much she trusted him. And she tried, but, having let her mind wander, her foot slipped on the loose-pebbled floor of the pool and again, un-nerved, she looked down to concentrate harder on her own safety.

But the surfeit of sensations around her were offering too much. She watched the ripples running out until, even before reaching the shore, they faded into the world of the unseen. For a moment she imagined where they might disappear to—a place of unknowing, a place where only unseen others could perceive them. Yes, for a moment she imagined the place where only gods could know the full and complete beauty of it all—the place of magic that lay beyond every horizon; the place of fulfilment and truth.

Then she tried again to step forward, breaking the momentary trance that had enraptured her, and this time she was successful. It took her a little deeper, and the water's surface met her breasts. She giggled as the veneer of it teased her delicate and sensitised skin. Her nipples hardened. She felt the thrill of it, and even though still captivated by the enchantment of it all, she managed to look up long enough to catch her lover's eye.

Cyrus lifted his hand and dangled his fingers above her mouth. Water dripped onto Bella's lips. She reached her face up to the droplets, as if she was a honeybee feeding on the nectar drizzling from within the shell-shaped petals of a beautiful flower.

She licked her tongue out and fed.

'You do love me, don't you,' she said, her tongue still resting on the edges of her lips.

'I do. Yes, I do love you.'

'You sound uncertain,' she said laughingly.

'Of course I'm not. You are a silly tease. You know I'm not. But I *am* uncertain about the *nature* of love—what love is as a thing-in-itself. And I can't understand fully what this feeling that I have, this beautiful feeling that I have because of you, for you, with you, this feeling of being in love, actually is. It's an experience, yes, but it seems an experience of my life that is somehow *beyond* my life. Even though my life is mine, it seems as if love, no matter how closely felt within me, is at the same time something beyond me. And how can that be so? How can something beyond me also be within me?'

She let go of his hand, curled up her fingers and used them to splash some water at him. It dripped down his face. He splashed her back playfully. She went to splash him again but, slipping on the pebbles, she fell backwards. Straightaway he reached out, caught her and saved her. Their wet, warm bodies clung to each other; their apparent existence extending no further than the sensation of contact between them.

But there *was* something that reached beyond that. And Cyrus had been right to puzzle about it. This experience, this love, even though it was within each of them, *did* extend beyond what they were. Through it, each of them was lost in the other, inhabiting the mind of the other, being within the existence of the other. And in this experience each of them was sharing the soul of the other.

Bella went to speak but realised that the sound of her voice, the need to move her lips that much, would intrude into the delectable, undefinable place of being that they inhabited. She smiled without looking up and knew that Cyrus too was smiling. They remained in each other's arms—in each other's love, each beyond themselves and each within the other.

The water's ripples produced by the movements of both their bodies barely reached the edge of the limpid pool—it was a horizon too far for the effects of their existence to influence. But closer, branches hanging from ancient trees reached down towards the crystal clear water—it was as if their graceful boughs were trying to share the magic of the moment that was taking place beneath their limbs. Except for the sounds of splashing and the laughter of the two lovers, everything was silent.

Some distance away, a young woman worked in her vegetable garden. Her name was Lotta. She was dressed only in a simple white smock of linen. She walked between her rows of produce, bending to touch them, to lift them slightly, to inhale their living scent, to look at them with the same tenderness and joy a mother looks at her children. And in these ways they were her children. She had planted their seeds and had watched them grow.

She had nurtured them. She had taken weeds from around their growing shoots so that they could be afforded all the nourishment available from the soil. According to their need, she had shaded some, and exposed others to full sunlight. She had walked between them in the evening, humming tunes to them and watering their roots. And as they grew, she had removed any weak fruit so that the strongest could better flourish.

Lotta stopped and pondered. She lifted some green beans in her hand, holding them as she would hold the dearest of things. She bent down and pressed them gently against her cheek. She smiled, filled with waves of love for the lives that she had helped grow to this perfection. She felt something of them within her and, with the same filament of the other that weaved its way into *her*, she travelled into that other and felt within *them*. But it was the end of her day and she must return. Although no other waited for her to come home with produce, she must return. She was her own provider and her labour was both a joy and a necessity.

The sun had passed its highest point as Lotta left her garden. She carried a bundle of beans, trailing her arms lazily as she walked, satisfied with her day's industry and the rewards that it had brought. She smiled and hummed and her steps fell lightly. A tree had fallen across her usual path and she was forced to take an alternate route. She had never been this way before and, as she walked, she looked around, intrigued by the novel images that the scenery provided. She did not want more from her world, but fortuitous perception of something different always exhilarated her. At this moment she had never felt happier. She imagined laying out her beans for preparation when she returned; her body thrilled with the anticipation of it. Life, and the sensations that came with it, were indeed the greatest gifts and she felt blessed with the best of them.

She turned her head to one side as she heard the excited barking of a small dog as it played with a bone. She peered between the trees and saw it gambolling around the edge of a pool. She smiled at its antics. She continued along the path, as it took her nearer to the water's edge. She caught sight of Cyrus and Bella and, instantly absorbed in their happiness, and not wishing to be seen, she dropped down to her knees, pushed the beans she was carrying into the large pocket in the front of her smock, and crouched behind a tree to watch them.

So now Cyrus and Bella were not the only two—there was another present. Behind the tree, whose branch tips yearned to touch even a ripple from the joy of the lovers, crouched Lotta. She peered around the sturdy trunk, holding her hands against the bark of it, pressing her cheek against it—feeling its natural closeness against her skin.

She watched the lovers. She was mesmerised by their happiness; envious of the loving sentiment that passed between, beyond and within them. She watched every movement of their naked bodies, and she followed the glistening, engoldened ripples that they caused on the surface of the water as they ran towards the edge. She was absorbed, feeling at every moment the sensation of her own existence, wondering about her purpose—its uncertainty, its peculiarity, its delectability. Although she knew they owed themselves to her—she was making them known through her perception of them—she had never experienced even a hint of the love-rich moments of engagement that Bella and Cyrus were now sharing.

She had never experienced anything like this for herself, and she was drawn in by her desire for it. She too wanted someone to stop her from falling, someone to play with her, someone to draw out the innocence within her. She needed another—so much she needed another. She saw that her life was exposed as empty of the emotional sharing that came with loving another. The conflict of needing something that she only witnessed others possessing filled her with pain. A tear ran from the corner of one of her eyes. It flowed down her cheek and dripped onto the muddy soil at her feet.

The small dog ran up to her. It carried a bone in its mouth. It crouched down, dropped the bone and wagged its tail. Still holding herself against the tree with one hand, she reached towards it with the other and rubbed its head affectionately. The dog made soft noises of appreciation and she felt aware of her importance to it. A strong sense of the other flowed through her. As if trying to pass a message, the dog nuzzled its bone repeatedly as it looked up to her. She smiled at it, and, realising what it wanted, picked up the bone and threw it to the edge of the pool. The dog rushed after it, splashing into the water enthusiastically in pursuit of its prize.

Cyrus and Bella did not notice it and again started playfully splashing water at each other.

Lotta, now flecked in a dark shadow caused by the slowly descending sun, pulled her other hand away from the bark of the tree trunk. The small dog came back and ran around her feet, dropping on its front legs, dipping its head and pushing up against her. She bent and patted it, again rewarded by its keen acknowledgement of her attention. It wriggled with joy and dropped its whole body to the ground. She stood up and moved from behind the tree. She glanced down at the dog, now lying on its back, turning its head from side to side. Another bone lay nearby. She placed her foot on it and the little dog jumped up, took it in its jaws and tried to wrestle it free. Lotta smiled, bent and playfully patted the dog before releasing her hold on the bone.

At the same time, as if woken from their engrossed reverie, Cyrus and Bella turned and looked around. It was as if they were suddenly again aware of a world that they had briefly left—as though they had been on a journey from which they had now returned. They could not see Lotta although they could hear the dog. Then she stepped forward and they both caught sight of her at the same time. Cyrus squeezed Bella's hand and with a freshened awareness of each other's bodies they both faced Lotta's approach.

Lotta was enthralled by the sight of the two lovers standing up to their waists in the glassy-surfaced pool. In a way she felt as if she was intruding on their privacy, yet at the same time it was her only way of sharing some of their love, their intimacy, their mutual engagement. In doing this she felt involved with them—part of their delightful world of love, knowing and desire. She could not stop herself from waving. As she did, she realised that she'd dipped her hands into her pocket and taken out the beans. Her waving hands were full of the beans she had taken from her garden, and she laughed at herself, feeling clumsy and silly, and filled with joy.

Cyrus and Bella, still holding hands, waded through the water towards Lotta. Lotta stopped her attempts at waving but instead took a few paces forward until she was standing right at the water's edge. Ripples ran out in delightful swirls from Cyrus and Bella as they approached. Lotta held out her beans as if she was making an offering to two approaching gods. Some of her produce dropped from her grasp and fell into the water. She bent to retrieve it but by then Cyrus was close enough to reach forward and stop her.

He held her wrist tightly. Lotta, still thinking of him as a god, thrilled at his touch. Then he increased the pressure and she felt a biting pain. Then he squeezed harder and she tried to pull away. Then Bella took hold of her other wrist and pinched her finger nails deeply into Lotta's skin.

Lotta pulled back as much as she could but it was useless. They held her fast and spread her arms out as if for crucifixion. Cyrus and Bella pulled her beneath the surface. Lotta coughed and choked, confused and fearful, not understanding anything that was happening. She gulped in water; it burned her lungs. She thrashed her arms and kicked out with her legs, but it was hopeless—she was overpowered and beaten. Then they brought her up above the surface. She gasped, her body still believing it could reclaim its grasp on life. But it was mistaken.

She shrieked as Bella bit deeply into her neck. Then Cyrus sunk his teeth into her arm and bit right through the flesh to the bone. Then another bite in her neck. Lotta was aware of redness everywhere. The clear water of the pool was staining red with her blood and she knew that with it her life was leaching away—in pain, distress and confusion her lifeblood was leaving her body. Amongst it all, she felt another breath being drawn in, but it was insufficient to allow her even to scream. She saw herself capitulating to the vicious attack; it was as if she was another watching her life being taken from her. She closed her eyes and listened to the gushing of the blood from her neck as it escaped her body, taking with it her life as it mixed with the churning of the water caused by her desperate thrashing and flailing.

Cyrus and Bella dragged their quarry up onto the shallow bank at the edge of the pool. They both knelt beside it, nodding first to each other to agree which piece each could have, before bending down and starting to bite into their victim, the body of whom was still warm and twitching with the remaining fragments of its life. They ate for a while then left the carcass, some of its bones exposed, some with flesh hanging from them. Hand in hand, they walked back into the pool where they began washing each other and joyfully ridding themselves of the bloody stains of their feast.

The small dog grabbed one of the bones that had so recently been part of the structure of Lotta—the structure that had supported her life, her joy, her industry, her hopes—and ran with it back to the tree where only a short time ago she had hidden enthralled and captivated by the lovers. The dog dropped the bone as if there was someone there to pick it up. But there was no one, and the dog ran back to the pool and plunged into the water in order to retrieve another and begin the game again.

Moments later, it emerged from the water, wagging its tail and gripping in its jaws another bone. Again it ran to the tree and dropped it. Again it looked to see if anyone would pick it up and throw it. Again there was no one. Again it ran back to the water to find another bone and start the game again.

And still, the sun shone.

CHAPTER 19

Thinking about...Socrates' Dilemma: good depends on evil

Again the machine came to rest with its accustomed sickening and sudden jolt. But this time, before it settled, its whole frame shook loosely and some of it threatened to break free altogether. Socrates was hanging onto the control lever, sweating and gasping for breath. He looked as if he would never recover himself.

Then, the screen flickered and IgnatiusM's voice spoke out calmly.

'It's amazing, don't you think, Socrates? Your adventures, no matter what they are, cause you to reflect—cause you to tackle questions about what is right or what is wrong, what is good and what is evil. And as you tackle them more questions arise.'

Socrates could not get into anything like a questioning mode. Instead, he wondered how much more he could take of the physical battering the time machine was handing out, let alone the psychological punishment that he was being dealt. What he had just witnessed had filled him with the utmost horror. Then the questions started. Had this truly been a human act? Were humans capable of such things? Could the path to true virtue really be via taking part in a life-form capable of such cruelty? And what sort of god would allow such a thing?

He slackened his grip on the lever and slowly eased himself into something of his calmer, more rational and enquiring form.

'Yes, yes, IgnatiusM, there is always more—further to go. But from where?' He eased himself back in the chair. His body was stiff with tension. The machine gave a final shudder, then all was quiet. 'Yes, how can I reflect without discussing the difficulties of the problem, without exposing alternate views, arguing the facts that they contain, and recording the flaws that they disguise? Reflection in itself is insufficient. I say again, wisdom can only come about from questioning, from examining, and it is only by this means that virtue can be obtained. Interrogation is essential, and virtue is the only quality worth pursuing by its method. But at the moment, my friend, my picture of virtue is obscured by horror.'

'Does that mean you turn away from it?'

There was a pause for thought.

'No, if it is an ingredient of living then I do not turn away from it.'

'Socrates, you are indeed very wise. But what about—' IgnatiusM broke off. He had noticed something—the appearance of the table with the teacup rattling on its top! Socrates stared at the table. He gripped the control lever just in case. Then the chair appeared. Then gGod appeared, this time looking a little the worse for wear—His hair was in uncombed disarray and showed no sign of the James Dean look. His suit was crumpled, His ruff grubby, His gaiters slack and His shoe buckles tarnished.

He cleared His throat, sat and, with a groan, settled back.

'In-laws! He sighed. What does it take to get a bit of attention! You'd think, wouldn't you, that if anyone deserved a bit of attention it was Me! All-powerful, ever-present, creative and all that! I'm gGod for gGod's sake! But no! How could that possibly hold a candle to the latest on the mother-in-law's haemorrhoids! I wish I'd never created them—haemorrhoids, that is! Sorry. Sorry. He reached for His teacup and took a fulsome swig. 'Sorry. Good to see you again, Soc. Sorry. Now what were you talking about?'

Socrates (setting aside his puzzlement at gGod's disordered appearance and not in any way wondering what He meant about in-laws, attention, and haemorrhoids) responded.

'Virtue. We were talking about virtue and how questioning is the best route to attain it. But also—'

'Ah, virtue,' said gGod, looking a little less ruffled as with long sweeping actions He stroked His hair back and began to reassemble something (at least the basics) of His sought-after James Dean look. He tipped His head to one side, quickly ran his fingers along the edge of his ruff and, His confidence seemingly boosted by the self-attention, continued in a much more self-assured manner. 'How should we examine it, eh, Socrates? How should you shape those questions?'

'Yes.'

'Well, let's see. Just sticking with your time, your era, provides some excellent approaches. I say *your* time though of course I mean that in a fairly broad sense; you wouldn't have known about all of them because they cover quite a span. There was Plato, of course (your own student, and very much younger than yourself). He was a wrestler, well you knew that, and he certainly "tussled" with the problems of what everything you know is made up of—"ideas" he thought.' He paused for a reaction to His wrestling pun but got none. He raised His eyebrows, stroked His hair again and continued. 'He, Plato, was on the right lines there—ideas, perceptions. Then, as always, there was Aristotle. Unfortunately, you never got to know him. Aristotle was a "peripatetic", he loved walking around, thinking, talking, wondering about it all while being on the move. For him happiness was the goal and a virtuous life was shaped by the plan to achieve it. You would have liked him, Socrates. Then there were the Stoics. You almost certainly came across a few of them in the Agora. They weren't walkers, not at all. They used to enjoy sitting around being stalwart about hardship and problems associated with living. For them, virtue could be found notwithstanding privation and physical suffering—the virtuous life was discovered not by aiming for happiness but by dealing with hardship. It's a good lesson, Soc. And, of course, there was the great Epicurus, tending his garden and puzzling out how in mortal life humans could avoid the terrors of anxiety. For Epicurus anxiety was the greatest obstacle to the fulfilling, happy and virtuous life. Eradicate anxieties and the path is clear, he thought. Clever man. Right on the button.'

Socrates began to feel more relaxed and, though still struggling to put the images of horror he had just witnessed behind him, took up gGod's line of enquiry.

'But what *is* this thing called "virtue"? How can we define it? Surely we cannot become virtuous without knowing what virtue is? We cannot *be* something unless we know what it is we are *being*? And where would we find ourselves in the absence of knowing virtue? There is only one place—if there is no virtue in life then evil reigns. Yes, surely there is only evil in the absence of virtue.' The image of Bella and Cyrus came back into his mind and he shivered. 'So I can only think that evil *relies* on virtue. And, as virtue is good so evil relies on good. But even though this seems the case, surely this is an ethical perversion! Something cannot be because of something else without containing the ingredients of what it is because of.'

'Ah, clever! But no, Socrates. Evil does not have to be in respect of ("rely on", as you put it) something which is not evil. If *I* did not exist then this might be a worry. But it is *I* who guarantees the good.' For a moment gGod looked self-questioning then, clearly receiving some positive internal affirmation, continued. 'There have been sceptics on this front. I will knock a few of them off and so take you through it.'

'Please do.'

'Right, so if I did not exist (which, of course, is not the case, as I *do* exist) as a supreme being (which I *am*) with all My divine attributes (which I *have*) then you would have to deal with the problem of evil. The sceptics claim that the apparently high level of evil in the world makes any claim for an all powerful and good god seem unlikely. This question was much discussed in your time by Epicurus and Plato, and continued to be discussed by others through the ages.'

'Please, tell me more.'

'The argument is this. If god (I use the generic term "god" so as not to cause confusion) is omnipotent then, by definition, he (this god, if he is male) could prevent evil if he wanted to. If this god is good then he (again I use "he" simply to keep things simple) would surely want to prevent evil if he could. If this god exists, and is both omnipotent and good, then he could prevent evil if he wanted to, and indeed, would want to prevent evil if he could. Why then, if such a god exists, is there so much evil in the world? Good question, eh, Soc?'

'Indeed,' said Socrates. 'Tell me more.'

'Glad you're on board, Soc. Well, responses to the problem of evil have traditionally taken the form of theistic arguments called "theodicies" (a term coined by a chap called Leibniz—long curly wig, but no beard).'

'Or moustache?' queried Socrates, now feeling fully involved.

'No. But his wig really was a whopper! Now, according to Saint Augustine (the "saint" title was one conferred by a religious following called "Christianity" on someone they considered had an exceptional degree of holiness, or likeness to, or closeness to god. What can you say!), evil is only the negative aspect of a pre-existing good released by the human activity of free-will. God (this god, that is) knows that ultimately out of free-will good will come. The evildoer will suffer and the virtuous will, in the long (or very long) run, benefit from their virtue. The purpose of evil is not to make you happy but to make you virtuous. In other words, you will "learn from your mistakes". In addition, because you do not see how much the evildoer suffers, the world is not such a morally substandard place as it might appear. What do you think of that?'

'I think—'

gGod was keen to press on and cut Socrates short.

'Saint Thomas Aquinas (yes, another "saint") thought that evil is accidental and caused by human beings as they exercise (male, generic) god-given free-will. God cannot be held responsible for something that he does not intend and he only intends that human beings should have free-will and not that, by using it, they should cause evil. At the same time, this god may permit certain evils that he believes are connected to his ultimately good purpose. But this purpose cannot be known to anyone other than himself. According to Leibniz, god has the power to create the best possible world. No world can be totally perfect and so god created one with the best possible balance of good and evil. Some good things are only possible because of evil (for example, compassion is only possible upon witnessing suffering) and god has calculated the balance of good and evil in all possible worlds and so has brought out the appropriate and best balance in the world that he has created. Without this tension between good and evil, many things that humans value would not exist.'

'Such as?'

'Creativity, for example.' Socrates felt this singular and undeveloped response rather weak. gGod continued. 'As a sort of bonus, because he weighs up the balance of good and evil, god is also just.'

'He certainly has his finger on things, this god,' said Socrates with a hint of sarcasm.

'He certainly does. Anyway, although the existence of evil does not necessarily prove that god does not exist, it does highlight the fact that suffering is an intrinsic aspect of human life. However, I'm sure you'll agree, there is little evidence to show that non-human life experiences anything like the same tendency towards pain and suffering as does human life. What does a spider think of his lot if he loses a leg? Does an amoeba feel pain when it splits in two to reproduce? It may be that there really is no evil in the world. It may only appear that way to you. It may be just your psychological perspective, and that perspective cannot adjudicate on the truth . So there you have it, Soc. Put simply, "evil" is there only according to the way you view it.'

Socrates pursed his lips. This was a strongly put (if weak) argument which for the moment he couldn't see a way around. Nevertheless, he decided to press on by sticking to gGod's last statement and pursuing the safe ground of definitions.

'But my question goes beyond the simple definition of evil. It is intimately entwined with action. I cannot imagine evil existing as a thing in itself but only as something attached to an action in the world. So, in saying that we cannot know what is evil unless we know what is good, we are surely defining one by use of the other. From that I would suggest (falling into the trap he had just described) that the perpetrator of evil must know how his actions lie in respect of the good.'

Socrates felt as though he had really hit the mark here, and leant forward to receive gGod's approbation. It didn't come.

gGod had to be honest with Himself, He never really thought of the idea of good until He had started to interact with Socrates. Why should He? As gGod, He was the only one and evil and good do not apply to only *one*. Good and evil are *applied* ethics. They cannot be without action. An action in isolation (that is, being the only one like gGod) cannot affect another, therefore cannot have any moral measurement. Such an action remains an un-applied and pure (meaningless) concept. gGod created the first man (with only Himself and God (himself) to measure things by) as it were, "in His own image", but man in the company of others (and without any intrinsic moral qualities) very soon started to experience the rough end of moral action. It was, after all, the first of the first man's children who killed his brother. No, gGod was not a good example of moral action, nor much of a knowledge base for moral interpretation. However, He *was* gGod, and He was not prepared to be viewed as having shortcomings in this argument. He changed tack.

'No, Socrates. Evil is ignorant of the good. Indeed, all evil acts are committed out of ignorance and are therefore involuntary.'

'So we should pity the doer of evil acts? Surely not.'

'You would not deny that you should pity the innocent.'

'No. Of course not.'

'And do you limit innocence only to the doer of good?'

'No, I would not do that.'

'Then you should pity the doer of evil more than the doer of good, for the innocent perpetrator of evil surely suffers more than the virtuous subject of his evil-doing?'

'I don't understand. Surely the victim of evil-doing will always suffer more. If that victim loses their life and suffers in the process of that loss, surely they suffer more than the one who brings about their suffering and death?'

'Yes, but the evil-doer who is innocent of the good, knows no good and so endures a pitiful life.'

'But life is a process, so surely if we encourage a virtuous self then it would lead us to a virtuous life and cause us to act morally to the highest ethical standards. It would bring us to the good whether or not we knew of it originally.'

gGod nodded thoughtfully and stroked back His hair. He was not prepared to concede the point (obviously as gGod this could not be) but (still a little pre-occupied as He was on the in-law front, and now seriously considering the idea of counselling) He was stuck for a response that would bolster His argument. He stroked His hair again and looked sideways as though He was catching His reflection in a mirror.

'I can see that this last day of yours is indeed going to be *most* fruitful of *all* days, Soc,' He started, clearly bent on avoiding any more discussion. 'It will provide some perspective, some idea of what can influence virtue or otherwise over time. Indeed, that's the purpose of this magnificent (though I say it Myself) machine. “Over time” eh?’ He provided a pause for approving nods but got none. Then, dispelling thoughts of gGladys and His in-laws, He again picked up the thread.‘Anyway, as well as being culturally influenced over time, anyone’s particular emotional definition of what is virtuous and good tends to be different from the estimation of others. Few humans get pleasure from exactly the same thing as others. Aristotle, for example, thought that there *is* such a thing as an absolute standard of virtue, but it is hard, even for Me, to see where this comes from. gGod, I suppose?’ He looked hard at Socrates in the hope of detecting a smile, but there was none—the joke, again, was lost. ‘Anyway, if there were such a thing, the application of such a principle could easily become (as Nietzsche —remember him, the one with the huge moustache—pointed out) simply an extrapolation of the wishes of humans under different circumstances and conditions.’ He took a swig of His tea. It had obviously gone cold. He stared at it as it emptied then re-filled with a fresh brew. ‘I think you should get IgnatiusM to start you off on another trip. Some more instances of what is virtuous or not would be most useful.’

Socrates looked more confused than ever.

‘Do you think I’m ready? I don’t really feel it.’

‘Yes, of course you are. And, I hope, willing! Remember, Soc, your last day now, at this moment, is shorter than it was before (this moment, that is). There is no time to waste. And no time—like the present!’

He drained His tea. It was obviously still cold; although He had refilled it with no trouble, He had forgotten to heat it up.

‘But—’ started Socrates.

gGod was now clearly occupied with other things.

‘So, good luck. And remember, if you need any help, just press the emergency button! That’s what it’s there for.’

And with that, an accompanying roll of thunder and a flash of light, He was gone. The table and cup remained for a few seconds, then they too disappeared.

Socrates looked confused. He had barely started to recover from his last trip, his question about virtue had been unsatisfactorily answered, and now he was expected to set off again with the unwelcome reminder that his last day was shortening by the minute.

'Ah! Ready again?' said IgnatiusM in a casually refreshing sort of way.

'Yes…er…yes…I suppose so.'

'You don't sound very sure. Is everything alright?'

'I'm not sure. No, I'm not sure everything *is* alright. I need to relax a bit.'

'Well, dig out another piece and we'll see where it takes us. Nothing like a bit of relaxing action to ease the mind.'

Socrates, obviously unconvinced by IgnatiusM's maxim, pulled out a piece of the jigsaw from his bag and held it face up to the screen.

'What does it look like?' he asked in a fairly uncommitted way.

'It looks good. Hold it up and look into it.'

Socrates pursed his lips, then trying to convince himself that action would indeed bring about a better and more easy state of mind, did as he was asked.

'Is that enough?'

'Too late to ask that, Socrates. We're already on our way!' shouted IgnatiusM as the urns started spinning, the dust started falling from them, and the machine began rattling and shaking. Rather red in the face and trying desperately to ease his mind of anxiety, Socrates barely had time to grip the lever before, yet again, he was under way.

CHAPTER 20

The Executioner

The law of the state was clear, categoric and unbending on the matter of the killing of another. The citizen's life was of prime importance: the state could not exist without its citizens, the citizen was not safe or provided for without the state—the two were inter and co-dependent. And so it had always been. If a citizen took the life of another citizen with intent, then that citizen forfeited his or her own life by execution. If the incautious or reckless action of a citizen caused the death of another then that citizen was imprisoned for life. If the death of another was caused accidentally by the action of a citizen, then that was considered a matter of luck and the citizen was not punished in any way.

Execution was carried out by an approved executioner using whatever means he or she decided on at the time. Between sentence and when the sentence was carried out the condemned was kept in complete isolation until the night before the execution itself when the executioner provided information about what was to happen.

Imprisonment meant the keeping of a guilty citizen in solitary confinement with tasks that, if completed to an expected standard, earned a meagre supply of food. If set tasks were not completed well, and food was withheld for long enough, the prisoner would die of starvation.

Crimes and their resultant punishment were dealt with strictly according to the state law and with no complication of mitigation allowed by judges of the council; all terms and definitions were fixed and were not open to any further interpretation. This system of certainty was applied to all other forms of law-breaking, loss or state-condemned ethical transgression.

All transgressions meant a period of imprisonment before the council judge passed sentence. One such prisoner's name was Herron. His mother, Edhita, had been barely more than a child herself when she bore him—a single act of naive sexual activity with an older uncle had spawned a child within. She was thrown out of her parents' house when her own mother noticed the signs of her daughter's pregnancy. Edhita lived alone in the woods for a while, in the daytime foraging berries and nuts for her food, and during the night sheltering under ferns. She had no idea what her pregnancy meant as her own mother had no other children and so Edhita had not had any involvement with the genesis or progress of human reproduction. She did not connect the sexual act with the child now noticeably forming within her—the two things did not link in her mind.

One day a pedlar passed through the woods. He drove a small and rickety cart drawn by an old, worn-out donkey. Needing a rest from the drudgery of travelling he stopped and talked with Edhita. He soon discovered her naivety and, entranced by her childish and simplistic approach to life, he stayed. His donkey died. When he tried to remove it from its burden of the cart, he found the left shaft had split and given way, and as he tried to undo the back loops from the girth strap, the singletree broke rendering the cart completely unusable. He told Edhita that he had once witnessed a stillbirth and could help her deliver her child.

They decided to stay with each other. With some money received from the sale of the broken cart, together with some items of bedding and washing still remaining from its contents, and what he had saved from his peddling of utensils, they found a room near the dockyard, moved there together and made it habitable. He was a competent fisherman and, when he was not working as a field labourer, he fished and often came home with food for the table.

When the time came he, this pedlar-midwife, delivered the child—a boy. Edhita had little idea what was happening to her, but when the child was held up to her, and looked at her, and cried, she was immediately entranced with him. She felt a surge of love that flowed between them. She just wanted to hold him and keep him close. She named him Herron after her grandfather.

Whenever Herron was asleep Edhita looked at him adoringly and planned a wonderful life for him: he would grow up well, he would be well fed, well educated and loved by doting parents. When old enough, she imagined, he was to be started on a career with prospects for personal satisfaction and reward. His life would be the living out of a wonderful dream. Every day she took him onto her knee, petted him, played guessing games with him by holding up her fingers, tickled him until he couldn't get his breath, and bounced him and threw him up in her arms making him gasp with joy. She called him "Hero"—her "Little Hero"—and her pedlar companion, who took to Herron as if he were his own, she called "Father".

Once, when Herron, still only a novice walker, was playing outside with an old knife, he stumbled and slashed his hand. As he fell he grabbed for the knife as if to steady himself and slashed his hand twice more. Clutching his bleeding hand, he ran crying to Father who was inside repairing a fishing rod. Herron held out his bleeding hand. Father took him on his knee, washed the wounds and held him close to help calm him. He looked at Herron's hand, now no longer bleeding. He noticed that the cuts had formed a rough "H" shape on its palm.

He held Herron's hand up.

'Look, my Hero,' he said. 'Your hand speaks your name. It is written. You are indeed your Father's Hero.'

Herron laughed and Father held him close and laughed with him.

Shortly after the incident with the knife, Edhita's hopes for Herron's future were dashed when Father was taken away by a naval press gang and he never returned.

After he had gone Herron and his mother became even closer. But she was poor now and, with no one to provide for them, she had to find washing work in order to keep them both in their squalid lodging. Herron watched her slaving over other people's dirty washing. He felt sorry for her as she worked: her sleeves rolled up to her elbows, her forehead beaded with sweat, her apron dirty and wet. But, even though he dearly wished for her to be saved from this daily drudgery, there was nothing he could do to help.

And time went by. As Herron grew up, the unending poverty and misery of dirty menial work continued. But amongst it all, his mother was always tender and kind to him, and even when she was exhausted from her labours she would, when they were over for the day, sit with him and play some of their old games.

Throughout all this, Edhita remained beautiful and her youthful appearance did not leave her as a result of her hard life. When she played with Herron they seemed, instead of mother and child, like two children, giggling and bunting each other, laughing and pushing each other in fun. It was truly love that passed between them, and resided beyond each of them and within the other.

As soon as Herron was able, he went to work at the docks and managed to bring in enough money to feed them both and save his mother from the drudgery of labour that she had undertaken for so many years. Now she used her time to clean their room, mend their tattered clothes and to attend to herself by washing her hair and bathing her body.

Edhita got into the habit of walking to meet Herron when he came out of work. Other workers would call to her and make comments to her on her desirability as she waited at the yard gates.

But she ignored them as she focussed her gaze exclusively in looking for Herron. When he came out she ran to him joyfully, embraced him eagerly and held his arm tightly as they walked back to their lodging.

Herron and his mother worked towards a hoped-for better life. But their plan foundered as a conspiracy of circumstances overtook it that would lead to Herron finding himself falling foul of the state.

One day he was dismissed from work early as there was not enough cargo to keep everyone gainfully occupied. This happened sometimes and when it did Herron would hang around the gates in case there was a sudden, unexpected demand for labour. That day, he waited as he had done before; he was known amongst the workers for doing this. But there was nothing. To begin with, other workmen had waited with him, but by the time he decided to return home un-needed, he was the only one left. All the time he had waited he had wondered why his mother had not as usual come to meet him.

After the dock gates finally closed, he left. He walked along the dirty cobbled streets, kicking absently at anything that lay in his path. The darkness was broken only by the occasional gloom of a working street lamp. It was a darkness that sheltered the evildoer from detection, that encouraged the breaking of the state's rules. But Herron was happy. He looked forward to seeing his mother again. For him nothing had changed since she had held him as a child on her knee. She was still young and filled with energy, always twinkled in his presence, was always ready to laugh with him, always keen to push him, and play with him. He smiled and widened his eyes as he thought of her and quickened his pace to be with her the sooner.

There was no working light in the road that approached the lodging where Herron and his mother lived. He heard shouting—screaming. He rushed to the door to their rooms which he found unusually open. He rushed inside. It was Edhita who was screaming. A heavy, brutish man was holding her arms outstretched and pinning her to the floor on her back. Her apron and skirt were pulled up and her legs were spread wide. The man was thrusting his hips between them. She continued screaming. The man shouted and gasped as he struck her with cruel blows to the face with his open hand.

The sound his clouts made pierced Herron as if they were the cutting of a knife. He rushed towards his mother. He grabbed the man and pulled at him, but the man's urgency for cruel sexual satisfaction kept him in place. Herron glimpsed his mother's face; no longer the playful smile that he knew, but instead the tortured anguish of a violently violated woman.

He reached back and pulled a heavy poker from the fireplace. With it he hit the man as hard as he could on the back of the head. And again he struck. And again. The man dropped forward. Blood spouted from the gaping wounds in his head. It sprayed over Edhita's tortured face. Herron kept beating the man with the poker until finally his lifeless body fell sideways and crumpled on the floor.

Herron could not avoid catching the briefest sight of his mother's distress: her exposed thighs, her crying blood-stained face, her loss of all that she was.

She muttered weakly.

'Hero. Hero. Darling Hero.'

Herron threw himself down, his face in his hands and wept with deep unremitting sobs.

In its code, the state made no allowance for circumstances that surrounded any transgression—this was the killing on purpose of another citizen. The trial was short. A judge read out from the code and proclaimed Herron's guilt. Herron was not asked to speak as there was no defence or mitigation admitted. He was sentenced to death at the hands of the state executioner who would, as was the custom, choose the method to be used. He was taken in chains to the prison and locked alone in a dark cell deep underground.

Dimios was at the end of a long line of executioners. His predecessor and trainer, Enoch could, he said, trace his ancestry all the way back to the first Enoch (who lived for nine hundred and fifty years). Indeed, he never tired of telling the story of his lineage to Dimios. The Patriarch Enoch, he related, was the son of Cain. Cain and his younger brother Abel were the children of the first man Adam, and Eve, the first woman. Cain was a farmer, Abel was a shepherd. They both made sacrifices to gGod. But gGod favoured Abel's sacrifices over Cain's and this caused Cain to be enraged with jealousy. He murdered his brother, and so with his victim's blood he contaminated the soil which he farmed. For this crime he was thrown out east of Eden to the land of Nod. And so the tribe passed down the art of dealing with those that killed others and he, this man Enoch, who was now passing on the role to Dimios, was at the end of this very long line.

Dimios felt as if he was in some way not entitled or fit to take on the job—he had been selected by good fortune and lot from the citizenry, and so had just come to it without any of his predecessor's background. He declined the offer of using the name "Enoch". But, determined to do his best in line with the responsibility it demanded, he took all matters relating to it with the greatest seriousness. He had been tied to rough and dangerous military service for many years, and when he finally escaped from that he had found himself geographically displaced, unable to adjust to working in any normal environment or to relate to others in any meaningful way. Whatever had been his previous life was no longer available to him. Only when he wandered into a chapel and joined the congregation there did he find a fresh meaning and impetus to bring value to his life. Yes, chanting and singing the praises of gGod made him ready and keen to do something worthwhile with his life. The leader of the congregation looked kindly on him and, seeing his potential for service, recommended him to the state penal service as a candidate for the pool from which the next executioner would be chosen.

Serving the state and carrying out its wishes was a great honour for Dimios. He slept on a stone slab in a small cell adjoining the execution room. He never took a day's rest. His meals were meagre and always cold. Each morning he dressed in the same way as the day before and the day before that. He wore a heavy black robe, a mask that covered his whole face, and black leather boots. He took great pride in maintaining the tools and equipment that he needed for his work and kept everything in the best order. When he was waiting for a condemned he read up on the history of execution, its techniques and effectiveness. Certainly he was not of the long line of executioners that could be traced back to the earliest Enoch, but because of his conscientiousness and self-education, he knew as much about the carrying out of the task as any executioner before him. As part of this carrying out, he (continuing the tradition) always spoke to his victims at length the night before the final act of execution.

And now he prepared for his latest victim.

On each wall of the execution chamber hung a plaque. A marked way forced anyone entering to follow along these walls. The first four plaques made a statement, the fifth asked a question.

When someone is hanged, the executioner has to release the trap door

When someone is electrocuted, the executioner has to throw the switch

When someone is killed by lethal injection, the executioner has to administer the drug

When someone is crucified, someone has to drive in the nails

Who is the murderer?

Dimios was used to reading the plaques every time he entered the chamber ahead of the condemned—it was a sobering reminder of the ethics of execution and of his role in it. And he was used to ignoring any questions or pleadings from the victim as they entered behind him. He ignored them at this point because he had spent the whole of the previous evening with them, answering their questions and explaining every detail of what lay ahead for them.

On the evening before the day of execution he had sat with Herron who had, according to procedure, been kept in isolation since the passing of sentence. Herron had remained in this situation without any opportunity to see another or find out about the wellbeing of his darling mother.

'Let me tell you what is going to happen,' Dimios had said.

'Please,' said Herron.

'First things first. For you, I have chosen hanging. I hope you approve?'

'What would have been the alternatives?'

'Electrocution, lethal injection, or crucifixion. Drawing and quartering, burning at the stake and decapitation have long since been withdrawn as acceptable methods.'

'You have chosen well for me, I think. Please, carry on.'

'Central to the event of hanging is, of course, the knot.'

'The knot?'

'Yes, in the rope that's going to be used to hang you. It's called the "Hangman's knot", or sometimes the "Hangman's noose". In some times past it was called the "collar". It's not exclusively a hanging knot. It can be used for other things. It's useful in fishing, for example. But its principal application is the hanging of a person —in this case, you.'

Herron nodded.

'How will it work?'

'The first thing is the construction of the knot itself. I use the classic hangman's knot where the heavy knot does the work of levering the head to one side. The number of coils in the knot is determined by the nature of the rope—its thickness, moisture content, greasiness, and so on—and of course the hangman's personal preference. I usually use eight loops, sometimes more, but, I can assure you, never thirteen—that would be unlucky.'

This was Dimios' standard joke, meant to put the victim at ease about the whole matter. It had never before caused amusement, nor did it this time.

'And how do you apply it?'

'Well, the knot of the rope is usually placed under or just behind the left ear, although I have found over the years (by trial and error) that the most effective position is just in front of the ear, beneath the angled part of the left lower jaw. I'm not sure why I favour the left but it has become my inclination.'

'What happens next?'

'The next is the crucial bit. If this doesn't work then, well, I'm afraid things don't go too well. But don't worry, I've done it so may times now that I have it perfected. For me, this is not just my job, it is my vocation.'

'Good, so what happens?'

'When you are released by the trapdoor, you fall—the "drop" we call it. When you are at the end of the drop you are pulled up by the rope, then the knot, carefully placed as I've said beneath the angle of your left jaw, pulls up the jaw and with it your head in a violent movement. This together with the abrupt yanking force of the now taut rope pulls your upper neck vertebrae apart. Just like that.'

'You've given it all a lot of thought.'

'I certainly have. I'm always particularly pleased with the way that this produces an excellently rapid death. Far superior to the more traditional position of the knot beneath the ear. I can see the point of it—the knot squeezing the neck arteries closed and so stopping blood flowing to the brain—but this does not always bring about a quick death. And that's what we're after, isn't it!'

It was as if Herron suddenly realised what was going to happen to him. The idea of losing the only thing that he had as a person—his self-existence—hit him as if it were a physical blow.

'Yes...er...yes, I suppose we are,' he said, but he knew he wasn't answering the question, he was simply mouthing words, making noises, exhaling breath, hearing his own stupidity.

'Do you have any questions?' asked Dimios.

Herron had only one.

'Do you know anything of my mother?' he asked.

Beneath his mask Dimios furrowed his eyebrows in a questioning frown.

'Your mother?'

'Yes. It was my mother that I saved from the brute I killed.'

Dimios furrowed his brow again.

'You saved your mother?'

'Yes. That is why I'm here.'

'What was your mother's name?'

'It was Edhita. She is the kindest woman in the world.'

There was silence as Dimios reached forward and took Herron's right hand. He spread it palm upwards. He pressed his fingers against the cuts that formed the rough shape of an "H".

'I will make it easy for you, child,' he said. 'You will be safe in my hands. And your mother will be safe. I will make sure of that. She will know that you died her hero, as much as you ever were. Hero. As much as you ever were.'

A strange pause ensued, made up of thoughts and words and recollection and puzzlement and realisation and identity, and the piecing together of so many things lost.

At last Dimios spoke.

'Your hand speaks your name. It is written. You are indeed your Father's Hero.'

'Father?' said Herron, barely able to speak through his tears.

'Father?'

Who is the murderer?

CHAPTER 21

Thinking about...gGod's perspective on justice

It was an abrupt and sobering end. Again, Socrates hadn't placed the letter-side of the jigsaw piece upwards—the events of the execution had troubled him so much—and so the return had been fittingly out of control. He was thrown backwards in the same way as before: roughly, neck-jerkingly, accompanied by flashes and bangs and the rattling of the whole fabric of the machine. He hung onto the lever with both his hands, his eyes staring ahead, and waited. It felt as if the whole thing was going to shake itself apart. After a while he wondered if something had gone terribly wrong. He thought of the emergency button (and all the worries that went with its use and abuse) and was (not withstanding those worries) just about to press it when the calm voice of IgnatiusM addressed him.

'I am puzzled, Socrates.' said IgnatiusM in a quiet, conversational way, seemingly unaware of the terrible events that Socrates had just been involved in.

'What about...my...friend?' replied Socrates, trying hard, though for the moment failing, to fall in with IgnatiusM's easygoing tone.

'I am puzzled why you do not avoid your own execution by escaping. I understand that this is a common and accepted practice in your time.'

Socrates tried to let go of the lever, but his fingers would not co-operate with his intention. He repeated IgnatiusM's question in his mind and forced himself to provide a coherent and relevant response.

'Yes…yes…it is both common and accepted.' Then finding his usual form, 'Though if you take this route you would have to leave Athens .'

'Is that your reason? You would not want to leave Athens?'

'No, though I would have found that difficult.'

'Tell me the reason then.'

'There are a number of reasons, compelling ones, and they are to do with my responsibilities as a citizen of the state.'

'Please tell me.'

Socrates was now well into the swing of things, so much so that he at last convinced his fingers to release their vice-like grip on the lever.

'If I was released what would I do? I would, of course, continue questioning. And so my inquisitive nature would bring me at odds with the authorities again. And I would not be able to stop, because for me this is the only true path of philosophy. But as I have said, I am a citizen, a member of the state, and as a citizen I believe that the dictates of the law should be upheld, and followed. And the laws apply to all. If I live guarded by the protection of the laws of the state then I must adhere to its laws.'

'You are indeed a man of strong principles, Socrates.'

'And also, if I escaped then this might cause problems for those who had helped me escape; they would be transgressing the law, and I would have been responsible for their lawbreaking. My own lawbreaking would thus be compounded.'

'But I understand that the authorities would have granted you clemency if only you had stopped your persistent questioning. Is that true?'

'Yes, it is. But, IgnatiusM, we are worth nothing if we stop questioning. There is nothing of value to be found if we do not scrutinise ourselves—our existence and our beliefs—as well as the beliefs of others. As I told the council at the trial when they made this offer—"the unexamined life is not worth living". Life is worth nothing if we do not question it. And I would not welcome such a life.'

'But would you not have liked more time to prepare yourself?'

'For what?'

'For death.'

Socrates laughed.

'I need no more time, IgnatiusM! I have been prepared for death for many years now. Much of my life has been dedicated to this preparation. I have puzzled over what life is about, and I have concluded that what it is about *is* death.'

'Then take out another piece and we will see what that reveals.'

Socrates, satisfied that this was enough discussion on the subject, fumbled in the now rather tattered bag that still hung from around his neck, bringing two pieces out at the same time and dropping one on the floor.

'Oh, I've dropped one!' he said, bending to pick it up. 'Where's it gone?'

'It must be there!' said IgnatiusM, clearly concerned. 'Whatever you do, don't lose any of the pieces. Every one counts! Can you see it? Socrates, can you see it?'

Socrates felt around where the piece had fallen.

'Ah! Yes, I've got it. Nothing to worry about.'

'Thank goodness! The last thing we want is to lose one of the pieces. Now choose which one you want to use and let's get started.'

Socrates looked at the two pieces, first holding one close to his face then doing the same with the other. This he repeated. He was obviously uncertain of any criteria to use in making a choice. But he was making a good show of trying.

'I think, this one!' He held one out. 'No, this one! No, I think the first! Oh, IgnatiusM! I can't choose! I can't choose! I can't think! I can't think, therefore I can't choose!'

Socrates went into a panic. He thrashed his arms about in a most uncharacteristic way then, in an attempt to control himself, grabbed the control lever, dropped both the jigsaw pieces and inadvertently pressed the emergency button.

Suddenly, gGod was there. He looked flustered, as if He had been woken or disturbed from something particularly engrossing.

'The emergency button again,' He said in a gruff, rather impatient tone. 'What's the problem *now*?'

'We have been discussing—'

'Yes. Yes,' said gGod with a scowl.

'Yes, IgnatiusM and—'

'You have been discussing. Yes. Go on. Discussing what?'

Socrates was finding it a bit difficult to assert himself in the face of gGod's clearly vexatious tone.

'Er...yes...punishment.'

'Very well, go ahead. I'm all ears.'

gGod shook His head to the side to ensure His hair was in place, and even though there was nothing to rest His elbows on, carefully dropped His chin onto his cupped hands.

'Well,' started Socrates, rather surprised that gGod hadn't bothered to bring His table and create Himself a cup of English Breakfast. 'We've been talking about my commitment to follow the will of the state. It all follows on from the events surrounding an execution that my last journey confronted me with.'

'Indeed.'

'Yes. And I have to admit to being a little confused. Perhaps you could help?'

gGod was still preoccupied with His other concerns: worries about gGladys, His in-laws, and the questionable success of His last counselling session. His usual easygoing nature had disappeared. He was not in the mood for tea. So, still in the back of His mind thinking about His own problems, He launched straight into a formal style of explanation that derived more from cold fact than sympathetic understanding.

'Why, we must ask first of all, do we punish those found guilty of committing crimes? Because punishments are typically not unlike the crimes that the punished wrongdoer has committed: fines are like theft, imprisonment is like kidnapping, capital punishment is like murder. And because they are enforced or inflicted by the state, they need justification—the state cannot act unless the members of the state are convinced by the rightfulness of that action . This is so particularly in a democratic society, of which,' He added with a now softening tone,'you, Socrates, are a strong supporter.' Then continued, 'where quite clearly they conflict (to some degree or another) with human rights and liberty. That great utilitarian thinker who we've mentioned before, John Stuart Mill, argued that everyone should be free to conduct their own "experiments on living" as long as they did not harm anyone else. Although in theory this view supports human individuality, in practice it can be an opportunity for the strongest and most ruthless to exploit the weakest and those at risk. With this in mind, state governments (democratic or otherwise) curb freedoms using laws and impose punishments for their transgression.'

'Yes, I'm with you there,' said Socrates, while at the same time realising that since gGod had introduced him to the time machine he hadn't had anything to eat or drink. 'Though, I'd like to add that since you introduced me to the time—'

'Good,' said gGod, pressing on with the only thing now in His mind. 'So the central problems of punishment are its meaning and its justification. Punishment usually involves the following necessary ingredients: it must be because of breaking the law, it must involve pain or some other unpleasant consequences, it must only be done to the wrongdoer, it must be intentionally administered (by others who have no bad feelings towards the one being punished, and have no personal gains to make from carrying such punishment out), and it must be done within the constraints of the state legal system. Do you agree, Soc?' He finished, now clearly mellowed back to His old self.'

'I wonder if I could…' Socrates reached over to the refreshment box that gGod had pointed out when He had first given Socrates the rundown on the machine and its controls. He pressed the lid and it opened easily. It contained a sandwich. He took it out.

'Would you like a drink with that?' asked gGod.

'That would be good. Yes, thank you.'

'It's done,' said gGod as He created a cup of hot tea.

Socrates tasted it. He had never drunk tea before and, after taking a swig, he rolled it around his mouth to acquaint himself with the novelty. Satisfied, he took a bite out of the sandwich. Again, it was a completely new experience to him—tuna and sweetcorn deli mix spread between to pieces of sliced bread—but he took to it eagerly. And now chewing the mouthful of sandwich and, stopping occasionally to savour the mixture of tastes, he continued.

'Do You…not think…that although we think that punishment might arouse feelings of…guilt in the wrongdoer, it may be more…the case that it actually hardens the…wrongdoer's attitude and alienates them even…further?'

'You have been studying the writings of Nietzsche, my friend.'

Socrates smiled obliquely. He was surprised that gGod wasn't familiar with his disbelief in the value of philosophy in the written form. For Socrates it "fixed" ideas and disallowed the important disputational nature of true, living philosophy—quite apart from the fact that Nietzsche did not live in his era, had never been translated into ancient Greek and Socrates wasn't too good at reading anyway. 'Remember? The huge moustache?'

That, he remembered.

'Ah, yes. Who could forget that.'

'Good.'

'But surely, facial hair aside, there are some things beyond our control. Some things that are determined.'

'Yes, some people believe that *every* human action has a cause beyond the control of the individual. If this is so then every criminal act would also have a cause, for example: genes, the environment, upbringing. In this case, the "determinist" would argue, that although there are "wrongdoers" they are not responsible for their actions because they do not make (un-caused) free choices. However, the determinist would still see the need for corrective action and would support reformist help for the wrongdoer or even the capital sentence (though this is only a short-term punishment for the wrongdoer—it is more importantly a way of ridding society of a problem member).'

'Genes?'

'Yes, sorry, Soc. "Gene" is a term introduced into the human vocabulary to describe the basic physical unit of heredity. It's the bit that causes people to have blue eyes or walk with a limp. Our "man", well, My "man", has genes that describe him in basic ways even though he appears at different times as apparently different people. Well, actually that's not genes, it's more My own miraculous power—I made him that way—but the principle is appealing to the inductively minded and can be usefully applied.'

gGod's description missed Socrates completely.

'Ah, I see. So, if you steal something that you want, and have a "gene" that predisposes you to steal things you want, are you responsible for your actions? Should you be punished for your crime or not? Are there any limits to being able to move the "blame" to a cause separate to yourself? And if—'

‘Right,’ said gGod, now getting fully into His stride, and already in response to Socrates’ sudden burst of questions giving forth with His own list. ‘Punishment can be justified in four main ways. The first, retribution, is a moral argument. The other three, as deterrents, in order to protect the society, and in order to reform the wrongdoer, are all utilitarian and stem from the thinking of… do you remember him, Soc…Jeremy Bentham and, of course John Stuart Mill?’

‘By “retribution” You mean?’

‘“Retributivist” theory is traceable even to before your own time, Soc, to the *Old Testament*, the Hebrew Bible, and the *lex talionis* (often referred to aptly as “an eye for an eye”). Simply, retributivism means that the wrongdoer deserves the punishment regardless of any beneficial consequences the punishment may have to the victim or society at large. In other words, those that break the law deserve to suffer—they must pay back society for their wrongdoing by their own suffering. The punishment is given on an increasing scale according to the increasing severity of the crime. When applied as *lex talionis* (might I add, also referred to as *jus talionis*, “the right of retaliation”, by, by now I hope, our old friend Immanuel Kant) the punishment should be directly equivalent to the crime. For example, murder should be punished by death. However, usually, when retributivism is applied, it is modified by exception (perhaps a wrongdoer is mentally ill), mitigation (taking into account the wrongdoer’s circumstances), and by standardised punishments being used where it would be ridiculous or socially unacceptable to apply directly equivalent punishments (for example, blackmail, rape and so on). However, retributivism is based on the human instinct of revenge and is considered by some to be too basic for a civilised society. Retributivism does not take into account the effects of punishment on the wrongdoer and as such, ignores the consequentialist moral purpose. Retributivism is also what you might call “backward-looking" (reviewing the crime which *has* happened) and, even though in many societies there has been variable interest in the plight of the victim, it can be considered to concentrate more on the wrongdoer not the "wrong-done".'

'And Your second heading, deterrence?' asked Socrates keenly, though still gasping from gGod's diatribe on the first.

'Well, deterrence is a strictly consequentialist (utilitarian) view, justifying punishment on the basis of its ability to discourage wrongdoing in the case of both the wrongdoer and others who know of the punishment. As with retributivism, deterrence is not concerned with reforming the wrongdoer; rather it is using the punished wrongdoer as an example to the rest of society.'

'That seems a sound view.'

'Yes, but deterrent punishment is prone to the criticism that it works whether or not the victim of the punishment is guilty or innocent (so some of the legal safeguards to protect the accused are not so important). On the other hand, it is criticised for not being truly deterrent, the argument being that certain crimes would be committed irrespective of the punishment, for example, the crimes of a psychopathic murderer. Or that certain punishments such as small fines, particularly for those who can easily afford them, do not deter anyway. These arguments are difficult to prove and so throughout time have remained politically and socially contentious.'

'I think it might be different if every punishment for *any* crime against the state were capital. After all, membership of the state is an entitlement based upon accepting to live by the rules of the state.'

'Yes, it is, though many would see that as *too* severe.'

'But…' started Socrates, unable to finish the point which was so close to his own situation.

gGod pressed on.

'Supporting capital punishment can be seen from the points of view of justice or utility. The argument from justice says that people deserve to be punished for criminal wrongdoing and in the case of the worst crimes (such as murder) the severest punishment should be prescribed. The argument from utility can take one of four forms: it is a deterrent (the criminal will not repeat the crime and others will be put off committing a similar crime), it is less cruel than life imprisonment, it satisfies the family and friends of the victim, and it satisfies public outrage. But there are a number of reasons for holding a view against capital punishment. Wrongly convicted (innocent) persons will sometimes be executed. Capital punishment is uncivilised (for example, if torture is considered uncivilised then why not "state murder"). The balance of bad effects on the criminal awaiting punishment may be worse than the effects on the victim or his or her family and friends therefore execution is not justified on retributivist grounds. Lastly, if, as some think, people do not act freely (because the world and all its causes are determined) such punishment is never justified. Not a view I can say *I* subscribe to!'

'And is there any argument for punishment as a way of protecting the members of the state?' asked Socrates, now being able to fit his own situation firmly into the discussion.

'Punishment based on the idea of protection of society is based on the consequentialist view that society is safer if certain (more often violent or sexually perverted) wrongdoers are kept securely out of the way. It is a view proposed by our constant reference point in this area, Jeremy Bentham. This method, however, often protects society from wrongdoers who pose no further threat. For example, even though it would be a good idea to imprison a serial and persistent rapist, it would serve no purpose to imprison someone who committed a once-off crime under specific and unrepeatable circumstances.'

'Such as?'

'Well, for example, the passionate murder of a particularly wearing spouse,' He said with a sense of undisguiseable personal involvement. 'Also, unless imprisonment is for their natural life, released prisoners, because they have been in the company of other practised criminals, can return to society better equipped to do harm, and perhaps better to evade further detection, in which case the protection effect would be reversed. Some believe that for punishment to be effective, and in order to protect the members of the state, crimes should be divided between those committed by persistent criminals and those that are once off, and should not take into account the severity of the crime at all. On this view, persistent criminals should be imprisoned for the rest of their lives and those convicted of once-off crimes should be fined. What do you think of that?'

'I favour banishment from the state. The state might protect the individual in return for the individual contributing and living by the laws of the state, but if that contract is broken by the individual, then the individual loses the right to be a protected member of the state.'

'Indeed, but the state has other obligations. For example, there may be a case for trying to reform the wrongdoer.'

'But why should the state bother to do such a thing?'

'The argument for reform is based on the consequentialist view that a reformed wrongdoer will not commit further crimes, so protecting the general public and allowing the reformed criminal to make future positive contributions to the society. However, it is hard to discriminate between wrongdoers who need reforming and those who do not, and wrongdoers who will respond positively to reforming treatment and those who will not. For example, a persistent thief might not respond to reforming treatment whereas a once-off wrongdoer may not need reforming. In practice, reform usually forms part of a punishment system that blends it with both deterrent and protective elements to satisfy consequentialist moral principles (that is, even though the punishment is severe, the state as punisher has a strong moral justification because of the reforming element). Reforming punishment may not necessarily be given on an increasing scale according to the severity of the crime, although, for example, because of the length of prison sentences, those convicted of the worst crimes can benefit from increased reforming facilities.'

'It seems to me that there is a muddle here. Surely reform is reform, and punishment is punishment—the two are logically distinct.'

gGod looked a little annoyed at being accused of muddled thinking and did not subscribe to the unproductive tautology used.

'Well…' He said, but not quite sure what to follow up with.

A fresh cup of tea appeared on the table and He took a welcome sip.

Socrates took advantage of the pause and powered on.

'What, I ask, makes it right that convicted criminals should be encouraged to study or learn trades while in prison when such programmes are costly and not afforded to members of the rest of society who have not broken the law and continue to contribute to the society's wealth?' He didn't give gGod a chance to reply. 'If members of the society were sufficiently well educated (and those with noticed pre-dispositions to criminality were purposely re-educated) then there would be no need for punishment. And we would arrive at the same point as before: anyone who could not abide by the state's laws should be banished from the society that constituted it.'

'But, Socrates, surely you are in favour of civil disobedience. Are you not in your present situation because of just that?'

Socrates nodded.

'I am,' he said soberly.

'Then you are in good company. Civil disobedience is a justification, on moral grounds, for breaking the law—a moral right to disobey laws that the civilly disobedient hold to be unjust. In human history there are many examples of the success of civil disobedience. It is an act of courage, Socrates. I applaud you. Indeed, it is because of admiration of your stance on this that you have been favoured with this very special last day.'

'For which I thank You,' said Socrates, adding "I think" in his mind, but not saying it.

gGod, now refreshed by His English Breakfast, and happy to receive thanks that He knew really belonged to God (himself), continued.

'Civil disobedience, as you know, requires a public act. It is not sufficient to break the law (on moral or whatever grounds) and keep it a private matter, although Henry David Thoreau (a person from a land not yet in your time discovered) suggested a private form of civil disobedience amounting to personal freedom based upon a high level of ignoring the state. However, the intention of civil disobedience, as has come to be commonly accepted, is to draw attention to some matter of public concern, not to undermine the law of the state itself. Acts of civil disobedience are generally peaceful. Civil disobedience has sometimes been confused with terrorism, but acts of terrorism differ not so much by the moral imperative inherent to the cause, but in the manner in which civil disobedience is approached—civil disobedience is usually a pacifist act, terrorism usually involves violence. Criticism of civil disobedience is usually either on the basis that it is undemocratic or that it starts down a "slippery slope" to lawlessness and terrorism. In a democracy, breaking laws made by elected representatives (particularly when the law breakers are small in number) goes against the principle of representative democracy. Most members of human society disagree with some aspect of the law yet abide by it as part of their contract as a member of that society. However, as the intention of civil disobedience is made public, it is often used to highlight "bad" law and press for change.'

'But surely *no* law breaking should be tolerated,' said Socrates. 'No matter how strong the moral principle involved and no matter how "bad" the law in question may seem, the laws of the state are sacrosanct. And if the state tolerates any unlawful questioning of them it will eventually lead to societal breakdown and anarchy. At the same time, some acts of civil disobedience may indeed be supporting the very reputation of the law that they uphold—the civilly disobedient suffering publicly under the laws of the state in order to make their moral case.'

'Yes, Socrates,' said gGod. 'And you are the (at present, still) living testimony to that. Can I get you another cup of tea?'

He didn't wait for a reply and disappeared directly.

Socrates stared into the space that He had left.

'Hello again,' said IgnatiusM cheerily. 'Still ready to take off again?'

Socrates' mind was reeling with the conversation with gGod about justice. It had reminded him of his current situation and brought into focus many of his dearly held views.

'Yes...er...ready...yes, I suppose so.'

'You don't sound very certain.'

'Sorry, I'm just a bit cluttered with thoughts. gGod is very wise and He knows so much. He has the benefit of knowing all things in time. It can be a bit battering sometimes.'

'Well, to be fair, He *is* gGod, after all.'

'Yes. But He seems to have His worries too. This gGladys (whoever she is) seems to be a constant source of concern for Him.'

'Yes, so it seems. She's the wife. And she's got relations, especially a mother. gGod didn't know what He was letting Himself in for when He created her. Anyway, are you ready to set off again? Oh, and this time, try and remember that the letters on the other side of the piece are most important, well, essential, for a satisfactory and safe return.'

Socrates was now used to the sequence of events: complete a journey, chat with IgnatiusM and gain knowledge and insights from gGod, select another jigsaw piece from the bag, hold it picture side up, stare at it, keep staring at it, pull the lever while holding onto the piece, hang on and wait for the turmoil of time-travelling to stop, while of course all the time hoping that somehow he would remember to do the right things to ensure a safe return.

So, he held the piece up, turned the picture side to face him, started staring, grabbed the lever, pulled it back, hung onto it and began waiting until the whole vibrating, shaking horror of the next journey came (hopefully) to a halt.

CHAPTER 22

Muttie—a worthwhile life must have meaning

Florence was eleven years old. She was an only child. Because she had no brothers or sisters to play with, and to fend off loneliness, she created imaginary friends. To Florence these friends were as real as any that anyone else had. And they were with her all the time. With these friends she played skipping games, or ran races, or just fell about laughing at the sheer joy of being with them.

On one sunny day in early summer, Florence ran along the dusty track between the houses, as she always did; in random directions, dodging from side to side to avoid being tagged by her friends, jumping with surprise and laughing when she was caught out. She swung her arms as if she was a windmill, she giggled and laughed at every part of the world she touched and saw. Florence was filled with joy and happiness. She side-stepped to avoid a particular friend who was just as quick and agile and often managed to get the better of her in their games. Florence lost her footing and fell over sideways. She laughed and kicked out to prevent her friend jumping down onto her. But she couldn't stop her!

'No! No! Don't!' she screeched. 'No! No!'

It was wonderful to live in this world of friends; always being able to play and feel the joys of happiness they brought with their company. Of all the games they had, her favourite was "chase and find". She loved the excitement of running away unseen as the chaser covered her eyes. She loved hiding, hearing her friend still counting eagerly until at last she was released when she arrived at the target number—it was always one hundred.

'Ninety-three, ninety-four, ninety-five…'

Florence would crouch down expectantly, squeezing her hands together as if wringing her fingers would somehow endow her with invisibility.

'...ninety-six, ninety-seven, ninety-eight...'

She would tense even more with the last few numbers, hoping all the time that her chosen hiding place would mean she would escape being found. At the same time she would be shivering with the excited hope of discovery, knowing then that the hand of her discoverer would be laid down on her shoulder, and she would jump up with shock, and turn and open her mouth wide, gaping with the surprise of it all.

'...ninety-nine, one...hundred!'

And she would crouch and wait, imagining her pursuer coming closer and closer. And her heart would pound. And she could hardly bear it. Then!

'Gotcha! Gotcha!'

And they would both break out with screeches and laughter.

And the finder's hand would fall again against her shoulder solemnly, declaring her "got", and now she would sigh with the joy of it—that feeling of contact, of being with another, of being within another. And as if overcome by the feeling of being within another, she would break away from the hand that held her and run away, shouting back excitedly.

'Now find me if you can!'

And so it was. But it was not quite as it was. For hide as she may, feel the joy of being found as she did, experience the excitement of contact that brought her so close to the other that she felt part of the other; in truth none of it was real—in truth, she was alone. No matter how much she was involved in her games, she was in reality the only one. And when she flopped down, tired from the efforts of her games, she fell into a silence of realisation, the existential peacefulness of accepting the truth of it—yes, she was alone.

One day, on the edge of a small woodland where she often came, Florence was gambolling in her usual way, dodging and ducking and shouting to her friends, when suddenly, she heard something, a different sound—the sound of a stranger! She had never known anyone else to be here before. She stopped and looked around. It was a footstep! To start with she couldn't puzzle it out. A stranger in her world of friends! How could that be!

She waved to her friends to duck down and she did the same. She squeezed her eyelids tightly together. The footsteps got nearer, breaking small twigs as they fell, scuffing the grass as they reached forward. And in the sound of the footsteps she realised the bulk of another, the heaviness of a reality that she was not used to. Still not looking, she ducked lower. The footsteps were now right alongside her. She could hear heavy, panting breaths. She tightened her eyelids until she felt the strain pulling her cheeks. She opened her own mouth in the hope that it would prevent her breathing from being heard.

Florence could bear it no longer. She opened her eyes. Two heavy boots was all she could see. They were brown leather, roughly made, one with a braided yellow lace, the other unlaced. They were almost on top of her. She wanted to attract the attention of her friends. She wanted to leap up and run away with them. But she was terrified and unable to move.

Suddenly, one of her friends broke cover and ran out of the wood and into the open. Florence froze. One of the heavy boots moved closer to her, as if its owner was turning to peer after the runaway. Still she couldn't move. Then a voice—a man's; strong but with something of age about it. Yes, she thought, it is the voice of an old man.

'Muttie! Muttie! Come here, boy! Muttie! Where are you!' Who was he calling, she thought? 'Muttie! Come here! That's enough!' It must be a dog. Yes, it must be a dog.

The calling went on. Eventually the boots moved and bit by bit went further away from the crouching Florence. The calling continued but got fainter. Florence took the risk of getting up onto her knees, just high enough to see what was going on. Her friends waved their hands at her, motioning her to stay down, but she ignored them. She saw an old man walking away through the wood, looking from side to side, still shouting. Slowly he disappeared amongst the trees and shortly after that she could no longer hear his cries.

Suddenly, Florence felt something against her leg. She jumped with surprise. She turned to look. It was a small black and white dog. It pressed hard against her, looking up at her expectantly. She didn't know what to do. It was so real! She looked around for her friends but they were nowhere to be seen. The dog nuzzled its head against her leg. It rolled onto its back and pressed its front paws against her foot. She wanted to reach down and stroke it, but she didn't dare. It began making whining sounds. She was entranced. It rolled over completely. She dodged down, still thinking it was worth hiding from her friends. The little dog, immediately excited by Florence's game, crouched down beside her.

They stayed there until it seemed safe. Florence jumped up but none of her friends were there. She was frightened. Her friends had gone. She started running through the long grass. She knew the little dog was chasing after her—she could hear its yapping and the sound of its paws treading down the grass. She turned. It stopped immediately and stared at her. She started to run again and it followed. She dodged to the side and it followed. She slowed and it slowed. And she speeded up and it did the same. She threw herself down, laughing and breathless. The little dog jumped onto her and started licking her face. Florence shrieked with joy.

'You must be Muttie,' she whispered, and the little dog licked her even more.

As they day drew to a close, and the sun dropped lower in the sky, Florence and her friends used fern leaves and moss to create a little bower near to a wide crack at the base of an old oak tree. Muttie took to it straight away and wriggled down to wait for the night.

The next day Florence rushed out to the old tree and found the little dog waiting. He ran to her keenly, wagging his tale and weaving sideways between the ferns. They played all day. Hide and seek with her friends took on a new character: racing to a hiding place with the little dog, trying to keep him calm as the counting went on, holding him close when someone came looking for them. The same thing happened day after day and the world felt perfect for Florence and her friends.

Their games became wider ranging, spreading first to the edge of the woods and then beyond. They ran up dusty tracks and hid behind hedges. Sometimes a stone wall acted as a shelter, or a fallen tree, or an abandoned piece of farming machinery. Once they ran into the garden of a cottage and were chased away by an angry lady with a broom. Wherever they went it was always with joy, and always with Muttie yapping keenly around their heels.

And the sun shone.

Flies buzzed in the beam-spanned roof space of the old cottage. The thatch had stood the years well, but two wet winters had caused some slippage and there were now two holes through which on sunny days, when the angle was right, shafts of light broke into the living quarters below. And it exposed the life-crippling poverty in which people can sometimes be forced to live.

The old man was one of these people. His name was Leof, meaning love. Many years before he had lived here happily with his young wife, Brona. She was very beautiful with long brown hair. They had fallen in love at first sight, and had, after only a few weeks, been married by an old lady in the village who looked after all matters ceremonial. They took over an old cottage that had been empty for many years and had fallen into poor repair. They both worked hard to make it their home. They had laughed and loved, made light of any worries or harms, and stared into each other's eyes whenever they needed the knowledge of being part of another through love. They had no children but they were always kindly to the children of others, never begrudging the happiness these children brought to their parents that had been denied to Leof and Brona. Leon learned to make simple boots and shoes and Brona made braided laces for them.

One late autumn there came a sickness to the community. They both became ill. Leof recovered quickly but daily Brona became worse. She lay in their bed unable to move. Although she could drink water she could barely eat. She became pale. Her beauty left her as her skin dried and became creased and wrinkled. Leof tended her as well as he could, but it was hard. As the winter set in and the weather worsened it became even more difficult. One day an old lady who lived a few fields away visited. She occasionally called around bringing cold broth. Leof welcomed her arrival, as much for the company as anything. She put her bag down on the table in the kitchen and stood back smiling. She drew Leof's attention to it and when he looked at it, it moved! The old lady stood back and laughed as the face of a small puppy emerged!

'He will be a friend for you,' she said, opening the bag and lifting out the little dog. 'I have already given him a name. He is "Muttie".'

'Muttie,' repeated Leof, and at the sound of his voice the little dog wriggled out of the old woman's grip and ran across the table to him. He stretched his hands out and straightaway it rushed in between them and wriggled with joy.

As time went on, and Brona became weaker and ever more frail, Leof and Muttie became inseparable. Leof delighted in the puppy's company and found his life, burdened as it was with

Brona's relentless decline, lifted and given fresh piquancy with every minute he spent with his darling Muttie. When time off from his caring responsibilities allowed, he would sit on a slope outside the house thinking about what life meant, while Muttie ran around his feet joyously or jumped onto his legs in sudden bursts of frantic delight.

Leof knew that Brona was going to die. But he knew their life together had been a happy and loving one. He believed he had prevented her from suffering and so her progress to death had been made as comfortable as possible. He did not fear death for himself or for Brona. When she finally died he buried her on the edge of the woods. Muttie sat beside him as he looked down into the grave that now contained her body. He reflected on the joy of life, picked up Muttie in his arms and walked back to the little cottage that was their home.

Several years passed and Leof and Muttie were as happy as ever two living things could be: each revelled in knowing the other, of being part of the other's life, of knowing the life that the other had. Then one day, in the woods, Muttie disappeared. Leof called him but there was no response. He walked in the woods for hours but could not find him. It felt as if his life had been ripped to shreds—he felt broken into meaningless living pieces. He wandered back to the cottage. All night he sat waiting, hoping that his beloved Muttie would return. The next day he wandered to all the places they had frequented together but still there was no sign. After a while Leof found himself sitting by the table in the cottage, his head in his hands, tears in his eyes and with a mind no longer capable of finding anything of value in his experience of being. He felt empty and hopeless. Life was not worth continuing with. He strung a rope up onto one of the beams of the cottage, tied a noose into one end, climbed onto the table, put the noose around his neck and stepped from the table.

The fall was not enough to break his neck and he hung for an hour slowly being strangled by the weight of his body on the rope. He thought of Muttie and felt happy to have loved him and happy to know that his own life was valueless without his dearest companion. Finally, Leof died.

Florence was approached by a farm worker who said that a man who lived in a nearby cottage had lost his dog and would do anything to have him back.

He pointed to Muttie and nodded.

'A little dog like this,' he said.

Florence didn't know what to do. She wanted so much to keep Muttie as her friend, but hearing that someone else needed him too weighed heavily against her keeping him. Muttie sat beside her, looking up to her and cocking his head from side to side.

'Come, Muttie,' she said, turning and running off towards the old man's cottage.

It was a happy journey. They arrived at the cottage. Florence knocked at the door but there was no response. Warily, she pushed it open and went inside. The old man's body was hanging limply on the rope. She started. Straightaway she recognised the brown boots with the single yellow braided lace as the ones that had stood by her as she hid from her friends and Muttie appeared at her side.

Muttie looked up at the old man and started whining. There was a roughly written note on the table. Florence picked it up nervously. Muttie continued whining as she read it.

"I find no point in living any more because I have lost my only friend—my special friend, my Muttie".

CHAPTER 23

Thinking about...self-willed death

Socrates hung onto the lever, the image of the old man's suicide the only thing he could see. It brought the immediacy of his own fate to the forefront of his mind. Yes, as he clung with tight-wrapped fingers to the lever, this picture of self-willed death was all he could think of—all he could see.

There was only a slight rumbling as the familiar table appeared, then the cup of tea, then the chair, then gGod, quickly disguising being caught in the act of combing His James Dean hairstyle by raising His eyebrows as though He had suddenly thought of something particularly interesting. He put the comb down on the table, affected an unperturbed mode, lifted the cup and took a sip of tea.

'And so, Soc, you are going to take your own life,' He said as if bringing Himself up to date with news He'd only just received.

'On behalf of the state, yes,' replied Socrates, keen to take up anything that distracted him from the old man's dreadful death.

'And so it will end—this is how your world will run away, eh, Soc? But in taking your own life will you have committed a right act?'

'Well...'

'I think it would be most apt to discuss the problem (current as it is, hot on the trail of the content of your last journey) of self-willed death.'

'Yes, You're right. I agree. Very much a good time.'

'Very well,' He said, looking longingly at the comb He had put down, and clearly struggling with Himself to hold back from picking it up. 'Let Me set the scene. Humans consider themselves to have a natural right to life (though, because it was entirely at My behest, we must view "natural" as also "gGod-given"). So, you may ask, are there any reasons why this should not include a natural (or gGod-given) right to death?'

'I would say there may be reasons, but I would find it difficult to uphold a view that this was universally applicable.'

'Well, Soc, the principle of protecting innocent human life is central to human morality. The view that under certain circumstances (say, unacceptable pain) it is preferable for a human consciously and deliberately to end its life goes against this central belief.'

'Yes, indeed.'

'As you know, in your time, the term "ευθανασία", "euthanasia" meaning "good death", originally had two distinct meanings: "active", involving the painless putting to death of someone suffering from a terminal condition, and "passive", involving not preventing the death of someone suffering from a terminal condition.'

'Yes, that is true.'

'But neither of these categories cover your situation, Soc. Yours is going to be more along the lines of what we might call "voluntary euthanasia".'

'This would indeed seem the best form, for if it is voluntary and does not affect anyone else, wouldn't that right be morally unassailable?'

'But questions hang over it: does it contravene some duty-based view, or fall foul of the utilitarian (consequentialist view)? The duty-based view says it is morally wrong to take any life (including your own, Soc). The utilitarian view says that if the killing brings about the greatest possible good then killing is the correct course. In your case, Soc, you would need to consider whether the "benefit" to you of losing your life (by killing yourself) would not create more "dis-benefit" to others in the future.'

'But, in order to honour the law of the state I am duty-bound to carry out its judgement. As a citizen of the state I must play my part in upholding its laws. If I do not do this then I dishonour my membership of the body that allows me to live my life fully under its protection. I am both a beneficiary of the state and a contributor to its existence. The state is because of me and I am because it enables me to be.'

gGod reached out for His comb but pulled back before He touched it.

'Yes, yes,' He said rather condescendingly. 'As you know, Immanuel Kant believed that humans should treat people as ends in themselves and not means to ends. In other words, they should respect their individual humanity, not what their existence might otherwise lead to. In order to fulfil this obligation, Kant's duty-based ethical theory involves a categorical imperative (a formal moral law based on reason that we've talked about already) that, in turn, would oblige you never to kill and that includes killing yourself. Again, as you know, John Stuart Mill worked out an ethical theory based on the consequences of action, not upon obligation to duties. This utilitarianism means calculating the potential effects of all the various courses available then, as a result of adding up all the possible happiness and unhappiness for everyone involved, taking the course that should bring about the greatest overall happiness. Socrates, picture the faces of your friends as they lie asleep in your cell. Do you think your death will contribute to their future happiness?'

'They are sad now, yes, sad to see me leaving them, losing my life. But that sadness is generated by the value that they may have had from knowing me. And perhaps in the future something I have said may be of use to them in their own lives. Even this act of committing my own life to death may help them solve something for themselves in the future.'

'But the *act*, Soc! What about the act itself?'

'The act is a selfish one. It allows me to play my part fully as a member of the state that has protected me. And it allows me to move from the confines of my mortal existence and become part of the virtue of true existence. It is the only wise act that I can undertake.'

'Soc, you are truly finding your form. It is as though the critically positioned nature of your own mortal life is bringing a fresh new sparkle to your thinking. Oh, what you could contribute to future happiness if you allowed your life to continue for a while longer!'

Socrates burst out laughing.

'A poor and teasing riposte, gGod! But You have brought me cheer.'

gGod sat back and stroked His hair. For a second He played with a curl that He had trained to drop down against the centre of His forehead. Although it was intended to put any witness in mind of James Dean, at the moment it held more of the early Elvis Presley.

Notwithstanding this conflicting concern, He restored His interest in Socrates' problem. Still, serious as it was, there was something about it that (perversely) caused him to strike a lighter tone.

'Then I have something that will complement your mood. Here!' There was a slight rumbling sound, then a glass and a corked, green bottle appeared on the table beside gGod's cup of tea. 'I have been inspired by one of humanity's greatest philosophers from many years in your present future, Bishop George Berkeley. Have we mentioned him yet? I'm not sure.' Socrates raised his eyebrows at how such a statement squared with gGod's supposed all-knowingness. 'Bishop Berkeley,' gGod continued, 'became convinced of the efficacy of the contents of this bottle.' gGod uncorked the bottle and tipped the contents into the glass. 'Here, drink it down. "Tar water, the drink that cheers but does not inebriate" was his slogan.' He raised the glass for Socrates to take. 'To your health, my friend. To your health. Be cheered.'

Socrates hesitated for a moment. Neither the appearance nor the aroma of the offered drink were particularly inviting, but a series of insistent, reassuring nods from gGod convinced him that it was the right thing to do and he took the glass, lifted it to his lips and downed the contents in one go.

'Mm…that was…' said Socrates, still trying to swallow.

'It is a question of making the most from what life has to offer,' said gGod. 'Being cheered by what cheer it brings at any one time is the secret. You have witnessed this. And the absence of it only accentuates its value when it is there available for the having.'

gGod smiled and, accompanied by a rustle of wind and a few flashes of light, He disappeared.

Socrates smiled and poured himself a second glass of tar water. gGod was (of course) right. The route to happiness, if not found on a continuously rising road, appears around corners, sometimes in dips, sometimes on hills. Each time it appears it must be seized. He sighed as a warm feeling of happiness came over him. He was pleased to know that he was dying knowing that he was doing it rightfully.

gGod's table, cup and chair disappeared.

'Do you have the next piece ready?' asked IgnatiusM. 'It'll be an easy choice this time as there are only two left.'

Socrates delved into the bag.

'Do *you* feel senses of happiness, IgnatiusM?'

'No, I'm afraid not.'

'Is that a sadness for you?'

'No, I don't feel that either.'

'Then what do you feel?'

'Nothing like that. I'm not alive in the sense that you are, so none of those emotional feelings are available to me. It's only being alive that brings those feelings—that makes them available.' A pause. 'So what's the next piece? Have you chosen?'

Socrates felt around the bag.

'There's only one piece, IgnatiusM. So no choices to be made. Where there is one there is only one.'

'You must be mistaken. There are still two pieces to go.'

'No, just the one.'

'Then choose that one, at least for the moment. But we're going to have to sort this out. There must be another!'

Socrates drew the piece out, looked at it back and front, then addressed the picture side with a solid, though cheerful stare.

Straightaway the machine stirred. Socrates gripped the lever with his free hand and, expecting to be thrown backwards, leaned into it. However, instead, the machine threw him forwards and he fell against the lever in a heap. The crashes and bangs, the showers of dust from the revolving urns, the dizzying movement of the rocking marble columns all contrived to disorientate him as again he was injected into another place, another time.

CHAPTER 24

Death—the old man's story

And the sun shone.

A heavy shower had passed and left a bright and full rainbow arching across the sky.

It was summer.

Birds were singing to others, hoping to attract a mate or to defend their territory. Insects were flitting through the warm air, seeking out the treasure of the next moment in their fleeting lives. Flowers were nodding, heavy with their fertilised seed, eager to release their burden and so continue themselves as parts of others. The world was radiant, glowing, eternal.

Hand in hand, a young man named Baldwinn and young woman named Annis walked along a dusty track that followed a descending ridge towards Blackwood. They were both barely tanned and the freshness and purity of their skin bore testimony to the fact that their bodies had not yet endured too many maturing years. Every few seconds they turned to each other and smiled. It was as if they were continually passing messages without speaking; as if they were continually saying silently that they loved each other, that their hearts belonged to each other, that they would be together forever.

But they did not truly know what love was, nor what it meant. As yet they did not realise that there were indeed many things they did not know, nor would ever come to know. The future for them was bound by the next squeeze of the other's hand or the warmth of their mutual smiles. No, they did not know what things might happen in a future much beyond these confining moments of their present. But they knew there must be something, and it begged to be discovered. And whenever there was an opportunity, in all their innocence, they tried to find out what it might be.

Ahead, they saw a figure sitting by the side of the track. They smiled at each other. Perhaps this was just such an opportunity. They squeezed each other's hand in unspoken agreement. They got closer. The figure was that of an old man, swathed in a heavy coat, his face clean-shaven but grey-bearded below his chin. They giggled at the sight of him and both skipped at the same time as the old man looked up and watched them approaching. Again they squeezed each other's hand—for exchange of love and for confidence—and when they got up to him they stopped as if they were one.

He looked up at them, his heavy-lidded eyes hard white, and reddened at the edges. He seemed to recognise them—as if he had been forewarned of their approach. He opened his mouth as if to speak, but it seemed difficult and he said nothing. He unfolded his cupped hands to reveal a small red and black ladybird. It crawled to the end of one of his fingers, spread its wings and flew up into the boundless sky. For a few moments it was out of sight. Then it appeared again, flew back to his hand and landed once more on the end of one of his fingers. It crawled into the palm of his hand. He looked down at it and smiled.

Annis nudged Baldwinn and pressed him forward.

'Ask him! Go on! Ask him!' she urged.

'He'll not be interested in our questions!' said Baldwinn holding back.

'Of course he will. He's old. He has seen more than us. He will surely know something of the future. Go on! Ask him!'

The old man looked into his hand and watched the ladybird as it nestled against the lines in his palm.

There were some moments of silence. Then, a tight squeeze of his hand from Annis and a bunting push forward caused Baldwinn to speak.

'Old man, you are…old. Yes, you must have seen many things. And because of this you must have become wise. And because you are wise, we have a question for you. It is something which concerns us greatly. Tell us if you can what we might expect from our future?'

The old man turned his eyes away from the ladybird and again stared up into the broad blue sky. The rainbow was fading. It was as if the ladybird had stolen its radiance.

'Yes, you are right, I have seen many things. And they are now all long gone. But whether I have become wise is another question.'

'But that is the past. We want to know of the future. Please teach us.'

The old man laughed.

'Very well. I can see straightaway that you are in need of teaching. Here is a first lesson for you, and part of any path towards your future and any possible wisdom. Although these things I have seen are in the past, knowledge of them now can help us look ahead.'

'How can that be?'

'Because we learn from our experiences providing that, when we remember them and how they happened, we take account of that knowledge and use it to shape our actions in the present. In other words, we become wiser, and in becoming wiser we act better.'

'So there is nothing in the past beyond that which is useful to us in our present.'

'What I have just described is what we do in our present that will affect our future. It is simply using the memory we have of the past. The past in itself will not tell you your future. Your future will be drawn from your thinking of the past "now". Look around. Can you imagine the drovers that have passed here? Can you imagine the bleating of their sheep being pushed along to the market by worrying dogs. You may wonder if the sheep realised their future —to be sold, then killed. Probably not. But we know that those that drove them did. That's an inescapable part of the way that humans live; knowing as well as possible the outcomes of things enacted in the present.'

'What would those people in the past have seen that affected them so?'

The old man looked down at the ladybird as it crawled to the edge of his hand then returned to its centre.

'Look down into the basin of earth that this ridge road encircles. See the darkness of it. No matter how much light might on some days be thrown down onto it, like your life, it still remains in a heavy shadow of the unknown future. Darkness! Darkness! That is what the future is. The blackness of unknowing. The blackness of the un-watched—the un-perceived. The blackness of the yet-to-come. Look again. See. Imagine this past that has now become present. Perhaps a medieval forest once darkened the earth there. And wandering souls felled its black-sapped trees in the hope of creating some sort of permanence—a permanence that would run out into the future. And the trees screamed out at their killing. And those that had destroyed them had, without regard for their living force, using their broken and injured limbs, created places to live; just hovels to begin with. And so human life infected the ground. But it was not all dark; it brought gaiety too. Yes, and optimism. And hope. Indeed, the future stretched out with beckoning hands. On spring days flags and ribbons intertwined with young girls' hair hung from the bare branches of the few aged oak and walnut trees that had been spared in the frantic urge for felling. And children clasped hands and, holding streamers, danced excitedly around maypoles. And their ecstasy led them to break away from the circling and, still hand in hand, to sweep and whirl in long lines between their proud and joyful elders. And those older ones were overjoyed by the youthful energy and spiritedness of their progeny that they knew for themselves could never be recovered. It is all there: past in memory, future always shrinking—a place of beginnings and a place of ends. Look! Look! That is the nature that has been ordained. That is the nature of existing in life.'

'Do you see more?' asked Annis, shivering because of the picture the old man had painted, but unable to leave the story half told.

'Yes,' said the old man.

'Then please tell us what you see.'

The old man drew a deep breath.

'I see the ancient ridgeway as it once looked down on the cluster of hovels. And I shiver. Yes, even in the warmth of the summer sun and draped with heavy clothing, I shiver with the sense of evil that emanated from it. I know that there much evil was done—the blackest of evil. The darkest and always irresistible aspects of human life were lived out there. The deepest part of this basin—in pre-history, was the dark floor of a deep ocean. There, where skipping maidens were stolen and never seen again, there, at the lowest dip of this damp sink, the foundations of buildings, even though stronger than the wattle and daub of their earliest predecessors, were still not able to hold back the insidious creep of wetness that ran within the ungodly sliminess of this infected soil. And over the years, their bricks became wet and flaky and water oozed from them like a fever-bearing sweat. It rained here at some time every day: since the first pole beams were erected by those earliest primitive settlers, since the dancing maidens had to run for shelter beneath the frames of heavy wooden trucks, since the flags that hung sodden from the wet-soaked branches had become rags to be stolen by predating magpies. Yes, since the beginning, the rain had borne down as if in preparation for another flood. *Another* flood? No, the one was enough. Such a terrible punishment. It would never happen again. But in *these* times I see no rainbow.

No, I can say no more. And all of this wetness, this soaking past has gone, consumed by the past future, by the insatiable now of the present. And, at the end of it all, I am sitting on a dusty road—an ancient man who, too, is covered in dust.'

Annis pulled at Baldwinn's hand, but they were unable to move. They smiled weakly at each other, trying to dispel the darkness that the old man had invoked.

'I'm sorry,' he said. 'My eyes are filled with tears. You bring too much light into my fading life. It has shaken my commitment to fulfil my obligation to…' He stopped as if from somewhere he had been instructed to stop. 'Look,' he continued, seemingly relieved but speaking with less certainty as if he had somehow lost hold on himself. 'Look, the sky now darkens. Another flash of lightning brings a heavy rumble of thunder, and already some patches of dust are yielding against the first drops of rain. Dust! I feel the dust in my mouth; it seems to fill it. I try to breathe but dust goes down my throat. I want to choke. I try to cough but I cannot get enough breath and instead I heave. My eyes widen. Look! Then a breath of air catches my face. Relief! All these images of rain and dampness and oozing and soddenness, and everything around me seems dried to dust.' He dropped his head and took several deep breaths. At last he seemed to have found himself again. 'And I think of death. Yes, *my* death. And I realise that I am inhabiting it. Yes, inhabiting my own death. Such a gift for me, and for anyone who witnesses it. In return for something I hardly knew I was giving, I have been handed something unbelievable—the chance to experience in my last few mortal moments the opportunity to know what will follow my death. For reasons I don't understand, I have been granted a chance to die and yet still use my living powers of perception. I have been given the chance to see what will come after my life has passed. For a short while I can use my living perceptions to know what is beyond. I can know within what is always beyond, before the ability to know anything for myself disappears.'

He paused. Now, Annis and Baldwinn's weak smiles had gone and a feeling of dread passed over them. The old man had painted a picture of life as past, and future being consciously captured within the few moments of his own dying. And this talk of a favour of some some sort. Given by whom? What had the old man done to deserve it? They shivered.

'It is over for me,' he continued, raising his hands towards them. 'And I cannot stop myself thinking about wrongs I might have done, or mistakes I might have made, or good things I might have lost or let slip by me. And I am thinking about where my life has led me—to one place only, here, to the experience of my death?' He stared at the young couple. 'This is common thinking for those about to die. But for me it is different—a world different. I know that for me there is so much more—the glimpse of eternity.' Again, he breathed deeply. 'When I see you, I see that through your love you have the secret. Nourish it. Value it. It is within you both, and for each of you within the other, and beyond that which you presently know. This unknown knowledge will lead you to the greatest of values—to the knowledge of all things, and immortality. You have asked me a question and that is the only answer I can offer to you.'

Annis reached out her hand to him. She touched his bare, grey-skinned cheek. It was cold, as if it were carved from ice. She pulled back in fear.

He turned his red-rimmed eyes up to her.

'Yes. I am dead! And in touching me you have just touched death.'

She shrieked and clung tightly to Baldwinn's arm.

'You can't be! You can't be!'

'It is true. I know the past because I am no longer constrained by life. I can see it all. In death we know everything. In life we only remember. In death there is nothing more to do—everything is simply being. In life we are always waiting for the next moment to occur—always having to act to make it sensible. In life we are perceiving. In death we are a perceiving part of all perception. Thank You gGod for this wonderful gift. I only hope that whatever I did that warranted this has benefitted You.'

'But you're still here! You're still talking! How can you be dead!' exclaimed Annis.

'This is nonsense,' said Baldwinn.

The old man smiled.

'Did you not feel death when you touched me?'

'I felt your coldness, yes…but…'

'That was the coldness of death.'

Annis could say no more. She clung to Baldwinn, overcome—caught in an unsolvable contradiction. The old man's ranting was both ridiculous and convincing.

They swung around to a sudden sound. It was a heavy cart being drawn by two black horses and heading along the track towards them. Its large wheels dug deeply into the wet ground and stirred up clouds of dust from the earth beneath. The horses snorted and reared back as they struggled to pull their burden up the rutted slope. The cart tipped to one side and a wheel became locked in one of the ruts.

'Look! They are here for my remains!' said the old man, now barely able to speak. 'And making a slow job of it.' He motioned to Annis and Baldwinn. 'Come close. Let us make the best use of the little time we have. Time!'

Annis, still clinging to Baldwinn, summoned up the courage to speak.

'What do you mean, your "remains"?'

'I mean exactly that. I have told you. I am dead. Look! They are coming to collect what my perceiving self has already left—my body.'

'This is nonsense! Your body is here, talking to us. You are not dead!'

The old man laughed. He motioned to them both.

'Come closer. Before they get here. There will be just enough time to tell you. I can still use this body even though it is already hardening with the rigor of death. You have felt the coldness of my skin. Touch me again, if you dare, and you will feel only the stiffening coldness that has overtaken me. Look! Look at my face and you will see the pallor that has spread over it. I am dead. Let us waste no more time. Ha! Time! Come closer. Closer! My voice is weak. The difficult track that waylaid the cart has given us the gift of a few more moments. Come closer.'

Nervously, and still clinging to each other, they did as he said, and bent even closer. Annis wanted to touch his face again and check what she believed she had felt before, but she didn't dare. It was as much as she could do to stare into his grey-skinned face.

'Go on,' said Baldwinn trying his best to offer encouragement.

'I lived for many years,' the old man said. 'I have seen many things. I have learned some things though I continued always to make mistakes. But in life everything was known only in the experience of the moment—anticipation and recollection scrambling around it like swarming bees. But when I died—yes, you must believe me, I am dead—it all changed. Instead of what was to come and what had been buzzing in the ungraspable swarm of my present, I saw every member of the hive, every single bee. The perceptions that I had known, the things I had brought into being because of my knowing of them were all available in one perceptual instant. Everything that has been perceived at any time by any perceiver is now available to me as part of that perceptive whole. And I am there. And I am also here because I have been graced with a few minutes in which I can use my dead body to pass this on to you. What a gift! Again I say, I only hope I deserved it and have done what was hoped would be done by its use. Learn from it. Believe it. Everything I say is true. Stay young.'

Suddenly, and with a crash, the cartwheel was released and the horses were able to move it again.

Annis let go of her grasp on Baldwinn, reached out and touched the old man's face. It was icy cold and rigid. He was clearly dead.

Two men jumped down from the cart. They told Annis and Baldwinn to step aside. Annis took her hand away from the old man's face and they both moved back. The men picked up the body of the old man, pushed it uncaringly into the cart, turned the horses to face back from where they had come and drove away.

And Baldwinn and Annis understood what the old man had said.

And they squeezed each other's hand.

And the sun shone.

And a rainbow glowed brightly.

CHAPTER 25

Thinking about…life, death, immortality and reincarnation

gGod appeared, already sitting in His chair. His haircut was clearly playing up and He fiddled inconclusively with the curl hanging on His forehead. He created a cup of tea and lifted it to His lips. He sipped at it and immediately put it down—it was obviously cold. He looked as if He was having a bad day that was showing no sign yet of improving.

'The emergency button again!' He said gruffly. 'What is it this time?'

Socrates didn't want to get involved in any of the normal civilities, nor in apologising for pressing the emergency button yet again (though he wasn't sure whether he had pressed it or not), nor in trying to find out what might have been going wrong for gGod (he had enough problems of his own without worrying about gGod's). All he could see was his own life depleting fast and in the time he had left he wanted more clarity. He still had so many questions.

He looked around, outside the now ramshackle, barely confining structure of the Time Machine. He hadn't given the world beyond the machine any attention since his first jolting acquaintance with time-travelling. Now, he gave it a few moments to soak in. It was all still there—the "outside" world, that is. *He* was still there, still in the courtyard at the end of the corridor of cells in the prison in Athens. Yes, he was still there. And he was still going to die. And soon.

He turned back and stared hard at gGod.

‘Is there a difference between “not being” *after* our life and “not being” *before* our life?’ he asked.

‘I don’t know what you mean,’ said gGod, clearly still irritated by things unknown to Socrates (things gGladys that had still not been sorted out) and not displaying anything remotely all-knowing. ‘How could you “not be” before you “became”?’

‘But a life doesn’t exist in the same way that it might not exist after death.’

‘A big assumption, Soc! And may I say, surprisingly uncharacteristic.’

‘Yes, it may be. But I am a little shaken by my latest trip. And, as You know full well, the end for me, my life, is becoming ever closer. And it has stirred up my less rational fears.’

‘That is natural,’ said gGod, now (with some divine effort) setting aside His own worries and offering some reassurance.

Socrates fired off a list of pent-up concerns.

‘“What is it to be alive?” “What is death and should I fear it?” “Is there a life after death?” “Could I return in another body after I die?” “What is the meaning of life anyway?” All these are everyday questions with obvious philosophical importance. They’re good questions. And reflecting on such things is what makes being human special. Being human *is* special. But I am thrown back onto my own thesis that the good life is the examined life and the unexamined life is not worth living. But the examined life is suddenly bringing with it new fears.’

gGod leaned back and reached for His cup of tea. It was still cold. He’d forgotten to refresh it! He reasserted His grip on omnipotence. The next moment it was hot and He took a sip.

‘Anything for you, Soc? Tea? Tar water? Anything else that might take your fancy?’ He held back on saying “hemlock” as He thought that at the present time this would be decidedly tasteless (“No pun intended”, He thought as He decided such a comment would be decidedly tasteless—no further pun intended, He thought before stopping the spiralling regress with a reassuring nod in Socrates' direction).

'No, thank You,' said Socrates graciously, but not wishing to be distracted from his current concerns and any progress that might be made in answering them.

'Very well. I know you are concerned, but there is no point worrying about what life means—just live it.'

'But it is close to over. There is hardly any more of it to be lived—not exactly the best time to start "just living it" surely.'

'But, my friend, you know that is only a matter of perspective —*temporal* perspective. Imagine the life of the flea in the Thinkery. How long did that have to live? Not long, I think. Compared to your life it would take up only a fraction of your span. But would the flea be daunted? I think not. And why?' gGod did not in any way encourage an answer. 'Because it did not *know*! It did not *know* how long its life was compared to yours, or whether it should be measured against some universal standard—the "universal life-measure". And that is because there is no such thing. You say it is "close to over", but the flea would be leaping over the moon to look forward to so much.'

'But I am not a flea! I am a human! And I have human concerns, and one of those at the moment is the shrinking of *my* future life-span.'

'Let's give all this some consideration. It is important. I know that. According to Henri Bergson (he had a very small moustache), life is different from all other forms of matter—it is creative in a way that inanimate life is not. Human life implies vitality, the urge to accomplish or initiate. Life, as a thing-in-itself, is represented by a complex organic structure able to utilise energy, maintain itself, and reproduce. But there is something that vitalises this structure, and I am the only one who knows of the vitalising ingredient that you could call "life".'

'Then tell me its nature. Please, gGod, tell me its nature. I cannot lose it without knowing more of it—the *meaning* of it.'

gGod threw His head back and laughed.

'Very well. Many of your co-philosophers, Aristotle, Saint Thomas Aquinas (I don't think I've mentioned him before—or maybe I have), and Immanuel Kant believed that humans are distinct from animals because they have a mental life that is rational—an ability to think through things in an ordered and logical way. It's an interesting idea.' gGod laughed again. 'It's true that humans differ from the rest of the animal kingdom in a number of important ways. Animals may desire but they do not choose. Animals have consciousness but not self-consciousness. Animals do not make judgements about the long-term future based on the past. Animals recognise each other but do not relate as persons (that is with some moral sense of justice, liberty and so on). Animals lack imagination (for example, they cannot speculate about possible outcomes). Animals have a limited repertoire of feelings. Animals do not have a sense of humour. Animals do not have speech (though they may vocalise). And in the world at large, animals do not generally have the same rights as humans (nor do they have the same duties of responsibility). And I know all this because I created them.'

'But I am a *man*! I do not want to know what *animals* are not! I want to know what *humans* are!'

Socrates was clearly not only anxious but irascible.

'I understand your impatience, my dear Soc. Let us deal with the matters, calmly, one at a time, and in this order: life, death, immortality, reincarnation, and finally the meaning of life. Though, forgive Me just wishing to finish the point I was making about animals. Ask yourself this. If a human being's brain were successfully transplanted into a dog, what sort of four-legged form of life would we be dealing with? If a dog's brain were successfully transplanted into a human, what sort of two-legged form of life would we be dealing with? Makes you think, eh, Soc?'

'Yes, it does. But I'm keen to move forward with the topics You've highlighted. Rapidly approaching death and so on. First, "life".'

'Oh, very well. Life is all to do with personal identity. The problem of personal identity, first proposed in a realistic way by John Locke is a difficult and puzzling one. Locke thought that for humans continuity of consciousness (that is, knowing your own part in the present and projecting it into the future) guaranteed your personal identity. And memory is an important aspect of this "selfhood". For example, take a human who is eighty years old and remembers when he was forty years old (sorry, Soc. I know you're not going to get that far, but it makes the arithmetic easier). When this individual was forty years old he could remember himself as a child. Now, let's say that he is eighty years old and he can no longer remember himself as a child. Is the eighty-year-old man the same person as the child?'

'If he can't remember it, then it would be difficult to say that that childhood was his.'

'Exactly. Memory seems crucial to what the human thinks of himself as being. But maybe this is misleading. Bishop Joseph Butler said that Locke's claim that human identity is guaranteed by a chain of memories is circular. He said that only claims on true memory could guarantee identity. However, because we needed a "self", an "identifier", in order to identify these claims, and this was what we were trying to prove in the first place, this so called guarantee gets us nowhere. Rationality, eh, Soc? Others have claimed that continuity of existence rests on continuity of body, or that the concept of bodily continuity is of itself no guarantee of continued identity.'

'This is a complex problem.'

'It is indeed. Imagine two humans, I could call them John and Jane. Yes, imagine John and Jane's brains are removed. John's brain is put into Jane's body and Jane's brain is put into John's. (I know this seems a bit extreme, indeed grisly but, you know, gGodly powers and so on). How do we now regard Jane (as the body) and John (as the body)?'

'This seems to bear upon "where" my "self" resides.'

'Yes, the notably beardless Ludwig Josef Johann Wittgenstein denied that there was truly anyone of whom we could ask the question "Who is that person?" But still it remains that even if Wittgenstein is right (or wrong), there is importance in the question "Who am I?" If I continue with my story of John and Joan. Before John's brain was transplanted into Jane's body and Jane's brain was transplanted into John's body, they were told that after the operation John's body would suffer a lifetime of torture and Jane's body a lifetime of pleasure. Should John feel anxious? What do you think, Soc?'

'I think I feel anxious just thinking about it!'

They both laughed and gGod, with a nod, encouraged Socrates to drink some of the tea He'd just created.

'Ah! English Breakfast, eh Soc? Nothing to beat it! Very well. Perhaps personal identity cannot be guaranteed by continuity of consciousness. Perhaps all that an "I" should wish for is that some of that "I" should continue.'

'In some guise or another.'

'Yes.'

'It seems without a solution.'

'It may be.'

'So we should move onto the question of death.'

'Ah, death! Death in itself is much simpler. Death is the final and irreversible end of life; your life, yes, but more precisely it is the condition "your" body is in after "your" life has ended. And this is not the same as "you" saying that "I" am dead because "my" body is dead. If, for example, your life is dualistic and consists in both your physical and mental existence, do both your body and your mind have to be dead before your life can be considered ended? Or could you be considered dead if you were permanently unconscious (with no apparent mental activity) even though your body remained alive?'

Socrates drained his cup of tea, put the empty cup down, and sighed heavily.

'So many questions! I think we've established in our previous conversations that "I" am not the same as "my" body. What we are concerned about with death is usually the cessation of all things that we know of as components of living things.'

'But it's not that simple, Soc,' continued gGod, unable to give up on His question-posing hypothesis. What about this? If you are pronounced dead, frozen for one thousand years then brought back to life, would you have always been alive?'

'Continuity! Mm. I suppose if the nature of my life was that it included a one thousand year freezing every now and again, then that would simply be the nature of living—in the same way that sleeping is part of living, and although not part of normal conscious existence, is accepted as something which does not break the continuous existence of 'me".'

'You're right, Soc. So that puts periodic freezing into its place. It is more the *fear* of death that worries the human. Anticipation that death leads to nothingness is an unavoidably disconcerting feeling.'

'But this is not a universal feeling', said Socrates 'I take the view that fear of death is irrational. If "I" could not experience anything after death then "I" have nothing to fear.'

'Yes, and Epicurus (wonderful beard by the way) said that death and you could "never meet"; because where you are death is not, and where death is you are not. Yes, and he was right. Any fear of death is truly irrational. Wittgenstein goes along similar lines.

He says that anticipation of death is part of being alive and that death itself cannot be an experience (because all experience is confined to life). The Stoics, for example (believing in physical and mental self-control), were good examples of putting this view into practice, facing their own death with undiluted calm.'

'However, there is some special quality about life that makes the loss of it of particular concern (for example, more even than the loss of our most treasured or valued material possession). We might fear loss of wealth because of the fear of the consequences of poverty, but we fear loss of our life because in losing our life we lose all potential. Fear of death is often the irrational fear of what it is like to be dead when logically the fact of being dead implies that we can have no knowledge of what it is like.'

'Sound logic, Soc.'

'Thank you. I would add that we fear many things because they are unknown (such as ill health, poverty, loss of a loved one, and so on.). We know with certainty that we will die (for me that seems a certainty very close at hand). Is it therefore less rational to fear death than fear the loss of something we treasure when we are alive?'

'Again, Soc, right on.'

'I know that fear of death is irrational. For example, we did not fear not existing before we were born, so we have no reason to fear not existing after our lives have ended. Against this, of course, the asymmetry of time means that although we can anticipate the loss of our own life in the future, we cannot in any meaningful way regret non-existence before we were born. At the same time, we can only experience being alive; we cannot experience not-existing (that is, "being" dead). Because "I" can only experience "being" alive, "I" cannot claim any link to whoever or whatever it is that is dead after "I" have finished being alive. "Who" (if anyone) or "what" (if anything) it is that is dead when "I" die must remain unanswered (and unknown). It may be that if we did not fear death (as a fear of loss), we would not treasure life, and without the fear of losing existence the things that we can obtain during our existence would lose their attraction. Coming to terms with a rational understanding of the loss that death brings about, together with the knowledge that we cannot experience death, rids us of unnecessary anxiety and places our life firmly and properly in the "land of the living".'

'You have thought a great deal about this, Soc. I congratulate you. I know it is a great cause of concern to the human (and at the moment to you in particular), and in many ways, I wonder if it was wise of Me to introduce it as part of human existence. I suppose I wanted to make life critical, valuable, and intense, and without an end to it none of these things could be achieved. Yes, I wonder if I have acted wrongly on this.'

'You should not reprimand Yourself, gGod. Death is not always seen as bad. Others may see the punishment by death of someone evil as good (though not necessarily good for an unrepentant subject of such a sentence—sorry to bring myself into it again!). Death may be seen as a relief from the pain and the suffering of illness. Death may be viewed as an appropriate conclusion after a long, successful and well-lived life. Death can be seen as heroic in that it is caused because of some particularly courageous action (though it is questionable whether all heroes themselves actually *feel* heroic). Death can be personally heroic inasmuch as we may face our own deaths with courage and fortitude. More radically, there may simply be times when suicide is preferable—death taking favoured precedence over life.'

'And that unavoidably brings us back to the situation I find *you* in, Soc: waiting out the last few hours of your own life that you will take by your own hand. And I can see that you are well prepared, and have come to understand the value of living that death brings about. And you have left open the door for some sort of future after death. And I would like to help you with that if you feel it would be worthwhile.'

'Yes, please. I have talked enough and would now welcome listening to Your thoughts.'

gGod stroked back His hair.

'When we talk of immortality we are talking about the continued existence of the person—that the personal identity of the individual continues beyond the lived life. Though we need to be careful here. If there is a continued existence of something of the individual (for example, a person's thoughts on something) this does not constitute immortality of the individual ("I" constitute more than just "my" thoughts, you would have to say). Neither can immortality be part of continued bodily existence. Some bodies are destroyed beyond the possibility of reassembly and some bodies could not sustain a continued existence anyway (for example, the very young, the very old, the very sick). Indeed, this applies to all bodies that die because at death bodies have died of something which precluded their continued survival in the last moments of their life. No, to think of immortality you must give up the idea of what you "are" now.'

'Yes, my dear (though absent today) student Plato holds (what he calls an "idealistic" view) that the soul is not material, occupies no place in space, and can therefore not be destroyed. I am inclined to this way of thinking.'

'I think you and your student are on the right lines there, Soc. Indeed, you may think that there is no point in continued existence unless it leads somewhere better than bodily existence. Immanuel Kant believed that there could be no purpose in the person acting morally unless the person was progressing towards a higher moral good (for which he or she would need an unending existence to attain). Some religions take a view that humans are caused to act morally because of the prospect of either heaven or hell. Rather silly, I'm afraid, but it can help direct people towards a virtuous life (even if it is for silly reasons). Others believe that the "soul" (as they call it) is reincarnated according to how you perform in each recurring life (I'm afraid Plato got onto this with what he called "transmigration" of the soul). Others again believe that you continue in some form of continuous experience. In human thinking ultimate liberation from the cycle of life can take a variety of forms (according to belief) ranging from a whole, unending consciousness to (whole, unending) nothingness. Most religions believe God (himself) and Me to be immortal either in that he (or I) is everlasting (exists at one and all times) or is eternal or timeless (exists somehow outside time). Following from this, many consider souls immortal in the sense that they last until God (himself) (or I) (if he, or I should choose) decide otherwise.'

'You provide plenty to hang onto there, though I am a little confused with the reference to God (himself) and You as if you are separate.'

'Well, We are, Soc. But that's nothing for you to worry about.'

'If you say so. Of course I find religious viewpoints unconvincing, though I am inclined to an eternal existence in some sort of "idealistic" world. But, to return to the basic syllogism: all living things die, I am a living thing, therefore I will die. This is true for bodies, but if "I", as a living human thing with a personal identity, am somehow different from "my" body, then this may mean that "I" might not die. Indeed, I might even have existed before I was born.'

'Plato and Aristotle both held that view (and much later, McTaggart), so, Soc, you're in good company there.'

'But I know I must be careful. Even though personal death is usually so emotionally and intellectually difficult to come to terms with, this should not give us reason to believe in continued existence (which is much more amenable to think about) over annihilation (which is not so amenable to think about).'

'Worthy caution, Soc. And so to our next topic, reincarnation.'

'This is very tricky.'

'Yes, a tricky problem indeed. In order to be reincarnated, something that is "you" needs to continue after your present body dies. In other words, although your body is mortal, something that you call "I" is not. To be reincarnated requires that something that you call "I" moves from one mortal body to another. It is difficult to imagine how this can happen: either the "I" can exist without a body for the time it takes to transfer to the other (in which case why does it inhabit a body anyway) or it needs to go to another body the instant the old one dies. In either case, to follow this line, you also need to decide at what stage in the life with this new body does the self begin to inhabit it. Is it when it is conceived? When it is born? When it is a few days old? And is it possible to apply any of these considerations if the self is to live in a very basic form of life (for example, a bacterium)?'

'Bacterium?'

'Yes, bacterium. Also, reincarnation implies that there are a fixed number of selves who must continue to inhabit a fixed number of bodies (if not, there would be bodies without selves, and on this argument that would never do). Such a proposition does not square with the commonly held idea (misplaced though it is) that life has evolved from origins which were quantitatively less or that the number of humans, for example, continues to increase (although humans could be a higher tier of existence for previously lower and more prevalent life forms). Though this would mean that the less evolved forms of life would be continually depleting in numbers. That humans cannot remember anything of any previous lives means either that they have not had any previous lives (which is most likely!) or that memory (in the form of a continuous memory) does not (for any reason) form part of their continuing immortal self. If memory is not part of their immortal self, it is, I have to say, hard to see how continued individual existence has any worth or meaning. And anyway, how can reincarnation into a lower life form (as some religions believe possible) be a punishment or retrograde step if the self remembers nothing of its previous life and therefore has nothing to compare with? And, as well, if it survives in a new body then we also have to answer the problem of the endless supply of new bodies to which it can migrate; after all immortality implies (indeed *means*) endlessness. As well as an endless supply of new bodies (be they human, bacterial or whatever)—'

'Bacterial?' asked Socrates, feeling a bit overwhelmed by this, another one of gGod's punishing diatribes.

'Very small living things. A bit like living atoms. The bacteria.'

'Not the bacterium?'

'No.'

'Oh.'

'So, yes, as well as an endless supply of new bodies—of *whatever* sort…' gGod's emphasis clearly underlined His irritation at being interrupted in full flow. '…the universe itself must also be endless. If the universe is finite then you cannot claim immortality. However, the question of such an endless existence might make us wonder about the point of such an existence anyway. Would it truly be to the self's benefit to exist endlessly? This would mean that there must be a supply of better bodies available for everyone in the end, and this seems unlikely as it would mean the annihilation of all *other* life forms, on some of which the better life forms (certainly humans) depend.'

'Like bacteria?' said Socrates.

gGod ignored the question.

'The question of whether existing like this would lead to endless tedium is also a concern. It is hard to imagine how continued life could hold much meaning when, as it progressed, it would come to know all that it had to offer. A bit like Me. All-knowing, eh, Soc?'

'Yes, You are, of course, right. But if that's the case, I'm forced to wonder if there is any point in making *any* post-mortem progress, as it would all be less than perfect. Endlessness of individual existence does seem pointless. I think You were right, when You created life, to give it an end-term.'

'Yes, Soc, and thank you. I like to think of human existence as you might think of youth. It is the case that young people have little true sense of their own mortality. The necessary youth of the combatant soldier is not merely a physical requirement. They know they are going to die but only in some rather remote sense. They often do not seem to link this with the deeply felt sense of awareness you may have in later life when you realise that you actually *are* going to die. I don't need to remind you, eh, Soc? However, religious belief and the plight of relatives and friends (and perhaps popular heroes) can affect how everyone reacts to this subject and this must be taken into account. Most things that you value have purpose. Purpose implies some end to a process. And, as we have seen, if immortality is simply endless this means that it is both purposeless and valueless. But it is not simply endless. It has more scope, more breadth. As you saw from the experience of the old man's death, he saw the true value of death—endless perception, in time and in extent. Immortality is the eternal knowing of all things without the burden of the person. As the old man left his body to inhabit the world of all-perceiving, so every living thing will attain its same immortal end. My message to you now, Soc, on your last day—now only a short time away from you administering a poison to yourself that will end your mortal life—is…stay young. Stay young and your death will be a good one. I know My purpose is beyond your understanding, perhaps you think what I am saying a little trite, but I assure you, it is not, and I do have a purpose, and My words are (of course) wise.'

CHAPTER 26

"Do pay it. Don't forget"

Socrates wasn't quite sure where he was. His meeting with gGod had knocked him for six: so many ideas, so many questions, so many answers. Answers!

He sat back in the chair. The machine groaned. Socrates groaned in sympathy. But at least it was over. No more jigsaw pieces. At last he could feel a sense of relief from the punishing business of time travelling.

'Just one last journey,' said IgnatiusM's calm voice.

'I though it was all over.'

'No, not yet. We need the last piece. We need to get on. Not much time left.'

'We've used the last piece, IgnatiusM.'

'No. There's still one to go.'

'No. The bag is empty. No more pieces.'

'It must be lost! The last piece must be lost! How could you lose the last piece, Socrates!'

'I haven't lost any pieces. I have used all the ones I was given. And now they've all gone.'

There was a pause.

'Very well, Socrates. We'll just have to go with what we've got. Look down at the pieces. Look down at them.'

Socrates gazed at the joined pieces of the jigsaw, and gradually, instead of the mixture of seemingly disconnected letters, he saw a barren and seemingly interminable landscape. He became absorbed. The next thing he knew he was sitting at a table opposite a tea-drinking gGod now graced with an impeccable James Dean hair style. And everything felt...well...different. He was actually *there*—this place was the place where he *was*. He no longer had the feeling of absorption in histories that his time-travelling had brought about. Nor was he caught up in the intervals of discussion and thinking that followed the last and preceded the next journey. No, instead he was now aware of a genuine first-hand experience of self; a proper awareness of his own existence—a sense of true being.

For a moment he heard IgnatiusM's voice again, reassuring him that he was indeed there, then it faded as it was replaced by the sound of a soft wind and the chirping of crickets. He felt a comforting and natural warmth around him.

'All the pieces might not have been placed, Soc,' said gGod. 'But you are now at the end of your travels, and at the end of your life. Let us finish our tea and walk together—let us follow the Aristotelean method and be peripatetic.'

gGod created a cup of tea for Socrates. They both drank their tea and then replaced the empty cups on the small table that rocked rather unevenly between them as they stood up.

gGod took Socrates' arm and led him ahead.

'This is a great moment for us both, Soc.'

Socrates was warmed by the sense of peace he felt, and the sense of companionship he was sharing with gGod.

'It is indeed a great moment for me—the wonderful end to my journey, the end of my last day. But why for You?'

'This is My last day too!' said gGod.

'Great goodness!' exclaimed Socrates. 'Why! What's happening!'

'Do not be afraid. All will be well.'

'Tell me. Reassure me.'

'Yes. I will, but I need to go back a little in god-time (I know that's a contradiction, but I think we both understand how it works by now). When I did the first man, you know, created him, I…

well…I…knocked one up, one of the other type, for Myself…you know…a woman…as a wife. Yes, for *Myself*! Selfish, I know.'

'Goodness!' said Socrates, taking hold of gGod's arm in a gesture of understanding and support.

'Yes, and as I was doing the creating I got a bit distracted—perceiving something I expect (as usual), I can't remember what—and, for some reason I still don't understand (I know, all-knowing!), she, this woman that I created ("Gladys" I named her, but she straightaway insisted on taking my name and being called "gGladys") came with relatives! Yes, relatives! Need I say more! You've guessed it. In no (god) time at all it all started to go wrong. Noah thought he had problems with Trixie! Remember? Well, he didn't know the half of it.'

'Oh!' exclaimed Socrates, tightening his grip on gGod's arm in as reassuring a way as he could.

'Yes. Imagine a typical scene. I've just got back, working hard perceiving and creating a few things, and this is what I'd get from gGladys: "Hello, Dear. My sister's here. Sit down. You'll be interested in this. Well, You'll never believe it but…". And I'd sit and all I'd be doing would be listening to endless talk about one of her sisters! Or the mother! Yes, she came with one of those too. And she'd always feature somehow in whatever the story was! She'd notice Me in the end and then I'd hear, "Oh sorry, dear. Done anything interesting today?". "Well…" I'd start, but before I could continue, she'd get back into her story and battle on. "Anyway, my other sister came round earlier. You know she's got a new…" and so on…and so on. And it all took Me further and further away from the sort of attention to detail that My task of perceiving needed. And a lot of things went to pot. And the counselling wasn't a success. And FX19! Don't mention FX19! Or kippers!' Socrates didn't. 'Anyway, I decided I couldn't take any more. And as God (himself) had got Me all set up in the first place, there was no one else to go to, and, well, it was only yesterday that I went to him and…'

For a moment He couldn't continue. He was choked with emotion.

'Yes, yes,' urged Socrates.

gGod cleared his throat and asserted Himself as well as He could.

'We'll, I went to him, and well, I…I…handed in My notice!'

'What!' exclaimed Socrates tightening his grip on gGod's arm with no evidence of a reassuring way whatever.

'Yes! "That's it!" I told him. "I've had enough!". Well, you can imagine. He was flabbergasted! It was ages before he spoke. "Very well," he said when he'd got his breath back. "But you'll have to finish what you're working on—Project Socrates". I couldn't argue. To be honest, I was relieved that he was letting me off so lightly. "Of course", I said. "Of course! But after that I'm throwing in My hat. I'm afraid you'll just have to find someone else to get on with what you want doing—and all the perceiving that comes with it! Oh, gGod! Or should I say, "Oh! Myself!" All the perceiving! I've had enough of it!" Then, to soften the impact of my resignation a little, I added. "But I'll throw in gGladys, her sisters and her mother to give my replacement some ready made company.". I don't know whether it was that or the general business of the resignation, but I have to say, I don't think he was best pleased. But I'd made up My mind—I couldn't go on!'

Socrates didn't know what to say. So he said nothing. There was a slightly uncomfortable silence. Then a more uncomfortable silence. Then, after an uncomfortable silence, he spoke.

'Oh…'

This seemed to relax gGod a little and He continued in a suddenly improved and less stressed tone.

'And already I'd found a nice place to retire to. I'll show it to you if you like.'

‘No, that’s fine,’ said Socrates feeling a sudden heaviness brought on by gGod talking of His own future.

‘Anyway,’ said gGod, keen to finish off His “duty” to Project Socrates, even if, as was obvious, His heart was no longer in it and His conviction was less than on the weak side. ‘We need to get on and finish up your last day, Soc. Let’s leave the machine—it’s done its job—and return to your cell and your sleeping friends.’

They turned to go. Socrates couldn’t resist an affectionate last look. The time machine sat in the walled courtyard bathed in the sunlight of a passed storm. But its use had taken its toll. The framework that held everything together was barely doing its job. The chair had tipped sideways at quite an angle. None of the four marble pillars were straight, one was fractured and looked ready to break. The urns that hung from the corners still rocked, but there was no longer any dust left in them and they rattled with emptiness. The square-shaped canopy that formed the roof was slack and had a number of tears. The originally brightly painted maidens with lyres, the men lying back on grassy banks being fed grapes by nymphs, and the gods in clouds watching from above, were now blurred and grey. The shiny rectangular plate in front of the chair attached at an angle, and the chunk of perforated metal that he had used to communicate with IgnatiusM hung down barely connected to its long arm. In front of the chair the long lever still stood proudly, resisting the worn-out-ness of the rest of the machine and almost begging to be drawn back for another journey. At its top the red light flashed intermittently, tantalisingly offering the use of the well tried emergency button. The self-replenishing refreshment box had fallen over and spilled out two uneaten sandwiches.

Socrates patted the emergency button affectionately. He looked at the gap in the jigsaw still awaiting the last piece. He turned and looked up into the sky. An upturned rainbow depicted the mouth of a roughly drawn smiling face. He smiled back, nodded his head in a final goodbye and raised a sort-of-half-knowing eyebrow.

A couple of stumbles in the dark corridor later and they arrived in the cell. They both looked at those gathered: all were sleeping soundly, some resting their heads on the shoulders or laps of the others, some lying flat out on their backs on the floor.

gGod ushered Socrates back to his original place on his couch. Socrates made himself comfortable. gGod then waved His hand as if He was declaring the denouement of a magic trick involving rabbits. The sleepers all awoke. They didn't stretch, or rub their eyes, or shake their heads, they just carried on from when He had sent them to sleep with not a sign of rousing their bodies back to normal consciousness or being in any way aware of anything unusual happening.

Socrates held out his hand and indicated gGod.

'You see that a new companion has joined us. He…He…'

gGod picked up from Socrates' being clearly stuck for an explanation.

'…is also a prisoner here, let out by my warders so that I may spend a little time with you all before I too must depart.'

That seemed to do the trick.

The others nodded to gGod in sympathetic acknowledgment of His situation.

Socrates turned to Crito.

'Crito, my friend, we owe a cock to gGod. He has indeed shown me everything I need to know—more than ever I could have wished. Let me call him "Asclepius" for He has truly given me the medicine to take me on my way. Yes, do pay it, for my debt to Him is great indeed. I am away now for life has finished with me, and me with it. My soul is already taking the hand of virtue. Yes, it has come. I reach out to it. I welcome it. Please don't forget.'

Crito nodded in sad acceptance of the chore of sacrifice that Socrates had give him.

'I will, friend Socrates. Even though I am surprised that you hold a deity in such high esteem.'

'There is none higher, Crito. Do not fail me on this.'

'I will not, my friend.'

From nowhere, there appeared a servant boy holding a cup of warm tea.

He stood before Socrates and, holding the cup in both hands, stretched his arms out and offered it to Socrates.

'Master. It has the hemlock mixed in,' he said before dropping his head in a sign of affectionate respect.

Socrates thanked him, took the cup, drank the tea, and lay back on his bed.

Crito moved aside to allow him to lie down fully.

'Carry me to the open courtyard. I need to do something.'

They did as he asked. They looked in amazement at the Time Machine. He indicated that they should place him in the seat of the machine. Confused as they were, they did as he requested.

He settled down and they all watched him as the heat of the hemlock spread slowly through his body.

And he looked up to them and smiled.

And they were astonished at how peaceful he looked.

And they were amazed at how young he looked.

And for a moment he saw the missing piece of the jigsaw trapped on the floor between part of the chair leg and some coiled wires..

And he reached down and picked it up.

And he looked at both sides and smiled.

And he offered it to the board with the letter-side uppermost.

And all the pieces fitted together perfectly.

And he died.

And everything was apparent to him.

And he saw that the final stage of the *C*-series contained only love. That the *C*-drive was tuned into the message of the letters. Now there would be no more crashing from the machine or its workings. Now, Socrates recognised the true nature of virtue and truth—an eternal, non-temporal, non-degrading series. The meaning of the letters was that nothing causes anything comprehensible. Everything is serial—it just keeps adding to itself. Even gGod had got it wrong. Changing His life would not alter anything; things would just keep adding into the series—perfection is simply the content of all things known at the same moment. Continuous perception and so the "causing to be" is unnecessary as all things perceive themselves and all other things in the atemporal-*C*-series. Reality is this. Virtue is this. Wisdom is the recognition of this. gGod had no need to keep perceiving. Things just *are*—eternally in the *C*-series, they *are*. Socrates realised that gGod could have got on with any hobbies He may have chosen, or with dealing with the seemingly ever-pressing marital matters without having to resign His role.

The *C*-series is what God (himself) called "god-time". Socrates realised that when any self is part of it (dead) then that self *is* within it. Like "space-time" it is a poor choice of term as it has no reference whatever to "time". Overall, love is the answer. Love as the experience of feeling beyond yourself and at the same time within another is the answer.

Like the ladybird flying from the old man's hand, Socrates flew away from life into death, and back again. Like the old man he realised what it is to die, to understand for that brief moment the wonder of eternity. All the stories that the time machine had told had matched the *C*-series system. Each placed piece had now become a permanent part of the series. And it is not a picture that can be understood. It is nothing intelligible. It is nothing that is a coherent whole. It is but a collection of letters all jumbled together.

Socrates realised that for him this meant virtue at last! He actually knew something! Not knowing had led him to true knowledge. In his last moment, he had experienced all the best, loving moments of his life in one serial blast.

So his virtuous death had brought him to a "timeless eternity" of existence where everything is known and nothing is in error. Everything was under the appearance of eternity—*sub specie aeternitas*.

He now knew that every part of everything shows that everything we know is indeed recollection; a strange recollection of all things that appear to have happened at the same time that they happen and are being recollected. Everything is in this sense recollection. Everything that he had seen in his time travelling experience had been a "reviewing" of all things both reviewed, seen and recollected at the same serial moment. All of it had been part of *all* life. Recollection is actually being part of the *C*-series of perceptions.

Socrates took a deep breath. For a moment he was filled with fear. He wondered whether he would be able to keep up with the pace of knowing everything, but as he became absorbed into it, and realised that he was still thinking in the wrong terms, he asserted himself over his fear, and the idea of apprehension quickly passed.

CHAPTER 27

Socrates meets God (himself)

God (himself) sat back.

'Well, it only seems a few moments ago since we were last together.' Well, actually, it *was* only a few moments since we were last together. Quite a lot can happen in a few moments though, don't you think? So, how have things gone (in the last few moments)?'

God (himself) made himself comfortable, and took a sip of tea from his cup (God (himself) had just created a table with cups and this time a full pot of tea so that they needn't run out). Socrates sat forward, keen to follow what was going to happen next, if indeed there was going to be a "next" in which anything could happen, and then if "happening" could somehow be outside time. He had been struck by God (himself)'s comment about a lot happening in a few moments and (finer details of the inconsistency of the implication of "happening" being reconciled with the implications of timelessness) felt aware of his experience having a strangely different pace.

'And you are?'

'Oh, Socrates! You are a card! God! I'm God (myself), of course! We've met lots of times!'

'We've met lots of times? And yet I don't recognise you.'

God (himself) laughed.

'Of course not! I'm *God (myself)*!'

'Oh,' said Socrates more than a little puzzled. 'I see...God (yourself).'

This wasn't at all clear. This "God (himself)" was obviously someone different to the "gGod" that Socrates had become used to.

And *this* God (himself) was there pouring tea from the teapot he'd just created just like gGod. But he was not using teabags straight into the cup! Indeed, he might not be using teabags at all; there were certainly no telltale labels hanging from the edges of the teapot lid. Very well, so it might not be gGod, but who was it? And how many "Gods" could there be?

'What escapades you've been having!' continued God (himself). 'Anyway, you're dead now. I must say I wasn't too happy about you taking your own life—sanctity of life and all that—but I think you've shown that you had just (-ish) cause. Not the sort of thing that should be repeated though. *Repeated* though!' he repeated to emphasise the witticism based upon the idea of being able to repeat death. It was lost on Socrates—completely. God (himself) tried again. 'Not the sort of thing…' but gave up. '… Well, never mind. Do you have any questions?'

'I'm dead now?'

'Yes, as a doornail.'

'But I still seem to be…well…here at any rate.'

'You're right. Death is not complete yet. Your body has died but for the moment you still have your own identity—you as yourself still "own" the residue of mortal life. But that will pass. You will lose your identity when you arrive, or should I say when your perceptions arrive in what I call the *C*-world. Then, you will no longer be known to yourself, other than knowing the perceptions of all others as they know your perceptions. And I'm sure you'll agree that will be pretty good. Marvellous, really, eh?'

'Miraculous, more like.'

'On the head again, Socrates—the nail! You are a veritable hammer!'

'So,' said Socrates still trying to catch up. 'You are God (yourself)?'

‘Yes. You might want to see me as the main God (myself), the big…whatever you can think of that’s as big as it gets. Kahuna? Cheese? Enchilada? Is that clear?’

‘So you are a…miracle,’ said Socrates, rather stuck for an object for his statement.

‘No! As you know, a miracle is defined as the act of a supernatural being that violates the laws of nature. In other words, a miracle goes against everything that you’ve ever known as evidence of how the world works. Well, I'm a supernatural being, inasmuch as I'm “super” to all nature—to all things. I did after all create *all* natural things. And all created things only know what I've created for them to know. I’ve been told that some humans who have thought about this, say that for a miracle to be real it must go against all inductive evidence, and so if a miracle happened it would be part of the inductive evidence and so its occurrence as a miracle would be self-defeating. Well, they didn’t take *me* into account! I am outside that body of evidence. So I can *do* miracles without limits without any problem. Though I don’t think I refer to myself as one. I hope this is all clear.’

‘Well, not exactly.’

‘Wonderful! So you are now in the process of becoming part of the final stage—the *C*-world. Feels a bit strange, I expect.’

‘More than a bit strange.’

‘Good. So it should. Now, to get on. As I said, you have a short period before “you”, as your perceptions, arrive in the *C*-world, so we need to make the best of them—last day and all that!’

‘I thought I’d *had* my last day! I’m dead, aren’t I?’

‘Well, yes. But, no. There’s still some of “you” to utilise. So let’s do it. Tell me what you have learned from your time-travelling experiences.’

‘What I’ve learned?’

‘Yes. Tell me what you’ve learned.’

Obviously this was not an instruction to be ignored, what with it being given by God (himself), the Big Kahuna (himself).

Socrates gathered his thoughts as well as he could.

'Go on! Go on!' urged God (himself). 'Go on! No time to waste!' he added in the hope of lightening the mood and making it a little easier for Socrates to press on. It didn't really help, but Socrates pressed on nevertheless.

'I have learned so many things. And now they all seem bonded together as if they have happened, that I recollect them, and that are happening and at the same time, that they have happened and are being recollected.'

God (himself) chuckled knowingly.

'Yes, please go on.'

'Well, in the way that I have just said, I have learned these things.

'I have learned that enquiry should not be closed by conclusion. Enquiry must continue to spawn fresh questions. If a conclusion is made then this can become entrenched in such a way that it is destructive (because of conflict and so on). Enquiry should never be halted. More answers expose more things to question. This can lead to a wisdom which can recognise virtuous reality. Logical questioning should lead only to "intuitive belief", and not to absolute certainty. Any claim for absolute certainty is destructive.

'I have learned from witnessing the happenings of the great flood that the goal of life is happiness; that the attainment of ethical goals relies on happiness.

'I have learned from my involvement with the dilemma involved in obligation to a friend, that attaining virtue in life's actions seems impossible. Obligation, duty and promise-keeping can all break down when self-interest breaks in. Decision making is always hampered by conflict and self-interest. But also from that, I have seen how deceit can lie at its very heart.

'I have learned from being there when the cruellest of things happened that the experience of love is both beyond the self and within the other. Within even the most loving there lurks the potential for terrible cruelty. The very best and kindest of humans can fall victim to untoward cruelty.

'I have learned from following the routine way in which a state can dispose of offenders against its rules that there is nothing clear-cut about how a state should deal with those who commit crimes against it.

'I have learned from the tenderest of feelings, that self-willed death can take many forms, and that there are justifications for upholding the individual's right to do this just as there are reasons why they should not. Such justifications and reasons range from the purely practical through the whole range of moral concerns to the far reaching consequential effects.

'And, most importantly, from being there when death occurs, I have learned that there is a period that sits between mortal death and being an eternal part of the perceiving system. This period is brief but an account of it helped explain the transition from the world of the physical perceiver (using perceiving apparatus and sense data) to being a non-personal, completely understanding part of the eternal serial world of the *C*-series. I have learned that life is only one part of the sequence of life, death and immortality.'

A pause. God (himself) smiled.

'You have learned well, my friend. Yes, you have learned well. In fact, I should say that you've passed!'

'Passed?'

'Well, "have become ready" might be a better way of putting it. "Ready to take over the reins" could be another appropriate expression.'

'Take over the reins?'

'Yes, from gGod. Take over the old perceiving business. I deem you to be ready, Socrates. More than ready. I deem you an outstanding and proper inheritor of the crown.'

Socrates was bowled over. He certainly hadn't been expecting this.

'Perceiving?' he asked weakly with little sign of being anything like an outstanding or even *un*exceptional inheritor of the crown.

'Yes, perceiving. Got it in one! See, I knew you were the right man!'

'Perceiving?' Asked Socrates again just as weakly.

'Everything you have known so far relies upon perceiving—upon being perceived. Everything in time is, in truth, only perceived under the false appearance of time—*sub specie temporis*, you might say.' Socrates wouldn't. 'But in order to be known it has to be perceived in this way. If it is not perceived in this way then it cannot exist. Things have to change (in time) to *be*. If this did not happen (in time) then nothing could be experienced: no humans could know anything and there would be nothing they could not know. But...but...and wait for it...' Socrates had no choice but to do so. 'But...outside of erroneous (though necessary for personal existence and so on) time this is *not* the case. When you break free from the world of time and enter the *C*-world then everything is known, if you like, in one big atemporal burst! And all you are is part of the perceiving process that outside time knows all other perceptions that have ever been and are being in one timeless moment. Now what do you think of that, Socrates?'

Socrates thought of saying something but decided to be exceptionally and crown-bearingly enigmatic.

'I see,' he said. 'And what has happened to gGod?'

'Here, I'll show you.'

'God (himself) took Socrates' hand and steered him along a gently sloping grassy bank that led down to a small, slow-running river. Socrates pulled back and God (himself) immediately recognised his need (well, if he couldn't, then no one else could)—he wanted to lie down comfortably on this perfectly sloped bank. God (himself) motioned with a broad, sweeping arm. Socrates lay back against the grassy bank. He stretched his arms back above his head and rotated his feet in slow circles. He knew it was going to be one of his very last sensations—that soon his self identity would disappear, and although the delight of this moment would continue and would be known as a *C*-perception, it would no longer be "his" to claim. God (himself) settled beside him and they lay together for as long as the experience demanded.

Socrates got up first. He smiled and stretched. He reached out and this time he took God (himself)'s hand to help him to his feet (he didn't seem too sure on his legs). They walked (slowly) down to the river side.

Socrates saw gGod. He smiled to himself. Yes, gGod had surely found His perfect retirement place—managing a small ferry on the slow-moving river, carrying those that needed to cross on his flat-hulled craft, poling across the stream, chatting with His customers, passing the time of day. Then, in between hails from those wishing to cross, he would, like Socrates and God (himself) at this moment, lie back on the perfectly angled grassy slope, stare at the clear blue sky and listen to the gentle plop of goldfish as they launched themselves into the welcome haven of the clear and ever-changing stream.

'It looks wonderful,' said Socrates, finding himself inadvertently squeezing God (himself)'s hand. He looks so happy—so at one with Himself.'

'Yes. He can have as long as He likes, too,' said God (himself) with a smile. 'I owe Him that.'

'Good,' said Socrates. 'Then that could be an eternity.'

'Yes,' confirmed God (himself) realising that he had made the right choice with Socrates. He used Socrates' hand to help lower him down to a sitting position on the river bank, stared ahead for a while then spoke. 'Yes, as long as He likes.'

A sense of wellbeing came over Socrates. He realised that meaning resides first in the living of a virtuous life, and then in being in the spiritual existence beyond it. Also, surprisingly, he realised that he liked goldfish (and quoits). For a moment he wanted to lie down next to gGod (who was just now taking another reclining break). Then he realised that he would only have to wait a short while and all wishes (including his own) would be fulfilled and complete. He waited for a moment, then smiled at God (himself) who looked as if he was about to close his eyes.

But he wasn't.

'I'm so happy you're taking over from gGod,' said God (himself). 'You've definitely earned it. I have to say, you have been truly exceptional.' Then, not giving Socrates a chance to respond, he carried on. 'Oh, and before you get too stuck into the old perceiving thing,' he said. 'I've got a surprise for you.'

Socrates looked appropriately surprised, at everything let alone what this surprise might be.

'Oh?'

'I bet you can't wait to know what it is!'

Socrates looked appropriately can't-wait, and not-knowing.

'No, I can't.'

'Well, with all the work that lies ahead for you, I thought you'd do better for having a companion: someone to come home to in the evening, someone to share your troubles with (not that there're likely to be any troubles), someone who understands the strains of your labours (not that you'll find them straining, of course)—in short, a wife.'

'That sounds good,' said Socrates unconvincingly.

'Yes! And here she is now! Her name is Gladys. Oh, and she's got her sisters with her. Oh, and her mother!'

'Oh, God (yourself)! You shouldn't have!'

THE END

Printed in Great Britain
by Amazon